September Christmas

Danae L. Samms

CONTENTS

1 MATILDA AND TESSIE

One of the hardest things I've ever had to do is live life. That's just because life is a hard thing. No one should ever say differently. In truth, no one really has it together or knows what they're doing at all. The best anyone can do is have a person in your life that helps you get through it. Two friends, hand in hand, moving forward with no idea what is happening. These friendships are only ever successful. For me, that friend is Matilda Day. Our friendship was one with no real beginning, it just always was. Like air or gravity, she was a constant requirement to my life.

We had a religious attendance to our Monday morning coffee in town. Scheduling for both of us made the trips to the little café a quick necessity. Matilda had a standing meeting each week with a local business to discuss logos and adds she was working on. She loved designing for them, but hating going in for the meetings. Coffee helped a little.

Resentment was displayed in her parking job that morning. Matilda could never parallel park. Usually one large wheel was up on the sidewalk, or a headlight poked into traffic. Sometimes it was both. Yet she would never dream of driving something other than her gigantic, black SUV; or "the tank" as she called it.

She treated the car like a military grade tank, and it almost was. In her ten years of driving it, the tank had taken out mailboxes, carried obscene loads of heavy, metal sculptures, and been climbed on by Matilda and Cat thousands of times. Despite the heavy wear and use, it still looked brand new.

That particular Monday, the SUV was crooked, and taking up two metered spots. I carefully parked behind her. The tiny Volkswagen was a blue speck in comparison. Just as Dad had so patiently taught me years before, I turned the wheel towards the sidewalk, backed in, turned it away, and rolled into place. The wheels rested an inch from the curb.

I remember that morning because I couldn't find my stupid pen. The refillable, polished ink pen had been a gift from me to me when I got my job. Since then, I had used it religiously over any other writing utensil in the office. Like a contortionist, I bent down to look under the passenger seat to see if it had rolled there. It hadn't, and I cursed under my breath.

Outside, I checked both of the meters the tank inhabited. Each had forty three minutes remaining. Matilda caught me checking the time from her spot across the street.

"Tessie, you're not a meter maid," she called.

I crossed over to her and sat down. Two cups of coffee had already been placed on the patio. Our usual Monday morning spot had outdoor seating exclusively from May to August. That morning was one of the first days they set up the tables outside.

"You're parking job makes mine look like shit," Matilda said.

"Well, it is shit," I teased. "It looks like Malibu Barbie parked next to G.I. Jane."

"I'm too weak to be a navy seal, and you drink too much to be a doll."

Matilda lounged in the chair like an aging king who'd grown used to his uncomfortable throne. A red flannel hung like a mantle over her graphic tee, and pink sunglasses rested on her head in her own sort of crown. All the extra fabric rumpled around her as she slouched. Every few minutes she coughed and created more folds. The sleeves hung down a bony arm to one hand resting on the table. Long fingers stroked the edge of her coffee mug. The porcelain cup was not much lighter than her skin.

By the time she was twenty, Matilda was used to people asking her if she felt alright or if she had eaten. So by that year, she hardly noticed it when anyone thought she was sick, although roughly a third of the time she was. Pale skin does that, and pale skin will seem especially white when it is framed by jet black hair. Judgement on if she was a Goth left over from the late nineties was another standard.

She couldn't help the fact her hair was the color of tar and constantly tangled. A savage war had lasted most of a lifetime between Matilda and her messy hair. Products, salon visits, and hair brushes had all been defeated by the persistent strands. After high school, she surrendered and accepted her life of messy hair.

Our table hugged the café wall, just barely out of reach of pedestrians. A young man close to our age jogged down the sidewalk across the street. I'll admit, he was handsome enough to catch attention from both of us; more so from Matilda.

She gave a soft hum of approval as he ran past us and stopped at the corner. He waited on the light to change, jogging in place. Matilda kept her gaze on him.

"Maybe I should go over there and say hi," she wondered aloud. "I've

2

been telling myself to get out there lately. That'd be a great story of how we met. I saw him running and I went for it.

"We swap numbers. We text. We date. We get married. He could spend his mornings running on my street while I answer emails. Our children would be mulatto and beautiful."

The light changed and the run disappeared into the morning crowd.

"Oh he's gone. In another life, my love," another cough ended the day dream.

"You should get that checked," I told her.

"Allergies," she sipped the coffee. "They always happen in the spring."

"It doesn't usually sound like that. You might have an infection or something." I knew she wouldn't take me seriously. Coughs and colds were a standard, but I still mentioned it.

"Good. Maybe I'll give it to these assholes in this meeting." Her eyebrows bounced from irritation.

For the thousandth time that morning I checked my bag for the pen. For the thousandth time it wasn't there. One clean legal pad, a memory stick, and my tablet were alone with a rough assortment of breath mints.

"What are you looking for?"

"My stupid pen," I grunted.

"Use one from your office," she said.

"I don't like those, and they don't match my grip or have a Margaret Atwood quote engraved on them." I dropped my bag on the ground in irritation.

"I'm sure it's just on your desk or something," Matilda's eyes widened, drawing in my focus.

I always thought all of Matilda was beautiful, but anyone would say her best feature was her eyes. Like two of my cars parked in a snowstorm, bright blue eyes lit up Matilda's entire face. When she spoke, they demanded to be seen. It was impossible to not make eye contact in a conversation. Focus was required to hear what she was saying and not be distracted by her sharply pointed eye liner.

Matilda knew this. Daily, she wore Coca-Cola red lipstick. The two extremes cancelled each other out, and you could take in her entire face.

Her prominent features drew in the most attention from anyone we came across. With my short brown hair and business attire, I usually faded behind her. Grunge flannel took more notice than a white button up and a black pencil skirt. Sometimes she offered me the same, red lipstick, but it never made much of a difference.

Anytime I tried to wear it, one half of my bottom lip took an extra helping of read smear. Making the distribution even, and only on my lips, was impossible. Matilda had a knack for perfectly applying the bright red color across her lips in one swift motion without the hint of an error.

That morning she wore the shimmery red lipstick. It was pushed into her natural, resting scowl as we scanned over the news highlights. Both of us lingered in the entertainment section.

"Wow, a bunch of celebrities got engaged this week. Mia Turner and Stanley Reed won't last."

"Does it mention Micah Farnham?" she asked as naturally as if she were asking which coffee was regular and which coffee was decaf.

"No, looks like he's still single."

"That's just because he hasn't met me yet." Her eyes were still on her phone.

"Obviously."

Keeping up with celebrities was a sort of guilty pleasure for Matilda; except she only felt guilty about it if she was around anyone besides me. In our teenage years her curiosity of stars was limited. Every so often she cycled through someone else, but her emotional, fan commitment of Micah Farnham lasted from when she was nineteen on.

I'm not sure she ever mentioned the one sided love affair to anyone else. She definitely didn't tell Liam about it; even though her brother was partial to inside jokes. He was allowed in on fun anecdotes, but most personal tastes were only between Matilda and me. Sharing any secret was a constant for our entire friendship.

Our first big secret came when we were seven. We snuck into the garage of her home and stole popsicles from the industrial fridge. It was summertime, so we ate them on the side patio. In the heat they melted all too quickly.

Matilda's orange shirt with the flower on it had three blue stains before we were finished. Panic fell over both of us. Mouths blue and purple from our conquest were stiffly closed as we realized the danger of sugar close to dinner. Frozen, we struggled with a plan. It was her first day in the new shirt, and it was stained with forbidden popsicle juice.

Together we raced upstairs and hid the shirt in the back of her closet. Toys and shoes were thrown on top of it into a permanent messy pile. A clean shirt was pulled from her dresser drawer, also orange to avoid speculation. I stood with my face in the corner while Matilda changed.

"Tessie, never tell!" she moaned. I didn't, until just now. At the bathroom sink we scrubbed our hands and lips. All traces of our snack were gone.

I don't remember actually meeting Matilda. I just know our family moved into the house across the street when I was young. This was before Tara was born, so I would have been less than four. One picture always stands in my mind of the two of us on Easter.

The actual day is a blur to me. I don't remember who took the picture. I can't even tell you what happened to the picture, but I remember it as clearly as if it hung in my bedroom right now.

We were both standing on the sidewalk in front of Matilda's house in our colorful dresses. A basket of plastic eggs was hoisted above my head while I laughed, probably at Matilda. She was holding her basket in front of her, properly, but she smiled big enough to show every one of her teeth. Simultaneously, her blue eyes were stretched open as far as physically possible. Her white skin matched a ruffled cardigan wrapped around a Sunday dress.

Despite the warm weather, Mrs. Day insisted she keep it on. Like so many other times in our childhood, Matilda was coughing and starting a cold. Any beginnings of symptoms sent Mrs. Day into a panic. She forced her daughter to drink orange juice and take vitamin c tablets.

Colds did not just make Matilda tired and snotty. They knocked her out for a week. Confined to her bedroom, Matilda left me lonely for several days. This pattern continued until sometime in our teenage years.

That Easter, the cardigan had succumbed to Matilda's wild lifestyle. Even in the picture you could see grass stains from her vicious rampage through the egg hunt in her front yard.

Since the Day home was a fair bit larger than ours, we spent a lot more time there than my house. Mom was constantly in their kitchen, jealous of the space and appliances Mrs. Day owned. The kitchen island was enough to make any cook swoon. Show them the extra fridge and freezer in the garage and they could faint.

Matilda and I were the classic, neighbor friends you always read about when you were young. Except, we didn't send secret signals through our bedroom windows. That was just because our rooms faced our back yards instead of the street between us.

The two story colonial was like a house everyone always secretly wants but only doctors can seem to afford. The walls outside and in were crisp white. Perfect black tiles lined the roof, and every window had black shutters. They weren't the kind you could actually close; they just looked really nice on either side of each window. All the rooms had hardwood floors, accented by squishy rugs that begged you to walk on them bare footed.

Calling the floors clean was an understatement. I would have been comfortable eating ice cream off of that floor. But I never would, because it was almost like the floor was too nice to eat from. It was nicer than the fancy china that sits in your cabinet on display and is never used.

Even now, I think I could walk through the place blindfolded. I could open that red, front door, and march right up the stairs to the "family space" where a thousand nights I fell asleep on a bean bag chair after a few hours of cartoons and candy.

I could walk across the hall into Matilda's room. She always insisted it was smaller than Liam's because he had three windows and she just had two. She didn't even believe the tape measure after we put it to the test.

I could circle the kitchen island and take you out to the side patio and glass table. Everybody had one of those tables in their life. The kind you sat around at two in the morning and talked about real shit. It was almost like the darkness gave you some kind of shield from the truth that came out and the judgement anyone in ear shot might have. Conversations held there usually never left.

In our semi-adult years, the patio became home to Cat, as well as his food and water dish. I was not there the day Cat took up residency on the patio. All I know on the matter is the story Matilda relayed to me later that same day.

For a few years, she had next door neighbors that commonly never spoke to her. Occasionally, we exchanged greetings with them as they entered or exited the home. They never offered more than that. Often, we saw their cat sitting on the glass table or one of its chairs, but as soon as you walked close enough to see him there, he jumped from his perch and darted out of site. For the most part he was just a streak of tan and white.

A year or so earlier, the neighbors decided to move. On the last day, Matilda watched them load a box truck and roll away. As the truck passed her house she waved from her spot on the front step. Since they had never spoken, she didn't care either way for their departure. That is until she glanced back to their driveway.

The tom cat rushed to the edge just in time to see the truck stop at the end of the block.

"Shit," Matilda cursed. She dashed across the yard and down the street.

In her socks, Matilda sprinted down the middle of the road waving her arms and shouting, "Come get your stupid cat, assholes!"

The signaling was impossible to miss, yet the truck turned the corner and sped away. Out of breath, she trudged back to the house with sore feet. Cat, as he came to be called, was still sitting at the end of the driveway.

Before evening, Matilda purchased dry food and two bowls. Cat discovered them beside the patio door, and took to napping on the glass table more often. He became the only being, besides Matilda, to be at the house more than me.

As well as I knew their home, the Days made it a whole different world at Christmas. Mrs. Day shrouded the place in garland and fake snow. Nothing cheap either. It looked like a spread from a house wife's Christmas catalogue. By the time we were in High School, she let us help with the decorating.

Just a couple years after we started helping with decorations Mrs. Day made us stop. Matilda was unwrapping glass figures of a Mr. and Mrs. Claus for the mantel.

"Who was Mrs. Claus before she married Santa?" Matilda almost shouted. "Santa has a thousand names, but she is just Mrs. Claus. She gets married, and that becomes her whole identity. I'll never do that." With a harsh thud the figure was set into place.

"Get married, change your name, or marry Santa?" I asked. I was always ready to encourage her declarations on society. Whether we were at home or having a classroom discussion at school, her responses typically lasted long enough to delay some form of work.

"The third one."

The sexist accusations continued on Father Christmas and Christmas. Before long, Mrs. Day shooed us away with an errand to run out of the house. When we returned, after two hours of wandering a store or five, she insisted our help was not needed.

A real Santa always floated through the party, passing out the gift Mr. and Mrs. Day had picked for that year. It was usually a magnet or coaster or some other useful trinket. The date and a note about the family's love and hope that you had a Merry Christmas covered the item in an ornate script. Sometimes, we would swing by Santa twice, hoping for a second gift. He never fell for it. But that was one of our poorer pranks.

More often, we stood on the stairs above the guests crowded along the edge of the living room and dining room. Different dads would be victimized by a BB tossed into their hair. Every time, they would touch their head in confusion, glance at the ceiling, and try to ignore it. If a guest had been particularly annoying to us, we would toss BBs into his hair until he was frustrated and moved to a different room.

Some required much less effort. Guests would find plastic bugs in their coat pockets on the ride home. Once we taped a picture of Ernest Hemingway to the underside of the toilet lid. That was fun for anyone who used the upstairs bathroom.

There was no stereo system in the house. A professional piano player sat down at the grand in the front room and filled the place with classy carols for the whole three hours.

In the dining room, the eight person table was pushed against the wall for an elaborate spread of food. The sides constantly changed, but each year the staples were five hundred Christmas macaroons, marshmallow snowmen, and Cherry-Life soda.

The Day family was rather strict with meals year round. When we were little, Matilda only had candy once a week. Soda was a constant no. The only day of the year she could have it was the Christmas party.

In our dresses, we were no longer neighborhood kids, but beautiful, sophisticated, grown up women. From the first of the parties I can remember, we twirled through the house acting like "ladies." Being the best friend of the host, I was granted a wine glass for my Cherry-Life. Whenever the table offered chocolate dipped pretzel sticks, we took them to the side patio. To a kid, we were enjoying French wine and cigars.

For a few moments, we could daydream. The cold air biting our cheeks and muffled party ambience placed us in a different world. Not always, but every so often when we stood on the patio shivering, it would snow. Snowflakes make Christmas magic stronger. Matilda would say any wish you made on the patio would come true. At five we believed it. By eleven we still played along. As adults we were smart enough to believe it again.

Tiny moments have a way of bringing back old memories. Matilda pursed her lips and the shimmer of red took me back to childhood Christmases for one quick second. I smelled the pine in the living room, and could hear the piano giving us a rendition of *Good King Wenceslas*. Downtown rumbles pulled me back to reality.

My coffee cup was getting low. I glanced around the outdoor seating for someone with the power to refill it.

"You want to see a movie tonight or something?" Matilda's attention was on the meter maid moving down the street.

"I can't the *Eternity* premiere is tonight."

"Watch it later," she coughed again.

"No, I'll see spoilers!" Our only disagreement came from the TV show I followed religiously. In its five years on the air Matilda had attempted to watch it ten times. Each time she gave up half way through the second episode. Not getting flustered by her completely wrong opinion of the best TV show I had ever seen was difficult. I changed the subject.

"So what did your client do this time that makes you want to give them a cold?" I asked as my cup was refilled.

Matilda gave a heavy sigh that lead to another cough. "They wanted to change fonts to something really ugly. I said no because it would throw off the hierarchy which would mess up the whole image. Also it doesn't match the rest of the poster. But they did it anyway on their own so the kerning is totally screwed and you can't read it. Now I have to go in on their computer and fix it."

"No idea what you're saying, but I'm angry too," I said.

"You would think years into this job they would just blindly trust me on things they know nothing about."

Indeed it had been years on the job. Matilda was in the small percent of lucky students who stumbled on a job right out of high school. She completely avoided college and things worked out well for her, I threw myself into the college world and ended up fine.

High school could not have been more different between the two of us. We were in the same school and grade. Every morning we carpooled there, went to class, and came home and did homework on one of our dining room tables. Yet, studies came much easier to me than to Matilda.

For the most part we were in the same classes, and spent the same amount of time studying our textbooks and notes. I was on the honor roll and received a few scholarships, she passed. Matilda never misbehaved to the point of irritation from our teachers. She just learned to fly under the radar and not be noticed. It kept her out of talks about college and career choices.

When everyone else was applying to schools and desperately searching for financial aid, Matilda applied for a single internship in graphic design. She showed it to me one afternoon after school.

As usual, we were at her dining room table. Mrs. Day had given us a plate of sliced apples and carrot sticks. Two used up water bottles rested amongst our scatter of notes and textbooks.

"What's Milton and Ford?" I asked. The printed application in my hands looked a lot more fun than any I had been working on.

"It's some kind of business in town that does stuff for other businesses. They were the only booth I visited during the job fair."

"And you would just do graphic design?"

"Yep. And they would pay me."

The average student applies for dozens of colleges and internships. If they're lucky, they will be accepted to their third or fourth choice. Matilda sent in one application, and was accepted within a week.

I stayed local with my collegiate choice, but not to be near my family or Matilda. As I was ordering a cap and gown for graduation, Mom and Dad were packing up our entire house.

Dad had been offered a promotion out of state. My parents moved me into a freshman dorm and then moved away, but my experience wasn't lonely. Every weekend I was staying with Matilda. We still saw each other almost daily.

Within a year her internship wrapped up and she was given a job. I purposefully kept my classes between 9am and 5pm in my sophomore year to match our schedules.

It wasn't choice that kept me in the same town for childhood, college and the first few years of my career. It was fate. I was supposed to be near Matilda all that time. She helped me think through class schedules, decide on dorms, and showed me how to shop for groceries.

Even as she worked professionally in graphic design her art didn't stop. Paintings were always found in the spare corners of the basement and in different closets in the house. When I moved into my first apartment she gave me a painting.

Those roommates had brought their own décor and furniture, but didn't mind me adding art to the wall. Matilda got me into the apartment through packing and carrying everything in the tank. Together we hung the canvas over the couch in the living room.

Purple and gold swirls mixed every which way. The frameless square took up most of the wall, and was all you could see in a room of beige.

"What does it mean?" one of my roommates asked

"If you have to ask, you don't really get it." They were in awe of Matilda's answer. Later I asked the same question myself.

"It doesn't mean anything, I just like the colors," she said.

After two cups of coffee, it was time for us to be responsible and go to work. I dropped cash on the table to cover both of us.

"You don't have to-" Matilda's objection was stopped by another bout of coughs.

"It's my turn," I told her. "Please go see a doctor."

"Fine, I'll go this afternoon." She gathered her things and stood up with me.

"Promise?"

"Promise."

2 THREE CHRISTMASES

Seeing my parents move away just as I began college wasn't too much of a shock for me. Like every other human I cried when they drove off, but I was quickly doing well. Mr. and Mrs. Day were available at a phone call, and their house took me in every weekend. Anytime I needed groceries or car help they were there. They even took me to the airport every time I flew out to Mom and Dad.

Our home town wasn't a gigantic, bustling metropolis, but compared to my family's new home it was New York in the nineties. Dad had taken a job in Allensville, which is just as boring as it sounds. In any of my visits there, the most exciting outing was a movie.

For the first couple of months, Mrs. Day arrived at my room every Wednesday with a home baked snack and a different sort of office supply. I soon had color coordinated pens, highlighters, and paper clips scattered across my desk.

At the end of the semester I loaded up my car and drove home. The space between my parents and me was about five hours by car or one hour by plane. Methods of travel home depended on finances and how adventurous I was feeling. Most often it was a road trip.

The first year of school passed pretty easily. Having the Day family at my disposal made the transition to college life simple. Every so often I was visiting their house to do laundry and eat a real meal. The Days were back up parents. Years of living across the street from us made them experts on Tessie Fletcher.

Without asking, they knew my pizza order, and often recorded the TV shows I enjoyed. As we reached adulthood, their rules on food began to relax. Matilda and I could have soda and occasionally cookies. Whenever we were watching *Pride and Prejudice*, they usually passed through the room. Either of them could quote any given scene along with us.

11

It was the end of my third year that I was called into the ER. Nothing is more sobering than a stranger's voice saying there's been an accident. I had finished my last final that afternoon, and had plans to drive home the next day. Those were immediately cancelled. Instead, Mom packed a bag and flew over.

Liam was gone. He had begun a career as a traveling nurse a year or so before. I can't remember where he was that night, but it was far. It took him a couple days just to get in. I was the one they called. At some point, I had been placed on an emergency contact list.

I can remember hearing my heart pound in my ears as I raced to Matilda's room. A nurse pointed me to an open door, and I was inside. She sat on the edge of a hospital bed completely frozen. All she had was a cut on her cheek.

"Dad was driving," she said as I walked in. Blue eyes had been glazed over. The usually messy hair was somehow messier and littered with specs of broken glass.

I gave her a hug, but she didn't move. I pulled a few reachable pieces from her hair. "Are you okay? Is anything broken?"

"Dad was driving." Her face met mine, but her gaze passed through me.

"I'm going to sit with you until they tell us something." I climbed onto the bed beside her. "Everything's going to be okay."

As the words came out of my mouth I knew I was wrong.

"Dad was driving." Her voice broke, and she grew quiet. A small tremor began in her shoulders.

I hugged her close, and we waited. A solemn doctor delivered the news. Matilda's whole world collapsed, and I couldn't find a single piece to pick up. The only thing I could do was hold her while she cried. We all experience growing up at one point, but at twenty one Matilda was forced to grow up very quickly.

The next week moved in a blur. Mom and I stayed in the guest room while arrangements were made. Mom made any call that was needed. Unsure of how to help, I just stayed close by and did anything anyone asked.

Mr. and Mrs. Day had been pretty active in a nearby church. When we brought Matilda home from the hospital, a spread of food was left on the table. She went straight to bed as Mom and I took inventory of what was brought in and placed it in the fridge or on the designated counter space.

By the next day, Liam arrived. Instead of waiting on a flight, he jumped in the car and drove. I remember him walking in through the garage, in sweat pants and a hoodie with baggie eyes. His face was contorted from hours of being awake. Even in his exhaustion, he made a plate of food and took it to Matilda's room.

She hadn't left it since she came home. I had gone in a few times to see if she needed food or any sort of thing I could think offer.

"No thanks," was the only answer I got.

Liam didn't ask what she needed. Instead he just gathered food and took it upstairs. After a few minutes he returned, the plate empty. Their stubbornness often banged together like two mountain goats, but when she needed it, her big brother won.

Those few days the two of us watched a lot of TV. I had known Liam as long as I knew Matilda, but the two of us were hardly close. That week we moved from awkward acquaintances to just acquaintances. Every so often Mom sent me on an errand. Liam came along.

"I want to help with what I can. I feel like I should be doing more as the oldest one," he explained from the passenger seat.

"You're doing a lot for her," I replied. Matilda remained in her room for the most part. The only time she ate or left it was at her brother's persuasion.

"Crazy to see you driving, and now you're half way done with college. You're always supposed to be my little sister's friend, not an adult," he gave a forced chuckle.

Despite the circumstance, Liam was good at staying calm and helping take care of things. Without him, Matilda might not have been able to move on at all. A few days in, we were in our usual spot on the couch and she finally made an appearance.

"What are you watching?" she mumbled.

"A crime show marathon," Liam offered a fleece throw. "Want a blanket?"

We sat together, learning about how to clean up after a murder without getting caught. Matilda spoke a few times, and that night ate with us at the table. Things began moving a little more smoothly.

In the time following the accident, I had unintentionally put any of my own thoughts aside. All of my focus was on Matilda and following the instruction Mom gave me. After Mom packed up and flew home to Dad, a pain formed in my chest. Liam had a few more days in town, and I thought it best to let him and Matilda have their time.

I arrived back at my apartment and found it very quiet. While I had spent all my time with the Days, my roommates packed up and went home for the summer. Very alone, the pain in my chest grew. It pushed outward and filled my whole body until tears started.

I wanted someone to talk to. Dad wasn't answering his phone. Mom was on the plane. Obviously I couldn't seek comfort from Matilda when I was grieving her parents. I slumped into the kitchen table and wept silently.

The absence of my back up parents was suddenly very clear and painful. The business of the week had kept me from thinking too much about it. Finally alone and free to think, I realized I missed them more than I had missed anything before. Just as painful, I couldn't fix it for my friend.

As my eyes began to dry, I desperately wanted comfort food. The kitchen was almost void of snacks. Final exams made all of us eat anything that didn't' require cooking. By sheer luck, I found half a sleeve of stale cookies in the panty. They weren't much help.

Beside them was a bottle of red wine. A few months ago one of my roommates had passed it off as a twenty first birthday present. It was yet to be opened.

My eyes were crusty and mascara was runny. I had no desire to venture out for more food. I opened the bottle. The first glass was good. The second was better. The third mad the stale cookies taste good.

Soon my head was light, and I realized I hadn't been crying for a while. I still missed Mr. and Mrs. Day. I missed them terribly, but I felt so much better. It would be easy to help Matilda act like a grown up.

Big life insurance policies helped Matilda keep the house. She stayed in her bedroom and kept every piece of furniture. Over the next few years piles of art just grew in corners and closets. She never touched a thing except the front room. The couch and piano remained, but Matilda added a computer. It became her graphic design office when her internship ended and full time job began.

She was working from home in a house she owned. There's not much that's more grown up than that.

Everything else was left alone. I don't think she ever emptied the dressers or the closet in her parents' room. When Liam had to clean out the house he must have found old shirts in the drawers that still smelled like Mr. Day's Old Spice.

Liam was barely there for the summer. After a couple of weeks in town he went right back to the road. He had planned on only traveling for two years to pay his student loans. After losing his parents he just kept traveling.

I stayed in town for the most part that year. Mom wanted me to come in for a visit, so I convinced Matilda to come along. On the road I did all the driving. She stayed quiet. Now and then I got her to chat with me or play a silly road trip game. The conversations didn't last longer than a few minutes.

My family sensed the difference. If we went out to dinner or on errands she followed. The whole week she was quiet and lack luster. Comments were nonexistent. The only time she spoke was to answer someone asking her a direct question.

When classes started again I kept my schedule in line with hers. Evenings and weekends we were still together. I managed to get Matilda out to movies and frequent stops. Sometimes we stayed in for *Pride and Prejudice*.

She talked, but only in small doses.

Like a candle when you blow out the flame, her life was gone. Nothing seemed to hold her interest or make her smile. That summer and fall she was a thin trail of smoke on a black wick. As it started to get colder, I expressed my concern to mom.

"I don't think I should leave her alone at Christmas." By then I was living in my first apartment. Half way through my third year I found a place with a few girls I knew distantly. A kitchen and my own space was a huge step up from a crowded dorm. I shut myself up in my room almost whispered into the phone.

"Want to bring her here?" Mom was cheerful.

"I don't know. She didn't love it when we came in before." I was worried, and my mother could tell. The closest blanket became my cocoon.

"Sometimes when someone goes through a loss it helps to change the routine for the holidays." I could hear Mom filling the kettle and setting it on the stove. "Would you want to take her on a trip?"

"What about you guys?"

"We'll be fine if you're here for New Year's."

The idea sparked my interest. My laptop was pulled closer to me and I began scrolling through the internet for ideas. We talked over a few options. Disney World was pricey. Leaving the country was impossible. Mom sipped tea and searched with me.

"How about a cruise? You could go somewhere warm and get a tan. That's pretty different for Christmas." She paused to think and hear my answer.

It was easy to find something doable. Excitement grew. We found the right options and looked at the final cost together.

"Tell you what," Mom said, "Your father and I will pay for it as your Christmas gift."

I squealed and thanked her.

Prepping for the trip was almost as fun as the trip itself. I got a basket and filled it with sunscreen, flip flops, sunglasses and a colorful towel. The next evening I drove to her house. She met me in the front room and I made her sit on the tiny couch.

"I have your Christmas present."

"In October?"

"It's not exactly here now. I'm giving you the prologue now." I placed the basket on the coffee table and pulled off the blanket that had been covering it.

She examined the contents and glanced up at me, "I think I'm lost."

"We're going on a cruise in December."

"A cruise?" A smile started to appear.

"A *lady pals* cruise," I tried to hype it up with a title.

"Okay, Fletcher. Let's do this!" She riffled through the box and her smile grew.

That semester was the hardest to finish. Every class was a milestone between me and our vacation. When it came time for finals I was in a rush. That wasn't my best academic year, but I don't care.

We started packing ten days before we even left. Matilda had treated herself to a camera that fall, and was getting into photography. All we planned for was looking cute for pictures. Being comfortable on vacation didn't seem as important as building up our Facebook pages.

Three swimsuits, two pairs of sunglasses, and at least ten cute dresses were shoved into each of our bags. Like romantic comedy stars, we marched onto the ship. A real, happy smile began to appear under her pink, bear shaped sunglasses.

Part of our packages included constant free refills for non-alcoholic drinks. We were each handed large cups shaped like toucans with our names across the bottom. As soon as we dropped our stuff in the cabin, we had to try all the soda.

Fountain drinks covered an entire wall. Matilda rushed through, reading the labels. At the end she turned back to me.

"No Cherry Life? This is barbaric!" I was silently hopeful that the absence of the drink would make Christmas go a little smoother.

Even without her signature brand, Matilda had a great time. I had planned our excursions and researched exactly what we needed for each one. She never thought to pack a day bag; instead she just borrowed sunscreen and other needed items from mine. I enjoyed taking on the role of pack mule.

The pictures did not disappoint. We had hundreds of photos on beaches and by the pool. Most of them had our heads thrown back in an old movie star laugh. Matilda trusted me enough to use the camera a few times. She insisted I did well on taking photos of her, but I think I failed to make her look as pretty as she really was each time.

It was worth the extra time we spent getting ready each day. I usually threw my short hair into a little ponytail while Matilda battled her black tangles. My hair had never been as long as hers. As soon as I realized how quickly I could take care of it, I never let it get long enough to touch my shoulders. The most styling came from bangs to hide the half inch scar over my right eyebrow.

In our cabin I watched Matilda fight with a spray bottle and comb. Her hair was a stiff mess that almost reached her shoulders.

"Why not chop it off?" I asked. "You'd still look good."

"What, and let the hair win?" she jerked the comb through a knot. "I won't give up like that."

She never did. Sheer determination got her hair brushed out each day, in her opinion that was always enough work. It was, she always looked better than me.

A highlight of the trip came on a night of one of the formals. We put on two of our best dresses and sauntered to the event. More than the usual amount of extra time was spent getting ready. By the time we arrived it was getting crowded, and most of the passengers were tipsy.

One group of two or three young men looked like they could only come from trust funds. No young adult from the middle class would wear cufflinks or tie a tie that well. They gave us an eye as we entered. We had no interest, and did our best to avoid them.

Our attempt wasn't successful. The small group found an excuse to move past us rather closely. One reached towards Matilda and pinched her butt.

In a direct, one-eighty degree spin, she turned to face him and snapped, "Hey, what the hell?"

"I like what I see," he smirked. Matilda didn't think it was funny.

"So just because you like something you abuse it? I'd hate to see the condition of your car, or your dick." Her words seared. The group went quiet.

"You should learn to take a compliment," the boy fumbled for words, and the group around him had little to offer for help.

"Oh, wow. You're so right." Matilda passed her cup to me. In one swift motion, she delivered a direct punch to his jaw. He went straight to the floor.

Matilda stood over him, like a queen on a throne, and called down, "Don't you like that? I thought guys wanted to show people they're tough and can handle a lot of pain. Wow, you should learn to take a compliment."

She turned back to me and grabbed my arm. In a second we were out the door and running. "We gotta hide before that prick calls security!" she hissed.

Together we weaved past any crowd and rushed towards our room. A toucan cup in each hand, I struggled to keep up with her pull and avoid spilling drinks. Somehow, we didn't stumble in our heels. In a moment, we were back in our cabin. Either it was fear, shock, or excitement, but we plopped down onto the floor and started laughing.

A quick snap had sparked her into life. In that moment, I knew my Matilda was back. Grief had knocked her down, but she was up again, and fighting harder than ever before.

By the next October, Matilda was back to normal. She was a homeowner, was working regularly as a graphic designer, and had sold one painting to a local business downtown.

We made a day of seeing it get hung up. Both of us dressed up for the occasion, and arrived in the morning for the event. Two girls in a quiet lobby applauded as a janitor made sure it was level. Afterwards, we enjoyed a celebration brunch with bottomless mimosas.

Matilda's skills were broader than painting. For her eighteenth birthday, her parents had given her welding equipment and converted the basement to a studio. In the years after, the equipment was handled very little. That year, she was working on sculptures a little more regularly. Quickly, Matilda was able to bend metal into dreamlike figures. In the summer one appeared in my old yard across the street.

Once or twice I saw her use it. I stood several yards away in safety goggles and earmuffs as an unrecognizable figure in a heavy safety coat and face shield bent metal with fire. After a few moments of bright light, she turned everything off and removed her helmet.

"Cool, huh?"

"Sure," I shouted, hands still protecting my ears.

The flame inside her was growing. Matilda was active in her career, made time to follow her art that was still just a hobby, and spent plenty of extra time with me. As her new life roared she longed to find happiness in every day, and share it with others. After dinner upstairs, she revealed her plans.

"I think I want to throw a Christmas party this year." We had just begun November, but by her parents standards, planning was already two weeks behind.

"Like a big one?" I asked.

"Yeah, the classic way we used to always have it. I've done pretty well this year, I can afford a party. Liam can come in, and we can invite everybody that used to come." Her plans were small, but her energy was strong.

"Okay, Day. Let's do this."

Within a week, Matilda had saved recipes and planned a menu. She was intent on making all the food herself and insisted it wasn't as hard as we thought. As difficult as food prep became, she never changed her mind on it, even when she was dipping pretzel sticks into chocolate at two in the morning.

One Saturday I worked on addressing envelopes as she placed stamps. Planning such an event made us feel high and mighty. Copying a long list of addresses onto envelopes was everything elementary school told me adulthood would be, so it was great to finally see it in action.

RSVPs came immediately. All of them were more than excited to have a Day Christmas Party again. My parents even decided to make the trip.

Mom offered to help with things each day until they all arrived. Even then she asked a couple times what else needed to be done after the party began.

I drove them all over for the evening to show off the outdoor decorations we had labored over on Black Friday. A clean line of bright, white lights flowed along the edge of the roof. Similar strands wrapped bushes in the yard and arched over the front doorway. Every window had small wreaths identical to the larger on the front door. I quietly admired our hours of labor, and hoped they could appreciate it too.

Dad and Tara glanced at it for a second before noticing our old house. They stood with Mom in the street, noting how different our house looked. The door had been painted, and flower beds replaced with gravel and stone figures.

"What is that?" Tara finally asked, pointing to Matilda's sculpture in the yard. In the darkness, the tangle of metal looked sharp and dangerous.

"I think it's a clown," Dad said.

"If it's a clown, it's terrifying," Mom stepped back.

"Aren't they all?" Dad began to turn away.

"I thought it was a rocket ship," Tara said, "Did she put that in their yard as a prank?"

I made a point to arrive early to help with the last of the setup. Matilda had also told me that my family would make the house look like it had more people in it. That way no one would be deterred if they showed up and the place looked empty.

It helped a little. Previous years of Christmas parties brought a house full of guests. Every room was crowded with people. When we were kids it felt like hundreds had shown up. In reality, there might have been fifty people. That night, people came and went throughout the evening, but the total was close to twenty.

Matilda had made plans for just as many as before. Somehow, her estimates were incredibly low. The invitation said we were going until ten; the food was gone by eight. People began to trickle out after that.

A rather disappointed Matilda took a seat on the steps just after nine. I joined her with encouraging words of how great it really was and how much her parents would have liked it. Liam leaned on the banister and gave her a half-hearted smile.

"You did good, sis."

Unable to give up, Matilda tried again the following year. The day after Halloween she had her plans going. Food plans and invitations were doubled. Once again, Liam flew in.

My parents explained that they couldn't make it. Time had gotten away from them that year, and Christmas made them extra busy. Apparently almost everyone else had the same idea.

Seventeen people showed up, not counting the three of us. At 8:30pm the house was empty again. We stood around the dining room table and examined the massive pile of food that had been left behind.

Matilda picked up one of the numerous chocolate covered pretzel sticks and examined the red and green sprinkles we had placed there the night before. "Well working hard is stupid," she stated before smashing the treat against the table's edge.

In January she still had left overs. After that night, Matilda didn't try for a party again. Each year, she packed a bag and flew to wherever Liam was at the time. We had our own gift swap mid-December, usually accompanied by dinner and a sleep over in festive pajamas. Afterwards I traveled home to Mom and Dad. Christmases had moved from meticulous planning to keep traditions alive into going wherever our loved ones happened to be that year.

3 A SHOT TO THE CHEST

I'll never forget that Wednesday evening. Like any other Wednesday, I was meeting up with Matilda. She had texted me that afternoon and asked for her place instead of mine. The location always swapped back and forth between my apartment and her house, but we always drank wine and talked over magazines.

We had no time to hang out since our Monday morning coffee. That was the standard. After telling her to go to the doctor, the only communication we had was texting until I made it to her place with wine and a random magazine I had selected from a news stand that morning.

Bad events have a way of making you remember every tiny detail about a day that would have been completely normal otherwise. If you asked about any other Wednesday, or "Winesday" as we called it, I couldn't tell you what we drank or what we read or even what we talked about. But that day I remember arriving at the driveway, Cat was cleaning himself and had one leg stuck straight up in the air. At the sight of my car, he bolted behind the garage. The main floor of the house smelled like fresh laundry. A stack of paper plates was sitting on top of the microwave in the kitchen. The clock still hadn't been set on the oven after a power outage three weeks before. I searched the front room for my still missing pen.

That week a minimalist painting of a green leaf on yellow was leaning in the hallway. New paintings emerged and shuffled around quite often. A stack of three waited at the bottom of the basement stairs.

As was standard, I walked into her house without knocking, a bottle of moscato under my arm. The house was empty, meaning Matilda was downstairs. I parked the bottle in the kitchen and headed to the basement.

A soft roar filled the air. Behind a tangle of metal, was a leather body and mask. At my entrance, the torch was shut off. Matilda lifted the mask off her face.

"Sorry, I got distracted by an idea." She peeled off her welding armor and rested it all on a hook.

"How's your week going?" I asked as I took my usual seat. A stool sat in one corner of the basement, as far away from the worksite as one could sit without hitting a wall. If Matilda got into a creative kick or was cleaning up down there, I sat on the stool. In the basement, separated by space and metal, our conversations flowed just as normally as coffee at a café table on the street.

"Well, I've had better. I went to the doctor, and he said something was weird." Matilda picked up a piece of shrapnel and tossed it into a sturdy garbage bin. "So I went to another doctor. She ran tests and sent me to another doctor. My insurance really hates me right now, but they finally found out what that cough is."

I don't know what I expected, but it certainly wasn't what she said. Somehow, she smiled when she told me. Her mouth moved, but the world around me was silent. The sound of my own heart pounded in my years and my mouth went dry. Matilda laughed about something, she was still talking.

I consider myself pretty lucky because I've never been shot in the chest. I can only imagine it hurts like hell. Your back would be bruised from the hard fall backwards, but you wouldn't notice from the pain of the bullet and the struggle to catch your breath. A pool of blood would blossom around you, turning your fingers sticky as you gasp and choke. It would be complete hell.

I would rather be shot in the chest one hundred times than hear my friend tell me she has six months to live. But in life we don't get to pick our pain.

The basement was suddenly cold. I took in every part of Matilda's pale face as my conscious shut down. Just like any other day, her eyeliner was thick and pointed. Red lipstick showed no trace of smudge. The icy eyes that usually cut into me felt like calming whirlpools beckoning me to look in them and find my reflection. With no other words available, I found myself saying, "What?"

"It only makes sense considering my luck," she walked around the work table and towards me. "Probably better all the shit is happening to me instead of being spread around to other people."

She wasn't panicking. People are always supposed to panic and have dramatic stares out windows. That's what Hallmark movies always taught us. I wondered if I should scream, but realized analyzing the shock meant not screaming.

"How did this happen?"

She leaned against a sturdy table and shrugged casually. I felt like she was talking to me about buying a new car instead of the unimaginable.

"Apparently my heart has been shit my whole life, we never noticed, and now it's giving up."

"What are we going to do?"

"It's Wednesday. You brought wine right? I have new magazines upstairs." She passed me and headed up to the kitchen.

Suddenly I was aware I had legs and turned to follow her. In the kitchen she began opening the bottle I brought. Instinctively I got glasses.

"Are you okay?" I found myself asking.

"Well, no. I'm not much for this earth. But, come on, Tessie, don't freak out about this. I know it's bad, but I don't want to just spend six months crying and fighting. Everything is going to be okay." She slid a glass towards me.

I didn't care that she thought everything would be okay. I wanted to scream, I wanted to cry, and I wanted her to do it with me. Either I was too well trained to say no, or her calm demeanor kept me silent, but I just obeyed.

My mind began to search through options and obstacles. These things don't happen. I just had to think of the right way to fix this problem and Matilda would be fine. There were thousands of treatments, new experiments were happening every day. One of them or maybe even a few would work.

"Can't they give you a heart transplant or something?" I began asking.

"They could," Matilda sat down in the corner of the couch and picked up a magazine. "But a lot of people need hearts, and they don't just pass those out like free t-shirts."

"So you could get one?" I sat down near her, still holding my wine glass. I hadn't taken a sip yet.

"I'm on a list, yeah, but the chances that I could get one in time are a fraction of a percent." She flipped through a spring magazine about bridal gowns.

The world shook around me like a small tremor. I drank the whole glass dry and fell into the couch. My head fell back, pointing my face to the ceiling. Thoughts both big and small were flying through my head in every direction. I tried to grab one of them and focus enough to say anything. Bones shook inside of me.

Shutting my eyes didn't help. More solutions began piling up. None of them were feasible. For a moment, I tried shutting my eyes harder, hoping it would put me back in my bed to start the day over again. This version wasn't right.

I'll admit, for a single second I wondered if I could get a copy of everyone on that list. Then how hard would it be to track down everyone ahead of Matilda and kill them off. Or maybe we could murder enough bad people that also happened to be organ donors.

As soon as the thought came to my mind I kicked it away. The wine bottle sat on the coffee table in front of me. Even with my hands shaking I could fill the glass.

"Well, what sort of things do you want to do? We can get everything done on your bucket list."

"I didn't write one."

"Why not? That's like dying 101." I felt my muscles begin to ease. The tremor stopped.

"Why would I make a big ordeal about a list and slowly scratch things off of it like a ticking clock? I love my life the way it is, and I want to have as much of it as I can." She picked up a catalogue from a store we frequented and tossed it onto my lap. "Act normal and read a damn magazine."

I struggled to turn the pages and read, but nothing made it to my eyes. Everything began to feel numb. The swirl of questions in my mind faded and slipped away. I couldn't form a sentence. Luckily, Matilda finally spoke up.

"Liam is in Michigan. I basically had to tell him over the phone, but it might take a few days to get out of his current job. A person dropping everything for you when you're sick is bullshit, I told him to take his time getting in. No reason why he should ruin his job for me."

I hadn't thought of her brother. Someone else was going to suffer from Matilda's absence. There were a lot of things I hadn't thought of, and I attempted to form the right questions to get everything in order. I knew there was a lot to be done, but I couldn't figure out just what.

"Should we take a trip?" I asked.

"Maybe day trips here and there," Matilda replied, "but nothing is coming to mind. There's so much we do already."

"Don't you want to go to Europe or Hawaii or something?"

"Everyone goes to Europe," Matilda refilled her glass. "I don't want to fall into the white, dying girl stereotype. My life isn't *A Walk to Remember*."

Most of the evening was my futile attempts at questions. I discovered nothing for Matilda's desires of her final days. Anytime I thought clearly enough to ask something, she shrugged it off with a half-hearted comment.

The magazine in my lap remained on the same page. The only movement I found was in refilling my wine glass every few minutes. Soon the bottle was empty.

Eventually I found myself following Matilda into the kitchen. She retrieved ice cream and toppings from different places and began throwing them into a bowl.

"Want some?" She offered me the chocolate syrup bottle.

"No thanks, I'm good."

"The uptick is I can eat whatever the hell I want. No point in trying to stay healthy now if my heart is a bust. I'm going to have donuts for breakfast every day."

We returned to the couch. The magazine I had before remained on the table.

"Wow it's getting late," Matilda noted. "Did you want to stay over? Or do you need to get home?"

Time began to exist again. I had been at her house for a few hours at that point.

"I should go home," I found myself standing up.

"I'll text you," Matilda called from her spot on the couch.

Just like that she sent me away. I wandered towards my car. She acted like nothing had happened. Life was supposed to keep going on like normal without this ticking bomb that could go off at any second.

Waiting for something bad to happen is like sitting in the chair at the dentist. You're stuck in a limbo that keeps you on edge. That filling is coming, but you don't know when. You distract yourself, and try not to think about all the pain ahead, but every small hum makes you jump. You're left to quiver in the slightly reclined chair. Their attempt to make you comfortable somehow making everything worse as you have nothing to do but wait.

After the atomic bomb Wednesday, Thursday I was in a complete, constant shell shock. Any time my phone lit up I jumped to answer it. What really shook me up the most was Matilda staying calm during everything.

I went into work looking like I had a rough hangover. It wasn't until the elevator I realized I hadn't touched my hair all morning. Despite the sun, I had on a trench coat that was usually kept for rainy days.

The doors opened to reveal everyone was already working. I was late.

Intertwining green, vines grew through the word, "Osiris," and turned into colorful plants along the top. The busy logo was everyone's first impression when they walked in. In its spot above the front desk it reminded everyone this was a company no one had heard of.

The receptionist gave me a usual greeting. I just smiled and returned it while taking my sunglasses off.

My supervisor's office was between the front door and my own space. Making my back as straight as possible, I rushed past at impressive pace for pointed flats. Glen still saw me. In a few moments, the portly man was in my doorway. The Bugs Bunny on his tie matched his own, toothy smile.

"Hey, Tess." I reviled his nickname, but didn't have the heart to tell him. That would be like telling a dog he can't go for a walk after he gets excited. After three years I had grown used to Tess when I was in the workplace.

"How's it going this morning?" Glen crumpled the paper wrapper from his hash brown and tossed it into my waste basket.

"I'm- I'll be okay. Just a lot is happening right now." The H made my voice crack. I checked my desk drawer; for the millionth time my engraved pen wasn't there. "I won't let it affect my work. Sorry to be late."

"Need to talk?" With four kids, three about my age, and ten grandkids, Glen had a knack for counselling his employees. I swear, once I came in and he was playing a game of catch with one of my coworkers.

With a heavy sigh I nodded. He closed the door and sat down.

Two years before, our company let us bring a plus one to the Christmas party. Still wanting to give a good impression and having no husband or boyfriend to speak of, I brought Matilda. All she had to do was comment the light up tree on Glen's tie and they hit it off.

Before the night was over, they were singing *Empire State of Mind* on karaoke. I stood in the back with Glen's wife Stella as we recorded it. Glen had insisted on singing Alicia Keys' part. Both of them stood on top of the reception desk, towering over the small crowd of fans. Matilda had forced her hair into an elegant but large bun. Christmas tree earrings matched Glen's tie. He spent the whole song pressing the button to keep it flashing.

"Next year's card!" Stella had to shout at me over Matilda's rapping. Their duet helped me get my promotion.

That memory felt so far away from my office that morning. I glanced out the window at the desk they stood on. Glen's tie was flashing, Matilda was dancing, and they both were laughing. I turned to see Glen's face broken.

"Oh god, Tess," he seemed a loss for words.

"I don't know what her plan is, but I might need to take a couple days here and there." My jaw began to tremble, but I fought to remain straight faced.

"Of course, whatever you need." He gave an understanding nod that felt like a hug. "You do whatever you need to help our Tildy."

"Thanks. Thank you." I wiped one eye just as a tear tried to escape.

He opened his wallet and pulled out a ten.

"Take a few minutes. Get yourself one of those fluffy drinks at the Starbuck down the street." His hand stretched across my desk.

"Thank you, but I really need to get started."

"No," Glen was blunt, "I'm not telling you as a boss, I'm ordering you as a friend. Take twenty minutes and get some comfort food."

"Thank you." I stood up and reached for my jacket.

"Leave that. It's seventy outside."

Glen didn't just comfort, he was stern enough to get you back on track and moving. I walked down the sidewalk, thankful for a substitute grandpa. So far, he was the only one who seemed to understand a crisis was happening.

"Oh shit," I muttered. I hadn't even told my mother yet. I checked my phone.

I couldn't call her in the morning. That would ruin her day. By the time I made it through the Starbucks door, my thoughts were collected. It was Thursday. I called my family every Thursday night. It would be best to tell her then right? Right.

My hands were both in front of me, one with my phone the other still clutching the ten. Matilda texted me and I almost jumped at the sound of the familiar bell.

Want to go to lunch at that place on 8th with the salads and the Paninis?

It was so casual, like nothing had happened. I responded, and plans were made.

A chocolatey, foamy, extra-large drink cooling my hand, I returned to our floor. Everyone's mood had changed. Gossip didn't exactly spread like wildfire. It was more like it rushed through the office like salmon swimming upstream. The experience began at reception.

"Hey, Tessie," he cooed, "Doing okay?"

"Yeah, I'm all right. Thanks."

Everyone I walked past had a sympathetic smile. Some tried to talk to me. I felt like a kid whose parents just announced they were getting a divorce. One person literally told me it wasn't my fault. I gave all of them a smile and thank you.

My pen wasn't in the side drawers of my desk. I slammed them closed in frustration.

I was never so thankful for an office. The window didn't help. Anyone who walked by it looked in and smiled at me. Eventually I gave my computer screen all of my attention. The morning inched by as I fought to ignore everyone watching me like it was the sadness zoo.

Lunch was a welcome relief. I power walked to the little bistro and arrived just as Matilda did. Without saying anything, I just hugged her.

"Tessie, please don't be weird about this," she said from my grip.

"I'm not trying to."

"What happened on your Forever show?"

"*Eternity*," I corrected. "They've made it to World War II."

I did my best to be normal over lunch. It was difficult. When someone tells you to "act normal" you forget any preconceived notion of what your normal is. You try too hard to relax or be cool, and end up looking like a moron, which is exactly how I looked.

My body kept slouching into the chair. I would catch myself and sit up straight again, just to have my body slip back into a slouch. Each time my feet bumped Matilda's legs.

"Okay, fine." she finally broke it up. "You may have one day to be weird about this. Then you're done." She opened her purse and slid a tissue and an eyeliner pencil across the table.

"Thanks." I didn't feel like crying. I really just wanted a drink.

Matilda examined her sandwich in her hands. "Paninis are just fancy grilled cheese. They're grilled cheese that's had work done. They're so pretentious."

"Do you remember that cruise we took right after your parents died?"

Matilda gave me an irritated look. "No. You'll have to be more specific. Which set of parents?"

"I was just thinking it was a lot of fun. You punched that asshole, and we had like a thousand awesome pictures." I picked up my sandwich and tried it.

"It was a lot of fun," she agreed. "You carried all my crap around each day."

"We should go again," I tried my first line.

"Eh, maybe. I enjoyed it, but I don't think I'll want to go again. Getting my butt pinched by another asshole isn't a high priority." She bit into the sandwich and a long string of cheese followed her.

"Then what are your priorities?" The second attempt to get her talking was less inconspicuous.

"To eat this panini," she said with her mouth full.

"Not right now. I mean like, you know." I nibbled at a second bite. Sometimes if I acted like a mouse she gave in, but melted cheese hung from my mouth in a mess. I looked like a bigger moron.

"To eat this panini." She finished the last bite and took a big swallow of her sugary drink.

I wasn't going to get the answer I wanted over lunch. Instead of trying again, I finished my sandwich and tried a different conversation.

"I had to tell Glen this morning. He was cool about it."

"Aw. I love that guy." Matilda pulled a brownie over and started in with a fork. "I should go in and say hi sometime."

"I got permission to take a few days where I need it here and there. So if you do think of something from a bucket list, let me know."

She paused, only her eyes turned up to me. Sharp blue cut me in half. Her disposal and control of my time got the attention I had wanted.

"So if I need you some afternoon to just eat an entire sheet cake, you'll drop everything and come over?" The brownie was abandoned.

"Yes."

A smile grew across her face. "This is the best gift ever."

I felt obligated to stay late at work. Getting extra things done then was like clearing up the time for taking afternoons or days in the coming months. By the time I was in my apartment, I knew Mom and Dad would have finished dinner.

White walls and wood floors felt extra quiet. Usual boards inside the door didn't creak when I stepped on them. The sun was still up, but everything was shadows and ghostly.

My dinner was three glasses of brandy. After the first one I called home.

"Hello?" Tara's soft voice answered.

"Wow, you know how to use a landline?"

"Well we've been discussing them in history class this week." Tara fired back, unfazed. "I think your picture is my textbook beside a dinosaur."

We chatted a moment before I asked, "Can I talk to Mom?"

"I don't know, can you?"

"Don't sass me, Fletcher."

I considered getting my second glass as the phone was passed off.

"Hi, honey." My mother's voice sounded like a lullaby. There was no stopping the sting in my eyes.

"I'm fine, but something's happened," I said.

"Tessie, what's wrong?"

Mom was always an unfaltering stronghold in a storm. Even if the world were falling apart, I know I would be okay if I could just be with my mom. When Mr. and Mrs. Day passed, she was on the next flight in. Matilda and Liam were saved by her phone calls and detailed planning. Arrangements were made without a hitch. We all cried in her arms. Everything was kept in order and went smoothly with Mom running it. She had a way of saying what was needed, but also keeping silent when that was best.

In a few quick minutes I had the news out. She stayed quiet for a moment before giving a simple, "Honey, I'm so sorry."

I fumbled around a few words before hanging up. I wasn't in the mood for more talking. Instead I had drink number two. The couch sucked me in, and I didn't move. Every sip of brandy was a burn in my chest. Sip after sip made the burn grow. I could feel it spreading into my stomach and up in my neck. Soon it would catch my whole body up and I would melt away.

After a few minutes, Tara sent me a text that read, *I love you*. Mom must have shared with her and Dad.

Thanks. I love you too.

The rest of my night was quiet. I couldn't make myself turn on the TV or read or even shower. Glass two became glass three. The burn in my chest lingered like a purr. Nothing made it grow or diminish no matter how many sips I took.

All I could do was wait for the next day.

Friday was an easier day than Thursday. I managed to get to work on time and not look like a mess. Seconds after I sat down at my desk, Glen came to my door. That day his tie was a palm tree.

"Stella made these," he said, setting plastic wrapped cookies on my desk. "She thought you could use them."

"Tell her thanks for me," I smiled at him. "And Matilda, she'll probably eat the most."

He slipped out with his big, toothy smile.

Matilda and I had a long standing plan of hanging out on Fridays. Activities ranged from going out and doing any sort of girl thing to staying on one of our couches and watching TV until we fell asleep. Plenty of nights were spent in downtown areas or restaurants, but movies at home were the most common occurrence. Usually it was the same movie.

The love affair we had with *Pride and Prejudice* felt as old as time itself. Like any middle school girl, Matilda and I read the book and loved it. When the film was released we saw it in theaters no less than three times. This was quite an accomplishment when neither of us could drive yet.

Within a few months we each had a copy of the DVD. Those first few weeks were just a trade back and forth of whose house we sat in to watch it. Before High School was done, we needed new copies from the scratches and wear on ours.

Together we had memorized most of the lines without even trying. Instead of quoting them while watching it, we sang along to the piano solos. "Da da da da dadadda" would fill the room. Mr. Darcy's hand flinched and our reaction was always a quick gasp. Sometimes when we were apart, and not watching anything, we even texted quotes back and forth.

Texting for the day was over everything but what to do that night. We talked about dogs and dresses. She complained about work. I promised her some of the cookies. Our conversations were the kind that never stopped. They just evolved to a new subject several times in a day. Somehow we still got work done.

After work I found myself changing clothes at home and going straight to Matilda's place. I turned onto the block and had to park in the street. My usual spot in the driveway was taken up by a gray Prius. Liam had arrived.

Growing up, Liam didn't hang out with us. He was just around sometimes. Like Tara, he ran with his own friends. Unless the subject was the size of Matilda's room, they weren't quarrelsome siblings.

Cookies with me, I headed up the sidewalk. The door opened before I could walk in as usual.

"Hey, Tessie!" a gray hoodie hugged me.

When you are a travelling nurse, or any nurse, tired becomes a state of being, and coffee exists in your diet more than water. Liam's eyes always had a little bit of a sleepy glaze, but like Matilda they were a shade of blue that split your body in half. Also like his sister, his hair was the same shade as fresh asphalt. Lucky for him, his skin realized the sun existed. Hospitals kept him from being tan, but he wasn't a ghost. He towered above me like perpetual adoptive brother.

Any understanding of personal space is lost after handling patients. We had zero contact over the past few years, and anything before then was simple pleasantries. Yet there we stood, in a long embrace.

"How have you been?" He asked, welcoming me inside.

"Great. Working. How's life on the road?"

Five years older, Liam finished college before I even started. In the time after, he had lived in Maine, Texas, Portland, and Miami. Every year Matilda flew out to visit him once or twice, but he never came in. Neither of us said it, but he had come in the second Matilda delivered her news to him. Based on his smell, he hadn't even stopped to shower. Despite Matilda's orders, Liam did drop everything.

"Can't complain. Always meeting new people and seeing other places. Pull a lot of weird stuff out of stranger's assholes."

"COOKIES!" Matilda appeared and took the plate. The power of the chocolate chips lead us into the living room. "Stop talking about butts. It's your only cool story and you've worn it out. Tessie has an important job in the business world doing… a thing."

"I'm director of new media and product integration," I explained, taking a seat on the white, leather sectional. It spread across most of the room, and had enough space for the three of us to lay back therapy style without invading feet or bumping heads.

"Whatever the hell that job is," Matilda started cookie number two.

"I keep our social media pages up to date. We have a photographer on retainer who visits the local farm for our company and sends me a shit ton of pictures. All year long I'm sorting through them and posting them and writing our blog now and then."

"So, you're paid to Facebook?" he asked.

"Pretty much," I shrugged.

"I could Facebook about superfood," Matilda had sunk into her corner of the couch.

"Superfoods aren't real," I explained. "I mean, it's my job to call them that. It's really just healthy food. But I get to do it from my own office."

"Well that's as grown up as you can get," Liam took a cookie from the plate.

Matilda playfully tapped his hand, "Hey, those are my cookies."

"No they're not. They're Tessie's cookies, she brought them." Liam turned to me, giving me all the power, and asked, "May I please have a cookie?"

"Sure, they're for everybody."

He took an extra two from the plate. Matilda turned to me in fake irritation.

"So besides taking stuff out of butts, what do you do?" I asked, trying my first cookie.

Liam leaned back on the couch. The house hadn't seen him in years, but it was like he had always been there. One hand ran across his head, rouge strands falling right back into shape.

No doubt Liam's hair was just as stubborn as Matilda's, but he never grew it out long enough to know for certain. It has a way of being aggressively straight in one particular direction: to the left. His lack of attention to styling it had always existed.

"I pick up people and move them from one bed to another, I give shots, I give medicine, I have seen more than enough naked bodies, and sometimes I get to do something cool like help reattach a finger."

"Do they ever have fun stories about how they came off?" my gory question grabbed Matilda's attention.

"No, it's usually just an idiot with a buzz saw."

We laughed, Matilda choked and coughed.

Instantly, Liam had a hand on her back. The other began feeling her pulse. He had gone from brother to nurse. I froze on the couch. Unsure of how to help, I just returned a half-eaten cookie to the plate.

Questions flew out of Liam like machine gun fire. Frustrated, Matilda shoved him aside and slipped into the kitchen. In a second she was sipping on water and glaring at us.

"It was a crumb, dumbass. I'm not going to die like that."

"I'm sorry I cared about you," his voice was blunt. "I'll never do it again."

Liam was exactly what Matilda needed in the dark days. Emergencies and medical attention were second nature, and he could deliver any care she needed. Equally as helpful, any time Matilda shelled out comments like a dick, Liam would dick right back.

4 7) PEPPERSBURG SUMMER CARNIVAL

Everyone had been called into the conference room for a meeting. Luckily, I had remembered to check my email when I brushed my teeth that morning. The company had hired a new Vice President for the north east division, and she was stopping by our offices. Extra effort was put into my attire. In my chair at the table, I forced myself to sit up straight and smile.

That day, Glen was wearing a Muppet tie. He introduced our new supervisor with his usual, excited demeanor. She half smiled politely and glanced down at Kermit the frog strumming a banjo.

"So here she is, our own Amelia Caty," Glen clapped alone as he moved to the side.

While a standard greeting and questions were exchanged, I let myself wander. Matilda had still behaved the same as always. My prodding for any big events she wanted to complete remained unsuccessful. Our regular, week schedule was held up with coffee mornings, lunches, and weekend nights. Occasionally, Liam joined us.

He had found a place in a local hospital. Under the circumstances of his time in town, they were keeping him there as long as needed. His schedule was always changing, but he joined us when he could. Besides his on and off presence, the only other change to our routine was how often we spent together.

Extra evenings were added to our regular hangouts of the week. Whenever Matilda wanted to do something else, she used dying as a trump card to make it happen. It worked the night before when she asked me to take her to the carnival that weekend.

"This is Tessie Fletcher," I jumped back to reality at the sound of my name. Glen was introducing me. "She's our director of new media and product integration."

"Hi," I waved awkwardly.

Amelia smiled and waved back. Her blonde, highlights wrapped into perfect curls. A multitude of them lay on her blazer collar, but didn't seem to move as she walked and shook hands with everyone.

We were excused and I returned to my office. A text from Matilda was waiting on the phone I had abandoned at my desk. Before I could read it, there was a knock at my door.

Amelia stood in the doorway.

"May I come in?"

"Please," I offered her a chair. She glided to it like a hovering ghost. I took a seat at my desk, unsure of how to speak to the new superior.

"I went through some of your work recently," she began. "I had no idea produce could be that fun."

I relaxed slightly. Tweeting about carrots and writing interesting posts around a single photo of organic asparagus had been a challenge.

"Thank you," I finally remembered to answer.

"I honestly laughed at the picture of the farm in the snow," Amelia smiled.

That winter, one of our farmers sent me an image of the fields covered by a thin layer of snow. The sun was setting, giving everything a soft, golden glow. Open fields, trees, and a barn were tucked in for hibernation. So I captioned it, "Shhhh, the farm is sleeping."

It got more hits than anything we had posted before.

"You stepped into this new position and just ran with it," she said.

"Thank you," I stammered.

"Considering your age that's rather impressive, even with a new spot like this." Her eyes glared into mine. I could feel her studying every curve of my face, trying to figure me out.

"Thank you."

"I've been looking over the work of different branches and this one really sticks out. A lot of it comes from the things you have done. You're clever, and that's working."

She looked she like already knew everything about me. I squirmed in my chair. Putting filters on pictures of vegetables for a few hundred strangers to see was easy. Your boss looking at it was like a teacher standing over your desk as you took a test.

"Thank you," I said again, forcing myself to hold still. "I try to do my best, but we have a great group here. Without pictures my job wouldn't happen."

"It shows. I can tell that you have a lot of potential."

"You're too kind, Ms. Caty. I just do what I'm supposed to do."

"Please, I am Amelia," Her smile began to feel real. "But with the effort your past projects have shown, you could go a long way. If you don't mind me asking, what do you want from this career?"

I held my tongue, searching for the right answer. Most of my time in college and after had been finding something I mildly enjoyed and then doing it enough to live comfortably. I never would have said I had a passion for my work; it was fun and paid the bills. But moving up never sounded like a bad idea.

"Honestly, I'm not entirely sure," was the best answer I could manage.

Amelia nodded. She found my response satisfactory.

"Well, Glen is just a couple years from retirement. And the corporate offices almost always promote from positions like his. Keep doing what you're doing and I wouldn't mind giving you a leg up."

"Thank you," For the first time in a few weeks life outside of the next six months existed again. I imagined moving around to different branches in a pantsuit like Amelia, or sitting behind Glen's desk and leading the people I knew.

She stood up and passed a card over. "I'm looking forward to our time together."

Again I thanked her. "I'm excited too."

My imagination carried me through the rest of the day at work. I saw myself settling into a home of my own, affording it with taking on Glen's position when he retired. The other idea was a corporate position in New York. Day dreams lead me back and forth between thoughts of possible futures. The work of the morning danced around the desk. New purpose drove me to make every small piece perfect.

By eleven, I remembered my weekend plans. Reality drew me back to the pressing matters. Specifically, I was glued to the one waiting at the end of six months. At noon I left for the day.

Per Matilda's request, we made a pilgrimage two towns over for the legendary summer carnival. As a child, Matilda visited almost regularly with her family. Venturing through the illuminous wonderland for an evening marked the start of summer break.

I didn't need to go home early, but I did. Matilda was staying over for the night, and she was ready to start a traditional slumber party as soon as I could be there. We still had sleep overs, because they were fun.

Late into the night were up giggling about anything. We talked about the carnival; Matilda complained about work, I didn't say anything about my new boss or the career she wanted to help me with.

"I wish they had a weight guesser," Matilda leaned into her pillow and stared at the ceiling. "You always see those on tv, but never in real life."

"There must be a shortage in the carnival barker career."

Silence filled the room. My mind slipped to work. For a moment I let myself think about the type of future Amelia had mentioned, and then I pushed it away. It didn't feel fair to consider something Matilda couldn't have. I shouldn't fantasize about a fancy life when she had the much bigger problem of dying.

I was letting her by with more here and there. The next morning she didn't finish her coffee during breakfast. Out of habit, she put the mug in the microwave and left for the shower.

Matilda never finished coffee at my place. A third would be left sitting in the bottom of the mug, and she would stick it in the microwave to come back to later. Only, she never did. A day or two later, after she'd gone home, I'd find an old, gross cup of coffee still in my microwave. A couple months before, I had nagged her about it.

"Just dump it out, you're not going to drink it," I had been a little blunt.

"No," she said, still placing the cup inside. "That's wasteful."

"It's not any more wasteful than me dumping it out in two days," I explained. "If you want more coffee later we can just make more."

"Let me shower and I'll come back for the rest. I'll warm it up."

"You say that, but you never do."

"Well, today is a new day, and I will finish this coffee."

She didn't finish it. Like every other time we both forgot. It didn't really matter that she left it behind. I just didn't want to mess with a cold cup of coffee later.

That morning as we got ready to drive to Peppersburg Matilda put away the unfinished cup. I didn't say anything. We had never fought over it or anything serious. I just felt obligated to let her do anything she wanted. She deserved more wherever I could give it considering how much she was losing.

Having fun like we were kids again was something that did matter. I had joined the Days at the carnival once. Details were a bit of a blur, but I remembered the intoxicating fun that came from every sense being overloaded from the moment you stepped foot on the grounds.

Walking through the front arch as adults felt just as magical. By mid-afternoon, the crowd was small, but the tents, food trucks, and rides still buzzed with life.

"That funnel cake is calling my name," Matilda sighed.

"Tickets first," I steered her towards the booth.

Keeping with tradition, rides still required small paper tickets. The excitement level decided the range. Lower level rides cost you one ticket, while the most exciting asked for five. In total, there may have been fifteen rides. Matilda bought one hundred and ten tickets.

Late spring gave us a warm day. The sun flooded the fairgrounds with light. Clouds seemed nervous to appear. The air had the kind of warm that made you comfortable outside, but you still wanted to drink lemonade and stand in the given spots of shade.

Matilda's hair was forced into a bun above her head. Her single pair of sunglasses appeared. Over each lens the pink frames took the shape of the eyes, nose, and ears of a bear. Claiming them to be the best sunglasses in existence, Matilda wore only the pink bears for years while I worked through dozens of pairs of aviators.

Bears adorned and flannel shirt tied around her waist, Matilda glided to the funnel cake stand. A roll of purple, paper tickets were wrapped on her arm like a bracelet.

That afternoon I followed Matilda like a puppy through the maze of canvas tents and chipped paint on metal. Still early in the season, the grass in the walkways was thick and squishy under our steps.

A daytime view of the carnival would seem a bit lackluster. Under harsh sunlight, the small imperfections of dirt and rust were amplified to ugly looks. A veteran of the Peppersburg Summer Carnival knew to arrive just as dusk began to settle in.

New signs stuck out every few feet. While the colors were the same, years of ware hadn't brought the same faded shade. It was impossible to miss that they wanted you to download the app specifically for the carnival. I reread the same notice upwards of thirty times.

Our hours passed like the chorus of a country song. My hair warmed up under the sun. Lipstick remained flawless despite cotton candy, funnel cake, and a myriad of other messy food consumed by Matilda.

After spinning rides and petting goats and ponies, I asked Matilda if we were riding the ferris wheel. Sitting in the center of the grounds, it towered above the rest of the carnival. It was the beacon of the fair, and logo printed on every shirt and hat. For the town of Peppersburg, it was an obelisk exclusive to the summer months.

"Oh no, Tessie," she instructed. "The ferris wheel is a no go until dark. I'm not letting you make the rookie mistake of riding the ferris wheel while the sun is still up. Now come on, we haven't gone to the cow tent yet."

Despite thousands of descriptions and retellings of the summer lights, I wasn't ready for the magic of them myself. A soft daze seemed to fall on us as new wonder broke through the fair. The same, hot metal world we had been wandering through all day was a brand new place after nightfall.

When the sun began to set, a switch was flipped and a thousand lights flickered on together. Walking in the middle of them, anyone could see as clearly as in the afternoon sun. Yellows, reds, and blues bordered stands and rides. The illumination completely reversed the look and feel. Visitors were taken from an open lot of sharp metal objects to a magical meadow full of sweet smells and sounds haloed in gold. First entrance would force anyone to just wander through in amazement.

"I'm only eating junk food tonight," Matilda declared, smothering a corn dog in ketchup.

"You say that like there's a time you eat healthy food." I scolded, but added just as much ketchup to mine.

"It's not my fault I'm dying. I'm going to enjoy this time and eat whatever the hell I want."

For a moment I imagined a list of nutrition information on all the food we'd had so far. No doubt we'd had several days' worth of sugar. I thought about food journaling and a tracker to match what you needed on a daily basis based on body weight. It wasn't something that I would ever want to do, but healthy people that followed the Osiris Instagram would.

In the colorful maze of attraction and green grass I felt my mind drifting to the future. As much as I struggled to remain present with the laughter and sugar, my imagination refused to be shackled. Thankfully, my lips listened and I kept the subject quiet.

My side of it, that is.

Like an unattended child, Matilda moved through the fair deciding what to do on a whim. Each decision of where to go next was executed the instant her mind thought of it. The day felt like happy chaos.

During my time with Matilda I could hear a rapidly ticking clock telling me the days were numbered and zipping past me. While I saw myself marching into new position and taking pay raises, I could see a cloud over each vision. I knew realization would come later of events and adventures we missed because we didn't plan for them. I saw myself in the future wishing we had done more in the time we had, and wishing Matilda realized it then.

I wanted to do everything possible as the time drifted by. Internally, I listed off things I wanted to see with her: mountains, cities, quaint bakeries on lazy afternoons. Simultaneously visions crept up of the future I could have. My mind wadded up the images and threw them away. This constant pull between my future, Matilda's short one, and desire to enjoy the hours we had together was ripping my mind apart. I silently struggled to align thoughts and focus on present matters.

No struggle like that existed in Matilda's head. The moment an idea was born she was putting it into action. There was no structure and my irritation was growing.

Matilda's smile remained unbroken. Pink bears had moved to the top of her head. Not wanting to tarnish the evening, I did my best to bring up ideas without drawing attention to them.

"Having fun?" she asked.

"Yeah!" I said. "Sorry, is my resting bitch face out?"

"A little, you might need more sugar."

"I'm good," I assured her. "I just want you to have fun."

We turned down an unexplored stretch of tents. Cheap games lured Matilda in, and soon we were in line for skee ball.

"I know you don't want like a bucket list," I struggled for the right words, "but do you have like a hit list?"

"Of people to kill? Not really. I feel like I've almost reached nirvana. Grudges and stuff don't feel like they matter anymore."

"That's very profound of you," I said. "But I mean something like a list of stuff you'd want to do."

"No. I don't really have one. I just want to enjoy the moment, you know? Be present. That's what all those moms post about doing."

Someone handed us weighted balls and the discussion was over for the time. I wasn't done. Dusk began to encircle the grounds. I asked if we should get in line for the ferris wheel, but Matilda insisted we wait for the lights to turn on.

Another tent drew us in. This time, a gentleman not much older than us was taking on a true carnival barker role. He and another man were passing out paper cups with red soda. A plastic banner above them advertised the homemade soda as "Memaw Maggie's Miracle Mix."

"Ugh. That looks horrible," Matilda nodded to the rough font.

She handed off cash and asked for two cups.

"Cures everything from hangovers to broken hearts," the barker declared as he passed our order over.

"I'll get back to you in a few months on that 'everything' bit," Matilda replied. He missed her comment. I heard it, and felt it like a pinch on my heart.

We moved aside to taste it and inspect glass bottles of the soda available for purchase. The same image from the banner was also on all of them. Matilda made her disgust clear.

"They need design help. Not from me, but they need it." She took a sip. "It's no Cherry Life, but it's kind of tasty"

Soon we were standing together in the longest line of the trip. Yet you hardly noticed. The same intoxication came over everyone with the lights. Time passed differently in the glow of this magical evening.

A clunk and squeal of old bolts invited us to our seats. We took them, our hips squeezed together on a thin, black cushion. In an instant we were raised up a few feet, and jolted to another stop as more adventurers were loaded into the cup behind us.

"This is only slightly worrying me," I confessed as we bounced upwards again.

"Oh ignore it. Soon we'll be moving smoothly and you can see the lights from-" Matilda's words were cut short by another jolted burst upwards. We both winced. "You feel the bounces a lot more as an adult."

After just a few more quick shakes, the ride was loaded and we began to glide smoothly. She was right, the clicks and whirs faded away as we rose up and saw the dazzle of the carnival laid out below us. From above, the rows of tents and trucks were clearer. Different colors showing the sections and options showed us blues for deep fried food and reds and pinks for games.

The sit made it to the top of the ride. Our amazement ended as everything stopped. The seat rocked freely, and I glanced around at others doing the same.

"The ride isn't supposed to be that short," Matilda said.

We each leaned over my side of the seat. Guests still in line below were backing up and looking towards us. All of them worried for our sakes, yet relieved to be on the ground. Two people who looked like they were in charge of things rushed to the operation controls.

"Oh shit," Matilda moaned.

"At least we're near the top. We can see everything." I pushed fear from my mind, but my voice betrayed me and cracked.

"We're also as far from the ground as we can be," Matilda said.

Together we leaned forward enough to catch sight of the ground. A mass tangle of thin metal bars and confused heads lay below us. We both snapped back up.

"I don't think anything is broken. The lights are off. It's probably just a power outage." I glanced at the still glowing lights coming from every other place around us. "A power outage that is only happening to the two hundred foot tall attraction we are currently strapped into."

"I don't think it's that high. Maybe it's just one fifty," Matilda leaned over her side of the seat. She caught herself and quickly sat back up. "We can go with two hundred that sounds right."

Guests were being ushered away from the line at the bottom. More employees, higher ups was our guess, were moving in. They gathered in a small group at the base.

"Well this is great," Matilda stated. "I don't even get six months. A dumbass carny mistake is what's going to kill me."

"That doesn't bother you?" I heard myself say.

"Well, I guess a little, but I was trying to make a joke," Matilda added a laugh at the end.

"So you're saying if we died right now there's nothing you'll regret not doing?" I was getting louder.

"What are you talking about?" Matilda's volume matched mine, and she turned her body to face me. In the close seat, she couldn't turn far.

"You're not doing enough, and you're going to regret it."

Matilda's eyes rolled and she sighed, "I won't be able to regret much, considering I'll be dead."

"God, why are you still joking about this?" I snapped.

"Why can't you?"

"Why can't you make a list of things for us to do?" I slapped my palm against the safety bar on each word. Several shrill clangs came with it; not exactly safe.

"I already told you," Matilda growled, her teeth set together. "I don't want a check list that I keep scratching off as I get closer to... it."

I took a deep breath, but my words still came out in a lecture. "We don't have a lot of time together. I don't want to waste a second of it because we didn't plan anything."

With a huff, Matilda dropped her sunglasses over her eyes and leaned back into the seat. I kept my face on her, gripping the bar between my fists. After a moment I leaned back into the seat, my arms crossed, and gazed in the opposite direction. I didn't want anyone seeing the sting in my eyes.

"I just think if your parents were here,"

"Don't talk about that," she cut me off with a snap. The early summer night grew cold as silence fell between us.

I bit my lip and gulped. Tears pushed to escape my eyes, but I wouldn't let them.

"I don't get why you don't want to talk about this."

"Because I don't," her voice broke over the words. "Can' you just leave it alone? Shit, stop controlling things. You can be so damn bossy."

I grunted; then bit my tongue. I felt the cut of her words and wanted to fire back with evidence against her being the bossy one or the bitch. I didn't say any of it. As the words formed together in my head, another part of me, calm and thinking of the future, stopped them. Matilda wasn't a bitch. I was, and I was mad.

Once again a future Tessie took hold of my thoughts. This future version of me didn't regret adventures to mountains or Europe or afternoons in a bakery, but instead regretted fighting with Matilda on one of our last outings together. I knew I didn't want to be her.

"I'm sorry," I began. "You may not care if you miss something, but I do, because I'm the one who has to live with it when you're gone."

Matilda ran a finger under her eye. Pink bears hid the silent tears she let escape.

"Tessie, this is my end. After this, my time is up and I never see you again." Her voice had grown hoarse in the struggle not to cry. "I don't want to fight. When Mom and Dad died it was a shock. I would give anything to have just one more day with them; just to hug them again."

Her sunglasses returned to her head, and she rubbed her eyes. I looked down at my lap and folded my hands together, pretending not to see the tear that rolled down her white cheek.

"I don't miss big trips with them," her voice came back and she continued. "I miss just being around them every day. We could die at any moment, but I have the pleasure and gift of these months. So I am going to do whatever the hell I want and spend as much time as I can with you and my brother. If I want small adventures on a whim, then that's what I'm going to do. But if I want to sit on the couch and watch TV all day then I'm going to do that."

"Okay," I whispered. Adventures and trips all faded in my mind. All I wanted was to be with Matilda. I wanted to sit on the couch, ride together in the car, and drink wine on the patio with her and Cat.

"I'm sorry I snapped," her voice began to break again. "I'm just so tired"

"I'm sorry I was so controlling," I said. "I love you."

"I love you too. I couldn't do this without you here."

"The six months or the broken ferris wheel?" I asked with a smile. It made her chuckle.

"Both."

We sat in silence for a moment, taking in the lights from our sky seat. Even though the ferris wheel broke down, the rest of the carnival milled on. People wandered through the maze. Only a few of them cast glances our way.

"It really is beautiful from up here." I said. "You were right to have us wait."

"At least we get to enjoy the view a little longer."

Something below us began to sputter. It was joined by a hum and our seat began to move. Others on the ride clapped softly as the lights flickered on. In a few feet we slowed to a stop, and once again began bouncing downwards as seats were unloaded one at a time.

The two of us remained silent. We gazed over the view of the lights, trying to enjoy every second of the view. All too soon they grew closer, the spectacle of their entirety diminished by our closeness. The bar was raised and we were unloaded. Our time was done.

A few employees apologized to us, and handed off coupons as we walked past them. My hands were filled with free ride tickets, game coupons, and discounts on more deep fried food. I flipped through the different options. Our lives must not have been in much danger if we could be bought with half off corn dogs.

"Want to use these?" I held them up for Matilda to inspect.

"Maybe," she sighed. "We can just walk and enjoy the night. If we see something we want, we'll get it."

We linked arms and made our way into the glow. Matilda grew quieter and slower as her fatigue began to set in. Yet she still found enough strength to give sassy comments to bland signs and point out cute men that passed us. Lights kept the world in a soft glow, making the entire night feel like a happy dream.

I don't think anyone on earth can really imagine heaven accurately. To me, it would be that night in Peppersburg. A navy blue sky softened by the glow of a thousand twinkling lights, and every person around us slightly out of focus as we migrate through the tangle of distraction. All of it falls into a never ending repeat of candy, laughter, games, and Matilda's arm hooked to mine.

5 11) THE BEACH

June had arrived. Mornings were warm enough to not bother with a cardigan. Walks on lunch breaks to nearby restaurants were happening every day. The summer sun warming the top of your head always makes things feel better. Matilda used to talk about her brain being warm enough to think when her hair got hot.

Feelings of infinite possibility roll in with nightfall. Cooler air falls down from starry skies. Matilda and I would sit at the glass table on her side patio and talk for hours. Each night, Cat would steadily creep closer to the patio, and watch us from its edge. He would wait, consider approaching us, and change his mind.

Everything felt open and free and sweet. Sometimes we even forgot about what was ahead of us in a few short months. Nothing existed but our words and the a few stars.

Since I was a teenager with a part time job, working in the summer was hard. Sitting at my desk that summer as an adult was worse. My legs felt suffocated in the pencil skirt and flats. Every few minutes I spun in my chair to look at the bright day trapped outside my window.

Recently, Matilda had been pulling me away in the midafternoon, or for an entire day, to do a different activity. The office took my absence without a fuss.

Projects ranged in oddness. She needed me once to get a new dress, insisting the shopping would take all day. Indeed it did. Another afternoon was spent eating an entire sheet cake ourselves. That one said happy birthday, but it wasn't her birthday.

Most of her adventures were food related. None of them took place at a lake or a park. They were nearly all indoors. Every time I looked out the closest window at the sunlight and itched for a fix.

All I wanted to do was sit beside a pool. With all the longing for summer sun, I said yes as soon as Matilda mentioned a beach trip. Instead of one day by a pool, we would spend two weeks at the ocean.

Matilda had already done most of the planning. Her organization skills were far better than her closet would have you believe. A house was reserved. Directions were mapped out. Desires and plans were clearly laid before me.

We sat together at her large desktop screen as she showed off the house's website. It was an adorable teal color with white shutters and windows. The place was designed to hold a couple of large families.

"They don't rent to single people. So I said it was Liam and me together. I just didn't specify that we were siblings and not a married couple. He'll be coming in for a couple days when he can get off work," she explained.

"How are you paying for it?" I clicked through pictures of sea shell decorations and an ocean front view.

"I borrowed from my life insurance policy." She recoiled at my look. "What? No one's going to use it."

More pictures showed a deck with a pool facing the ocean. Another deck a couple floors above it was screened off, making for mosquito free evenings. The highlight for Matilda was how far apart the houses were spaced. There would be no need to worry about noise as the closest home sat half a football field away.

"I do have a list of demands for this trip, Tessilda." Matilda spun her chair out like a supervillain.

"That's not what Tessie is short for."

"I don't care. Number one, we drive your car with the top down. Number two, we drink and get tan and at night we have deep, soulful conversations on the deck. Number three, at some point we go skinny dipping, but only in a pool because ew."

She was the one who talked me into the Volkswagen bug when I decided to get a brand new, grown up car. Matilda had always wanted something small and cute, but needed the black tank she drove for hauling art and supplies.

Just a couple of short years before we had stood together in a dealership. This was just a few months after I got my promotion. The car I had known for high school and college was aging, and not long for this world.

"Come on, you can afford it and you're only young once," had been her words that pushed me into a yes. That entire morning we were shuffled around by a salesman. I asked all the right questions my parents told me to ask. Luckily, my old car helped on a trade in.

While waiting on paperwork, we had a look at a bright sports car parked on display inside. It was a candy apple red that had been waxed to a color only art students could see. It looked more like a jolly rancher than a fast car.

"Tessie, dare me to lick this?" she asked, tapping the hood with her knuckle.

"Why would I dare you to lick a car?"

"So I can tell the story about it later." Matilda hadn't stopped tapping her knuckle on the car's hood. The steady pulse was on the verge of drawing attention.

I didn't actually dare her to do it, but she did. A smudge of lipstick and an impression of her tongue were left behind. The event ended up making an okay story. I guess you had to be there.

That afternoon I glanced at the sparkling pool that would soon witness my horrifying, naked body. If Matilda wanted to skinny dip, it would be happening. I agreed to her list of demands.

Work became even more difficult to focus on. I changed the background on my phone and desktop to white sand and blue waves. They only distracted me more. I had been counting down the days until we left from five different spots across my desk.

One afternoon, when seven days were left until our trip, Amelia appeared at my door. A continual riff of ukulele music had been playing in the back of my mind, and I jumped at the site of her.

"Hi, Tessie." Her smiles were getting more believable.

"Hi, I'm sorry did we have a meeting?" I quickly closed several pictures of palm trees and a web page. The new swimsuits I didn't need vanished.

"No, just checking in on everyone. I enjoyed your picture this morning. I'll always see troll hair when I look at asparagus now."

"Thanks," my mind jumped on track. "I had an idea, could I run it by you?"

"Sure," Amelia closed the door and took a seat. My thoughts lined up in order and I sat up like I was giving a presentation.

"I've been wondering, what if we made an app?"

"An app for a food supply company?" She wasn't turned off, but she certainly thought the idea was odd.

"We could appeal to the healthy crowd. It could have a nutrition tracker, a place for a food diary, and links to the stores that sell our food, because it's the best option."

"It could show someone their closest farm, people love local." Amelia was nodding.

"And we can always sell ad space," I added.

Amelia smiled. She told me I could work to something bigger, and I brought her a good idea. It was small, but it could grow.

"Write up your best ideas and send me an email," she explained. "I'll help you write a pitch for some of the big people. If they like it, we'll go from there."

"Great," I smiled back. Amelia stood up, more than satisfied with her potential protégé.

"I'm excited to hear about this," she headed toward the door. "I've got some things to discuss with Glen, why don't you come with me?"

For a moment I relished the admiration my boss's boss had given me. My mind slipped into a daydream of a fancy job at a corporate office. It would be the kind of thing I could brag about at a high school reunion.

The two of us walked to Glen's office. He rolled back in the chair behind his desk, happy to have me along. Framed photos of children and grandchildren covered every open space. My mind went numb as my eyes traveled across the room. I sat quietly as the two of them talked about promotion and production and other words with percentages attached to them.

Day dreams of walking in high heels and weekends in a big city appeared. I started to want it even more. An exciting future was possible, simply from an idea I had.

"We'd need a slide show, Tessie why don't you make it for us?"

Hearing my name drew me to attention. Glen had been speaking, but I had no idea what he said. I just nodded.

"Perfect. I'll get the information sent to you," Amelia said.

I blinked and saw the palm tree on my screen. In a sort of highway hypnosis I was back in my office, scratching a note about making a PowerPoint presentation. Plans of a fancy life moved to the back burner to simmer while thoughts of warm sand and waves rushed back to the front of my mind. I added the note to a group of others with similar reminders.

A trip as simple as two weeks in a beach house still required a significant amount of stuff. Both of us needed flip flops and tote bags to carry everything out in each day. Matilda stocked up on sunscreen, and insisted only fun towels with cartoon characters or superheroes could be used.

It's funny how your friend dying will make you spend money on anything. I just agreed as she tossed three different Superman towels into the shopping cart.

This continued with a plethora of other vacation items. Beyond towels, our cart was filled with sand mats, baskets, inflatable beach balls, and sand toys. Eventually I lost track of what Matilda was picking out and just followed her with the laden buggy.

I began to hate going to work in the morning. The load had increased that week. All I wanted was to spend time with Matilda. My pictures of water and sand taunted me.

Countdowns said we were three days from leaving. I did everything in my power to focus on the job before me. Classical music was on in a low purr, and every distraction or decoration had been banished from my desk to the empty drawer in the filing cabinet.

My eyes happened to drift to a pile of loose notes left behind. In the middle of them, my own words reminded me, "presentation slides."

"Shit," I whispered.

All the information I needed was in an ignored email. A second look to a calendar confirmed my worries; everything was due in the middle of our beach vacation.

In a moment, I rushed down the hall to Glen's office. Several coral pink flowers greeted me from his tie as I entered. Against a grey dress shirt, they stood out like five flares.

"Hey, Tess! What can I do you for?"

Just by entering his office unplanned, I was treated as if I were visiting royalty. He turned from his computer and greeted me with a usual, open mouth smile.

"That presentation Amelia asked for, it's due during my trip with Matilda." I let a puzzled frown take over my own face.

"Oh shucks, I know you're excited for that." A similar frown appeared on his face. Glen knew about the trip right after I did and happily gave me the time off. He added on an extra day to recover from the drive back.

"Would submitting it while I was out of town be an issue?" I planned my words carefully.

"I don't see why not. You just got to email it in, and Amy's not coming into our offices that week. Or, if you wanna pass it off to me before you go, there's nothing wrong with submitting it early."

Absolutely nothing had been done yet. Even if I dropped everything else and worked only on this stupid presentation I wouldn't finish before I left. I told him I would email it, and his happiness was unwavering.

"Thank you," I waved and slipped out. As quickly as public appearance would permit, I power walked back to my office.

With the velocity of an Olympic diver, I jumped into the information and set to work. Ignoring all else, I rushed into the project, desperate to finish it as quickly as possible. It wouldn't be done before we left, but I wouldn't let it take over our trip.

"This looks like one of those cartoons where the same outfit is hanging over and over again." Matilda examined my work clothes hanging in the orderly closet. One section was dresses, another was blazers, and another shirts. Along the floor shoes were lined by style, and above everything winter clothes were packed in labelled boxes on the shelf.

That evening we were packing up my suitcase. I sat on my bed, surrounded by an open case and scattered shirts, shorts, sweaters, and shoes that Matilda had selected.

I remembered sitting together in my old apartment. Matilda judged all of my clothes as we prepped for my interview with Osiris the next morning. Four or five options were tried on. She had me test them for mobility and how well they hid pit stains. All the while she gave me practice questions for the next day. She was the reason I got that job.

"Do you own a color besides white and black?" she asked, flicking through hangers. Her comment pulled me back to the present.

"Says the person who only owns flannel." I glanced at the red plaid shirt that was tied around her waist. Similar selections were scattered all across her bedroom. Hangers in the closet were stuffed together with clothes that exploded outwards. One set of drawers was never completely closed. Most likely her stained shirt from the popsicle crisis was still in the floor covered by an Everest of jeans, shoes, and more flannel.

"I'm also wearing a band t-shirt. Don't hate. I put on a blazer for a new client the other day."

"Why don't you get onto Liam? He only wears scrubs."

"He's a nurse. It's allowed." A few loose shirts were tossed onto my bed.

Packing together was important. We both agreed that the excitement of getting ready should be shared. So far, we had packed enough clothes for two days, and had three fashion shows. Unlike planning for our Christmas cruise, we decided the beach should be almost exclusively comfortable clothes.

The entire contents of a beach resort pamphlet was scattered across my living room. Everything was still bagged from multiple stores, and nothing was organized. The night before we left the two of us sat in my floor unbagging shit we forgot we bought and roughly grouping it all into piles.

By some miracle, it all fit into my car: flip flops, sun hats, those stiff beach mats you lay your towel on in the sand, travel snacks, and a trunkful of other stuff. A margin of space was left in the back seat for our suitcases.

"Why couldn't we take the SUV?" I asked, closing the trunk as carefully as possible.

"Because it guzzles gas like a son of a bitch, and it's not cute." Matilda replied, climbing into the black monster.

I promptly pulled up to her house at nine the following morning. Before I was up the sidewalk, Matilda was out the patio door with her luggage in tow. Pink bears covered her eyes, and the camera hung around her neck. She plopped an auto feeder full of cat food and a second full of water in Cat's usual spot.

"Wait! Pictures start now!" she pointed me back to the car. I lowered the roof and tossed her bag into the back seat with mine.

"I thought we were dressing comfortably and not cute."

"Yes, Tessie, and I am documenting every second of it, because you're going to be glad you have these pictures when I'm dead. Now give me a summer catalogue model laugh, one hand on the car, now pop your foot up." I followed the instructions as she listed them and clicked. "Now lean into a flirty pose that would make a Greek god want to get you pregnant."

She looked through the photos and showed them off. Matilda knew how to work a camera and make anyone look good. I had thrown on sorts and a baggy tee shirt then pulled my hair into a short ponytail. No intention of cute was put into my wardrobe for the drive. Those pictures were much better than the mirror had been that morning.

"Now that's the picture you'll show your kids someday and they'll say, 'mommy you look so hot I see why Daddy knocked you up.'"

The blue bug peeled out of the driveway and we were off. Road set before us like an unending adventure, every second together feeling more fun than the last. Vacations let your mind wander into a thousand possibilities and a promise of fun if you're willing to let it happen. My fingers gripped the steering wheel. Despite it being something I touched every day, that morning it felt completely different and so much better.

Matilda began playing music, keeping it loud to match the wind blowing over our heads. It's funny how we can age and change, but a smell, a song, or a place takes us right back to a moment we had been in years before. You open a book of memories and feel the way life used to be, not that it was better before or now, just different. Hearing those songs as we drove south took us back.

For a moment we were seventeen again. We giggled at the thought of boys and worried about eye liner. Old songs made us feel like we were driving home from a movie in Matilda's then brand new SUV. Pieces of jewelry and articles of clothing I hadn't thought about in years were suddenly clear images in my head.

Songs came on that I hadn't heard since adolescence, but we could still sing every word. After twenty minutes we raised the top back up. Our singing continued, but gradually lost energy. After an hour Matilda spoke up.

"Okay, this is getting boring now." She flicked off the sound. "Let's play a game."

"How about bed, wed, behead," I offered.

"Ah yes. Henry VIII." She leaned back and rested newly manicured feet on the dashboard.

"Okay," I thought for a moment and said, "Micah Farnham in *Antony and Cleopatra*, Mica Farnham in that WWII movie, and young Micah Farnham from those episodes of *Days of our Lives* he was in."

"I would wed him from the WWII movie because he's in uniform and beautiful. I would bed the young one, he wouldn't know much yet, so I don't think he would be ready for marriage. And behead him as Antony because he was crazy." Matilda pointed red toes towards the windshield.

"See I would have married the *Days of our Lives* one."

"Really?" Two pink bears looked my way.

"Yeah. He always wore a button up shirt, and they just do it for me. Now you pick three for me."

For a moment Matilda stared straight ahead, her bright, red lips opened slightly in thought.

"Okay, the guy from that cowboy show."

"Justin Smith," I answered.

"The guy from the dark and gritty superhero show you watch."

"Chris Winter."

"And the guy you liked in ninth grade."

"Jess Beast," I sighed in embarrassment and exasperation.

"Yes. The cowboy, the superhero, and the nerd," Matilda smiled at her choices.

"Wed Chris Winter, the superhero," I had my answer immediately, "because he's just got it together. Bed Justin Smith, the cowboy, and behead the nerd."

"You would kill Jess?"

"It's just a game," I reminded her.

"His poor family," she feigned sorrow.

"I have to pee," I said taking an exit to a rest area.

A friend in college once told me that a road trip has a way of making two acquaintances awesome friends, or ending a weak connection between people. Luckily for Matilda and me, it only made us stronger. Advice when planning a road trip with anyone, know each other's pee schedules and plan accordingly. Knowing stops will make a world of difference.

We eventually reached a quiet period. Matilda had taken to flipping through a wedding magazine she had brought along, and I was playing the alphabet game silently. We hadn't started a fight, I just forgot to mention I was playing it myself until I reached K. At that point it was a challenge to finish it without help.

"You have to talk to me for a minute," I finally said. The silence started getting to me.

"I'm so glad I won't waste money on a wedding." Matilda's eyes stayed on her literature, but she complied with my request. "These are way too expensive. Why do you pay so much for a dress you wear less than a day? You can't even pee when you're in it."

"I wouldn't know, I haven't done it."

As our destination grew closer, the landscape began to change. Rough underbrush bordered the road as trees thinned out. The sky opened up and felt almost bluer. A hint of salt and ocean filled the air. Our GPS told us we would arrive within the hour, but we could tell before the robotic voice mentioned it.

We elected to stop for gas before we were trapped in the coastal section of homes. An old gas station coated in friendly character and rust appeared. Soon the tank was full and we stepped inside the store to stretch out legs.

I browsed a row of candy bars, debating how soon unhealthy eating could happen. Thoughts were shattered by shrill, quick scream.

"Oh my god!" Matilda had frozen in a spot across the convenient store.

"Are you okay?" I joined her side.

"They have Cherry Life slushies." Matilda stood still in excitement. She rushed to pull the largest cup from the selection and fill it.

Soon we were back on the road with a full tank of gas and slushies the size of our torsos. The Cherry Life slushies were a staple for the area. Anytime we left the house the rest of the trip we each had another one.

The house was a turquoise embodiment of cute and relaxation. White legs held it off the ground, and it gazed over a private pool to a vast stretch of sand and ocean. Salty air drifted inside, and the soft white walls bordered by squishy carpet made me want to curl up and take a nap in the middle of the floor.

Stern, iron will and stubborn arms helped us empty the car in two trips. Straps cut into my shoulders and forearms as we marched up the white washed steps and into the front door. A gigantic pile of crap was left on the kitchen table as we went back for everything we needed in our bedrooms.

Upstairs, Matilda and I selected bedrooms with adjoining bathroom between them. Three other full bathrooms were in the house, but we ignored them for the most part.

I began filling the empty dresser drawers and closet with the things I packed. Matilda started to as well, but ended up dumping almost everything into one large drawer before taking a seat on my bed.

"We need to get food," she reminded me, sprawled across a comforter decorated with palm trees.

"Make a list. It's vacation, so we're eating whatever we want."

"That's why I like you, Fletcher." She whipped out her phone and began typing up an assortment of food.

I carried shampoo, soap, and a few other toiletries into our bathroom. Each bottle was extra-large. I always planned ahead on sharing.

"Did you pack enough for me too?" she asked, suddenly realizing how many things she had forgotten.

"Yep," I called. I could hear her sigh with quick relief.

"Thank you!"

We struggled back into the car. After a few hours inside of it, returning to the aqua bug was almost painful. Even for a quick trip to the supermarket. We moaned in unison as the car backed from the driveway and took to the road.

Inside the store a cart was loaded down in a few minutes. Then we kept finding ways to fit more in. Mixes for cakes and brownies were surrounded by frozen pizzas and easy made bags of vegetables to steam. Nutrition thrown to the wind, we piled in graham crackers, several kinds of cookies, and a few bags of marshmallows. I tried to add in rice cakes, Matilda immediately removed them.

"You said yourself, this is vacation." Their place was taken by two bags of potato chips.

In our journey south, we had reached an area common for Cherry Life. Matilda pulled three cases from the shelf and shoved them into the bottom rack of the cart.

"Is all of this going to fit in your car?"

"It should," I promised. "We can hold shit in our laps if we have to."

Eventually we decided we had enough to keep us happy for breakfast, lunch, and dinner. Matilda had glazed through the alcohol, gathering what she needed for margaritas and insisting she knew how to make them. I followed her and scooped up whiskey and wine.

Late afternoon now upon us, we opted for an early dinner. I unloaded our multitude of bags as Matilda put frozen chicken nuggets on a pan. Before long, our fridge and cabinets were full. Bottles of liquor took up residence on the counter corner, and Matilda used them as our food was finishing up.

On the back deck, we sat on Adirondack chairs with dinner and margaritas. They didn't taste exactly like ones I had in the past, but Matilda did all right.

Waves tumbled over themselves to reach the shore. For once, we grew quiet and listened to the sounds around us. Despite being the middle of the summer and the highpoint of vacations season, the beach was almost empty.

Matilda had carefully selected a private area, almost free of tourists on purpose. I glanced on either side of us. The closest houses were still more than a hundred yards away. Back decks similar to ours were empty.

The calm of the evening felt like a prelude to the days to come. Warm weather, food, and good times shared together.

The first few days of our vacation passed rather similarly. Mornings were a heavy breakfast from our enormous stash of food. I found myself paring waffles with fruit most days to deceive myself that I was making healthy choices.

We piled on sunscreen, Matilda extra generous to her white skin. Every summer outing we took across the years brought the same phrase, "I do not tan, I burn."

Our first morning we pulled on new swimsuits and examined each other's choices. Matilda had bought a navy blue and bright pink polka dot two piece. I was standing in plain black.

"Tessie, that's your swimsuit? You look paler than me."

"Yeah, so?" I snapped the elastic resting high above my waist.

"I didn't know something that plain existed. I'd hate to see what your lingerie looks like." She draped a baggy, white cover over her shoulders and back.

"I don't own any lingerie," I replied.

"Yeah, and you won't anytime soon dressing the way you do." A large, sun hat came to rest on her head, and the pink bears appeared over her eyes.

Our bags laden with books, towels, and a set of speakers; mine with a snack, we headed to the water's edge.

It's impossible not to enjoy a beach. As soon as the warm sand hit the bottom of my feet I couldn't stop smiling. Distractions seam to fall away when you stare into the steadily crashing waves.

We set up our chairs just above the water's edge and took to enjoying our view. Most of our time those days was spent just sitting, occasionally speaking, and enjoying being together. Sitting quietly doing nothing are some of the clearest memories I have.

My chair was low enough for my hands to touch the ground below me. Fingers slowly dug into the moist sand and rolled it through my palms. Soon two holes the size of my fists sat on opposite sides of my hips.

The last lick of waves reached our chairs with tide's movement, and filled the fresh spots with new pools. All too soon, the water disappeared into the earth. They were private ponds that existed only for a second. After a few minutes, the sand began to swallow the chair's legs. I stopped digging, and the space under my hands began to level. All traces of the private ponds were quickly gone.

I cast a glance to Matilda. A moment before, we were remembering our high school math teacher. We hated math, but loved the kind, Portuguese woman who taught us.

Spare hours and study halls were shared around her desk. Will power was the only thing that got Matilda through high school math. Together, with our teacher's extra tutoring, we battled through information we never used again.

In her large sun hat and excessive sunscreen, Matilda wasn't likely to change her snow white demeanor. I glanced her way from my chair. Matilda's arms had never been large, but then they were especially small. In the recent months they had grown slimmer. If any muscle or fat hung on her bones it was tissue thin.

"I'm hungry, but the house is so far away."

Her eyes shadowed by the pink bears and voice completely silent, I thought Matilda had drifted to sleep. Without a word, I slipped my hand into my own bag, retrieved a box of wheat crackers, and passed them over.

She thanked me, and I recalled our cruise from a few years before. Several times a day I loaned her sunscreen, a charger, hand sanitizer or some kind of snack from the bag I packed each morning.

Common sense would have anyone else reminding Matilda to pack her own bag for those excursions off ship, or even then when we walked each day from the house to the beach. I didn't, because I didn't want to. I didn't want her to pack her own bag with a water bottle or a snack. I wanted her to ask me for some of my water or some of my crackers because I liked being able to help her.

If I couldn't fix her body or get her a new heart then I would help her in any other small way. Even if that way was giving her crackers or driving her to the gas station just to get her favorite flavor of slushie, I was going to do it. The whole time I hated myself for not being able to do more. Screw endocarditis.

"God, I'm going to miss you," I heard the words slip from my mouth.

"I know."

"I don't know what I'm going to do."

"Don't talk about it. Just enjoy right now," she almost whispered.

Matilda's jaw broke through several crackers at once. Her rhythmic chewing, that would normally drive anyone up the wall, added to the music of the ocean side.

"Want one?" She offered me the box.

I glanced down at my hands. Ten thousand grains of dark, wet sand clung to my fingers.

"Yeah, but my hands are gross."

"Here, open your mouth." Without a thought I complied, and a cracker was wedged in between my teeth.

"Thanks, babe," I mumbled, trying to chew at the same time.

"Eat more," she shoved three more into my mouth. "They're good."

I giggled at the forced food, not just from Matilda's silliness, but the sudden relief she brought. She felt things getting serious and found a way to make us laugh. My weak moment was ended by her quick action.

The crackers didn't last long, especially when we decided to splash in the water and get knocked over a few times by the waves. Within the hour, we gathered everything and returned to the house.

After showers, we each had a sandwich and sat before the large TV in the living room. Matilda settled on a movie channel, but was asleep the second her sandwich was finished. I used the quiet opportunity to sit with my laptop.

A good portion of the project was finished. I looked through what I had done so far, and thanked past Tessie for her work. The few hours required to finish lingered ahead of me like a dark cloud.

Every second with Matilda was now precious time. I glanced at her lumpy figure on the other end of the couch. She didn't stir when I draped her in blanket. Even asleep, I was happy to be with her.

After a good hour of devotion to my work, I let my body lapse back into vacation mode. Heavy eyes made me put my laptop on the coffee table, get my own blanket, and give into the tug of sleep.

Before long, a shove woke me up.

"Let's go get slushies," Matilda yawned.

Most days were the same. We stayed by the water until early afternoon. Lunch was a sandwich, and then Matilda napped while I struggled to finish the presentation. Each day it was harder to work on. I soon went from meticulously checking every aspect three or four times, to rushing through it once and agreeing it was good enough. I then moved on to the next piece.

Eventually I drew up an email. I listed my ideas for the app; a food diary, information about local farms, where you could find the organic, best options of food that only Osiris provided. I wrapped with a quick signature and hit send.

Evenings were a different form of dinner on the balcony. We pointed chairs to the ocean, and kept our plates on our laps. Our position was exactly like the morning, only a few hundred yards inland.

Friends require outings and adventures on a regular basis. Best friends can sit and do nothing for long periods of time and completely enjoy themselves. Matilda and I could do nothing, fart, and still have a great time together.

Later evenings we sat on the bed in my room or hers, and watched old sitcoms. Matilda often dozed off during episodes of *The Golden Girls*. I took the chance to return to the work on my laptop.

The project grew from a standard annoyance to a large pest. Like a mold growing in the corner of the ceiling that refuses to yield to any amount of products or constant scrape of a tool. I hated it, and more so hated the thought of going back to work when we got home.

The only relief was in the email Amelia answered.

Looks great. Let's talk about a pitch.

About a week in, a finished product sat before me. It was far from perfect. I didn't care. Half of our vacation was close to over, and each day I had devoted sacred time to the piece of shit. I saved what I had and sent it in before shutting off my computer for good.

I nudged Matilda awake, and told her it was time for slushies.

That evening was slow. Matilda complained about being tired as soon as we returned from the gas station. The sun's work on our backs didn't help.

We took the chance to lather our shoulders in aloe. In loose tank tops, we turned on a fan in Matilda's room and drew the curtains. The extra air flow and lack of sunlight took us from a midsummer day to the gentle chill of an autumn evening.

Pride and Prejudice was on. With our red slushies, we settled in for what might have been the ten thousandth viewing. Matilda and I could have quoted the entire film on our own. It was almost a third friend to our group. Like always, we reacted to the lines and sassy moments. We gave rough, "da da das" in time with the elegant piano music.

Then something struck me like one of the cold waves from the fan. Would such a solid tradition even be imaginable in a few short months? Without my best friend, could I ever turn this movie on again without feeling completely miserable? Just like our time together, my opportunities to watch Lizzie and Mr. Darcy were numbered.

A swelling filled both of my eyes. I closed them tight, refusing to let tears pass when Matilda could see them.

She didn't, because she said, "Promise me you'll never love a movie more than this one."

"Promise."

As the first week wrapped up, we were in higher spirits. One evening, Matilda had more energy, and was ready to kill someone for a decent seafood meal.

We had grown accustomed to watching sitcoms older than us every night. That evening was promising an eight hour marathon of one of our favorites. The retirees of Miami felt increasingly more similar to the two of us in our time at the beach.

Matilda was feeling drinky. I was always feeling drinky, so encouraged it when I saw it in her. Not wanting to worry ourselves with finding safe transportation, we decided to stay home for our seafood night, and ordered take out.

Within an hour, we were each carrying four boxes of crab legs, hush puppies, and affordable lobster. The styrofoam was balanced together in a delicate heap in the back seat of my bug for the drive home. Only one stop was made for more pineapple juice and coconut cream.

I organized the feast on the coffee table in the living room as Matilda worked on her off brand margaritas.

"Liam just texted! He's on his way here to spend a couple of days!" She had to shout over the blender. Shutting it off was not an option, in her opinion.

Watermelon flavored margaritas paired nicely with our crab legs. *The Golden Girls* slowly began to fade ahead of us as two glasses became three and then four.

Our minds began to stray from the show and we turned nostalgic. A few years before, we had invented our own form of the game twenty questions, but instead of guessing something we just came up with twenty intensely personal and sometimes awkward questions that we had to answer. It was a game best saved for a time when judgement was watery and memory of the answers was questionable.

Questions about old crushes rolled into stories about terrible dates. Our attempt to count to twenty was abandoned by laughter and encouraging ourselves we had ended up much better than the men that turned us down in the past. The list of boys was very short, so it was easy to roll through them and convince ourselves we were much better without any of them in our lives.

"Didn't one guy keep talking about getting shots?" Matilda had moved from the couch to the floor.

"No, it was acupuncture!" I was still on the couch, managing drink four. "I kept poking my salad and everything he said made me grimace but he wouldn't shut up about it."

Matilda laughed until she belched. Then we laughed together.

The pitcher was empty. We moved back to the kitchen.

"I thought I heard something about that guy you dated in high school. Like recently I saw it somewhere." I jumped up and sat on the counter, certain I could not stand on the floor.

"Jeremy?" she rinsed the blender in the sink.

"Yeah, I think he's in jail now." I slid the pineapple juice and coconut cream to her.

"What? No he isn't," Matilda tossed ice into the blender along with rough guesses of every other ingredient. After pouring new drinks and taking a gulp, she pulled out her phone and struggled to stalk Jeremy online. She violently tapped the screen.

"Need help?"

"I can do it! I just have to find him." Buzzed Matilda could not do it.

"Right, I only use social media every day at work, what would I know."

Instead of finding her old fling, Matilda got distracted by a quiz. She sent it to me, and we both sat quietly in the kitchen finding out which continent we should live on.

"We're not going to finish that rum before the trip," I nodded to the large bottle

"I'm not doing rum shots. Get the tequila."

A lime was sliced and we each threw one back.

Matilda returned to the rum and the blender. Without standing up, I reached into the cabinet behind me and got new glasses. They rested on the counter and were soon full. Distracted by our memories and piña coladas, we stood in the kitchen for a few minutes, or maybe a couple of hours, talking. We moved through a couple more shots. The timeline got fuzzy.

"Wait!" Matilda interrupted her own story, she had been on the verge of walking out of an Italian place when her gentleman caller said he didn't care about paintings. "I know what else we need to do. And I am just buzzed enough to do it."

Changing clothes was a brand new challenge of the night. Stumbling through our bedrooms trying to complete the task was in itself should have been a warning we were in no state to do anything, and that any idea was a bad one. After a few minutes, we were on the back deck by the pool.

The world slowly rocked around me. I gripped the wood of the deck with my bare feet. As my body steadied, I realized I had been the wobbly one. A fresh, salty breeze came off of the late high tide, and did nothing to sober either of us. If we were going to be rash, it needed to happen right away.

Even in the warm air of the night I shivered, feeling only the large, baggy tee shirt on my skin. Matilda had loaned it to me from the sleeping clothes she packed. Soon it would be gone, and I would be bare before no one but Matilda and the moon. A second glance to the dark balconies on the houses either side of us confirmed there were no other witnesses.

"I'll go first," Matilda offered, "it was my idea."

I couldn't bring myself to watch. There wasn't enough rum in the world to make me do that. From the corner of my eye I managed to tell she removed her own large shirt and draped it on the banister. A heavy splash greeted Matilda to the pool. I finally glanced her way. She was crouched in the four foot deep water. Dry, black hair fanned around her shoulders.

"Let's go, Fletcher."

I nodded, waiting for her to turn away. My own shirt fell next to hers on the banister, and I quietly slipped into the water. It felt no different to wearing a swimsuit.

"I think short stories and romantic comedies embellished a little," I noted. An inflatable raft drifted between us, shielding all but our eyes from each other's view.

"It is a bit drab." Matilda's face scrunched in thought. "Maybe it's because we're in a pool. Doesn't this usually happen in a lake or something?"

"I'm not going into the ocean," I stated. "That's how *Jaws* starts."

"Well we're here. We might as well enjoy it." She stuck a foot out of the water, examining it as if her nakedness made it different. "At least we'll have a great story for later."

Sure, Matilda.

Our conversation looped back to old crushes and awkward dates. She did leave the Italian place after her date said paintings were dumb, but not before ordering a second bottle of wine and the largest dessert they had. She took the bill herself, and dropped plenty of cash on the table.

"Don't worry, I've got it," she explained, standing up from the table. "I sold a painting the other day."

Most of the memories had been exhausted at that point. I didn't have a story to top her last one, at least not that I could think of in that state. I thought about my piña colada, melting on the kitchen counter. Half of it was left. I missed it, and wondered if it missed me.

"Guys?" a voice from the deck broke through the darkness.

I slid into the water until only my eyes and the top of my head were visible.

"Shit!" Matilda pulled me behind the raft with her. "How did you find us? I haven't heard from you since you left!"

"GPS," Liam stepped forward. I was thankful we left the back lights off. "Also Tessie's car is parked in the driveway."

"Leave!"

"Those are mine," he pointed to the shirts we had abandoned moments before.

"Go inside! And wait in a bedroom that isn't claimed until I come get you!" She yelled, standing up and shielding herself with the upturned raft. I sank deeper into the water.

"Why? Are you having girl talk or something? You left the TV on by the way."

Frustration boiled over, and Matilda screamed. In a flash of white, she jumped from the pool and ran up the stairs after her brother. Unintelligible screams came from both parties until the slam of the back door silenced them.

Drawing the raft closer to me, I waited. The shirt was waiting about twenty feet away. All common sense gone, we had forgotten to bring towels outside with us. I remembered the shirt wasn't Matilda's and decided I never wanted to wear it again.

The door was across a deck, up a flight of stairs, and another short deck away. In a hurry, I could run inside within a couple seconds. Then what? The downstairs bathroom only had hand towels. A hallway, kitchen, living room, and a set of stairs would be crossed before I reached my room. Liam and Matilda could be in any of them. I debated with myself on what to do.

"Tessie!" Matilda was my savior.

She dashed down the stairs, wrapped in one the large Superman towels she had bought for the trip. From shoulders to knees she was covered, and I was grateful.

"I locked him in the half bath," she held a towel out at the edge of the pool, "because it doesn't have windows." I rushed to the security of a cartoon Clark Kent.

I followed Matilda up the steps and into the house. As we passed into a light shadows on her back became prominent. Bones were beginning to push through the skin as she steadily became slimmer.

Inside, we walked past the half bath. A chair from the kitchen table was propped under the handle, keeping Liam inside.

The morning woke me with a splitting headache and a tossing stomach. Both doors to the shared bathroom were open, and I could see Matilda sprawled across her bead.

Pale legs crossed the comforter until her feet hit the corners of the mattress. Black hair was completely hidden by a stack of pillows. Face down, her butt and back were all that were visible. Thankfully, she had thought to pull on shorts and a tank top before crashing. I glanced down, and was relieved to see that I had too.

I stumbled out the door and down the stairs. A blurry figure that I concluded was Liam was having cereal on the couch. I hurried past it for water from the kitchen.

"Good morning," he half smirked.

"Morning," or something similar to it, was my reply.

Very little happened that day. Once or twice Matilda and I wondered to the kitchen for water or coffee. Burned toast was all that accompanied it. The doors between our bedrooms stayed open. Luckily we never had to rush to the toilet to barf. Not a bad hangover, except for the feeling of complete misery.

"Tessie."

"Hmph."

"You dead?"

"No. Are you?"

"Yes."

This exchange happened a few times. I drifted in and out of consciousness. At one point we stated we were done with alcohol. The resolution lasted until a couple of nights later.

The rest of the week was a delightful blur. I remember the taste of Matilda's stupid margaritas, the feel of fresh air on the deck, and the joy of being together. Mornings were spent by the water, where we rubbed our feet in the sand and let the waves knock us over. Our bodies faded into deep sleeps in the afternoon. By evening, we were over eating, drinking, and laughing at fresh moments and memories long past.

After the circumstances surrounding his arrival, I was careful to avoid Liam unless Matilda was nearby. She didn't bring the matter up again. It's quite possible she forgot most of the night and what happened. I'll never know for certain.

Vacations have a way of becoming a drug. The time away puts you on your own relaxation high. As soon as you're home you itch for more. Despite how much we slept and lounged by the TV, I felt exhausted prepping for the week when we returned. Making the change back felt like picking up an anvil and carrying it on my shoulders.

The largest cup I could find was filled with iced coffee, but it hardly made a dent in my fatigue or complete hatred of the day ahead of me. In my final steps out of the apartment, the drink was doused with a shot of whiskey. That made a small improvement.

Settling into my desk, I swallowed hard and turned on my computer. The background of the ocean and palm tree taunted me. I covered it with work. Projects lay before me like methods of torture. Work that I once skipped through with a smile sounded less pleasing than being tied to a rack.

An hour into organizing my pain and planning a coordinated attack on it, Amelia appeared at our reception desk. She was soon in my office, and closed the door behind her. The click of the handle echoed in the room.

"How was your trip, Tessie?" She smiled down at me.

"Very good," I smiled back.

"The beach, right?"

"Yes, I've never felt more rested." I half lied. My own take on Irish coffee was helping me through the morning.

"Well," she took a seat. "I hate to start your first day back like this, but I have to be honest."

I froze. Amelia wasn't mad, but she looked slightly annoyed. Curves in her face pointed to disappointment. The expression was common all too often on my mother's face. Usually over Tara, not me, but that's a debate for another time.

"What day did I tell you I needed the power point you were working on?" She gazed into me. I scrambled to come up with the right words.

"The presentation you gave was on the 25th, so I sent it to you on the 24th."

"Yes," she glanced away. My answer wasn't what she had hoped for. "But I wanted it on the 23rd. You were a day late."

I kicked myself. Words of apology formed in my mind. I considered claiming that I was misinformed. Before I could give any answer, my superior spoke again.

"You were out of town, obviously you were distracted. I still was able to use everything, you did some great work. However, I know you can do better."

"Thank you." Maybe I wasn't in trouble.

"I'm not trying to reprimand you on your first day back." Her words made me sigh with relief. "I know you can do better. I want to see you do better."

"Thank you," I said again. "This sort of situation is not common for me."

I paused, trying to defend myself. Even if this wasn't a scolding, I still felt like I was in serious trouble. I ended up using Matilda's trump card.

"My best friend is dying. That was our last trip together, and now we're down to the last few months." My eyes stung, and I bit my lip to maintain my expression.

"Honey, I know and I am so very sorry." The sly face was overridden by a compassionate expression.

I sat quietly as she peppered me with more encouraging words. She wrapped up her speech with an encouraging phrase that she must have decided was satisfactory. Our conversation shifted to the trip. I told her about the house and the food.

Amelia was at our branch that day for routine meetings. She stood up to excuse herself for them. Before opening my door, she stopped and looked back at me.

"You need to think about your future here."

6 8) THREE DAYS

"I don't get why I can't come over at all or even call you."

"Because, Tessie, I love you, but you can be a huge distraction." Matilda dropped Liam's duffle bag by the front door. "That's why you can't text either."

"I have to know you're okay," I argued.

"If something is wrong I'll call you," she offered.

"But what if you fall and pass out and you can't call because you're unconscious in a pool of your own blood?" I raised my eyebrows the same way my mother always did.

"I won't fall down the stairs or leave anything in the floor to slip on."

"Please defend me on this," I asked Liam as he descended the steps.

He stopped two steps from the bottom and loomed over us. In this declaration of three days to herself, Matilda had told Liam to leave the house. He didn't want to. Matilda insisted that I could take him in during the time. I didn't want to.

"Please agree with me because you're my brother." Matilda crossed her arms.

"I'm kind of with Tessie on this one," he said.

"Ha!" I shouted.

"Hey, quick question," Matilda interjected. "Who here is dying and by that right should be given just about anything she wants?"

Liam glanced my way. That week Matilda had not asked for anything as far as where to eat or what pastimes we should take part in. Not once had I been called away from work since we returned from our trip. She was due for some demands. We were due to agree to them. The two of us realized this together.

"Why don't you just text one of us now and then so we know you're okay?" He dropped a backpack on the floor between Matilda and me.

"Fine! But you're both ruining my creative process." She rolled her eyes. Slightest requirement of mature behavior pushed Matilda to frustration.

"Consider it payback for kicking me out of my childhood home."

A new pile of blank canvases had appeared by the front door that afternoon. Beside them sat several piles of fresh paint and brushes. The supplies seemed to take Liam's place.

"I'm not kicking you out. It's just three days that I need the house." Matilda explained.

"Besides, you're staying with Tessie, not in some hotel."

"That might be worse," I admitted.

"Now it's time for you both to leave," she said waving us out the door. "I don't want to see your faces unless it's an emergency."

The two of us shuffled out the front door and onto the stoop. The door began to close behind us. Matilda stood in the last few inches to see us off.

"What time can we come back Sunday?" I asked.

She leaned inside to look at the wall clock.

"Six in the P.M. We'll call it a very late brunch and have donuts." She paused, and glanced towards the kitchen. "You should bring donuts."

I nodded, making the mental note. We both moved towards our cars. Matilda lingered at the door.

"Have fun, I love you!" I called from my bug.

"I love you too, but don't enter my property again until you have jelly donuts!" Matilda slammed the front door closed. The brass knocker bounced with a shudder.

Any excitement I had for having Liam stay in my apartment for three days was delivered for Matilda's sake, and slightly for his. The two of us had only ever been together when Matilda was around. Without her, there was little to do or talk about.

On the drive home I struggled to come up with topics of discussion. Besides nursing, I couldn't think of anything he liked. I had no idea of sports teams or movies or breakfast preferences. Our recent interactions had been veiled in silence.

Not much had been done with any of us since Matilda bursting out of the water in her pale, nakedness to chase Liam inside the house. I tried to shake off the thought of the fifteen year old who mowed the front lawn standing twenty feet from me, as I struggled to skinny dip.

Awkwardness appeared the moment we entered my front door and it refused to leave.

Liam sauntered into the living room and took a seat at the couch. I remained in the kitchen, searching for something to do or a topic that could end the quietness. After a few minutes I came up with something.

"Have you had dinner?" I asked from behind the refrigerator door.

"No." His eyes were on his phone.

"Want to order some food?"

"I actually have to get to work," he stood up. "But I'll see you in the morning."

"That's when I'll be heading to work. There's food and stuff so help yourself to anything." I gestured to the cabinets.

"Thank you."

The next morning all I saw of Liam was a rumpled lump on the couch. I woke up for work to find him asleep after a night shift.

With Matilda quarantining herself from the world, I had a considerable amount of free time on my hands. Work was void of distraction. For the first time in months I was ahead on projects.

Amelia had paired me with a graphic designer to make some images for a pitch. She was beginning to make plans to bring a few people to our branch to hear me talk about the app. I should have been more excited.

The designer had sent the first layouts to me. The food journal page and store locator were done. Everything bore the colorful Osiris logo on top of the page. I spent the morning shifting through them and approving the work. Then they were sent on to Amelia for a final approval. I didn't dare set up something for a pitch with board members that she didn't think was perfect.

I still found myself worrying. Images of Matilda falling down the stairs, being hit by a car, or slipping in the bathroom kept appearing in my mind. Even though I knew they were ridiculous, the thoughts had me worried. Like a mother who just sent her first child to school I fretted over Matilda, and kept thinking of worst case scenarios. By noon I broke down and texted her.

Are you okay? You've been quiet.

Almost instantly, she answered.

Dammit, I'm fine. I'm working.

Shortly after, a second text from her appeared.

Thank you for your concern, I love you.

Too. I replied.

Knowing any conversation with Liam would be full of the same awkward stance as our short time together before, I stayed late at work Friday night. Time was passing quickly with my mind focused on my desk and my computer screen. Distractions helped me count down the hours to seeing Matilda again.

I wondered what to do with my free time after work. Always having Matilda text me throughout the day kept my evenings and weekends planned out for me. I was stumped. I told myself an evening home alone would be a chance to catch up on rest, but I knew before long that would be my only option.

That day had given me a taste of my future in just a few short months. I hated it. Ideas for what to do were nonexistent. I had no life without Matilda. Besides her, the only people I talked to were my family. I would need to make new friends or start using a dating app to find someone to spend time with.

Those ideas repulsed me. I kept asking myself what should be done until my mind was exhausted. Thinking of the future at all was painful. Once again I let my mind slip into fantasies of a shiny, big corporate job in a new city. Imagining it made me feel guilty. Then more pain.

I pushed everything into a closet in the back of my mind, telling myself today was what I should focus on. I told myself to enjoy a night at home for once. Soon I would be busy again.

My late afternoon, quick dinner was wearing off by the time I headed home. I found myself fantasizing about ordering Chinese food and eating it alone on my couch. Wine pairing was selected when I opened my door, only to have my hopes shattered by Liam on my couch.

"I thought you were working again tonight," my excitement of being alone fell apart.

"No, just a few hours today."

Our statements were both blunt. Slightly annoyed at having to share my evening, I struggled to find a way to make things lighter between us. For Matilda's sake, I knew I needed to be friendly towards her brother.

"Do you want some Chinese food? I haven't had dinner."

"Sure," he smiled, glancing my way.

I placed an order for takeout food, but remained in my kitchen after hanging up. Around the counter I found different things to look at or move around in the illusion of cleaning. I pulled out my phone to complain to Matilda, and then returned it to my pocket without sending anything.

Liam remained on the couch, staring at his phone. The bed sheets and blankets he had been using were neatly folded on the coffee table. Thumbs danced across a screen for several seconds, spelling out a long message. I wanted to ask him who he was texting. The only people he knew were here or demanding she be left alone to make art for three days.

He was my guest. I knew I should be nice, but I also just wanted to eat my food and watch TV. Seeing no other way around it, I decided to address the situation that was making any interaction uncomfortable.

"Sorry," I spoke up. "I feel like Matilda's moment at the beach pool is making this weird."

"No, I see naked people all the time," he was nonchalant. "If I had seen you naked, though, that might be awkward."

"You're not wrong." We remained at opposite ends of the apartment. Both of us searched for a topic to discuss. Liam's eyes fell on the five empty wine bottles next to the stove.

"Are you one of those people that keeps the bottles after you finish them?" he asked.

His assumption was better than the truth.

"No. Those are just last week's bottles that haven't made it to the recycling bin yet." I sighed. "But I'm opening more, do you want some?"

As we waited for our food to arrive, we drank moscato and asked each other about work. Out of politeness, we each pretended to be interested.

"I hope the couch is okay," I finally said. "No one's ever tried it before. The only person who ever stays over is Matilda, and she sleeps in my bed with me." I avoided eye contact by pouring a second glass.

"Oh," slipped out quietly. I felt a judgment pass over me that had appeared several times before when our friendship was inspected. Meticulous looks from anyone who didn't know Matilda or me would often come to the same assumption.

"We're not lesbians," I explained. Often that response required proof. Usually I just had to show one of the many pages of information Matilda had on Micah Farnham. That always worked.

"Oh I didn't think you were." Liam was on his phone again. "Not that it would be an issue, but Matilda hits on any man that's, I don't know, breathing."

I checked the time. It had only been ten minutes since I ordered dinner, but the choppy conversation made it feel longer.

"Do you like working here?" I circled back to work.

"It's nice being somewhere I have friends." His answer made me pause. "Friends" was a plural response, more than just Matilda. If I was his friend I was doing a shitty job of it. "Most places are work, laundry, food, and watching *Eternity*."

The clouds parted. A new wave of opportunity flowed in. In one leap I moved from the kitchen to the living room.

"Oh my gosh, I love *Eternity*!" After several seasons of enjoying the show with no one but an internet community, having someone to enjoy the show with was almost unbelievable.

"I haven't seen any of the new season because Matilda won't watch it." Liam's voice had become as loud as mine.

"I have them all recorded!" My arm flailed against the coffee table as I reached for the remote.

Soon we were both settled into the couch for a night devoted to the TV. The only pause in the marathon came when the food finally arrived. Everything was quickly resumed.

The immortal characters we had been following had arrived in the 1940s on the cusp of the Second World War. Two believed that their group should remain passive and avoid conflict, as they had been doing for the last thousand years. Another wanted to fight. The fourth was stuck between the two positions.

"I lost count of how many times I tried to get Matilda to watch it," I said as I skipped through a commercial break.

"She doesn't watch much besides reality shows." Liam replied. Like me, he had been subjected to marathons of deciding wedding dresses and remodeling houses. I enjoyed them more than he did.

The only silent moment that followed was during commercials. I started skipping through the first break, and Liam spoke up.

"I'm glad we found something in common. I don't think I've liked you this much since before you guys stole my boomerang."

"I forgot about that," I lied.

When we were nine and Liam was fourteen, he had a pen pal. They wrote letters, and at one point the pen pal went to Australia and sent back a wooden boomerang from the trip. Liam refused to use it. Instead, it sat on display in his bedroom.

What were Matilda and I to do but wait for him to leave the house, steal the boomerang, and throw it ourselves? In the backyard we tested it out. I tried several times, and it landed in the grass a few feet away. Matilda took one turn, and it soared around us from right to left in a crescent moon shape.

Mesmerized by the flight path, we stood completely still. Any thought of the boomerang's destination was gone, and with it our intent to catch it. Then it hit me in the face.

Mom drove me to the urgent care center with Tara in tow. While we sat in the waiting room my little sister patted my arm and tried to tell me jokes. I had three stitches; Matilda wasn't allowed to watch TV for a week.

I touched my bangs, making sure they were still hiding the tiny scar.

Late into the evening we were absorbed by our favorite show. As much as you love something, it's refreshing to share it with someone else who loves it just as much. Watching the show with Liam made me notice more details, gasp aloud, and keep a better commentary.

Chinese food disappeared and was replaced by cookies. Wine turned into hard liquor. Slowly the couch began to absorb us both. By the end of the evening only a handful of episodes remained.

Sometime past one I turned the TV off. Slightly dizzy, I made sure to drink water before moving to my bedroom. Liam was an unconscious lump in my floor. Exhaustion had claimed him before alcohol did.

Creaky floorboards led me to my bed. After struggling into some pajamas my white comforter absorbed me like a giant pile of marshmallow fluff.

Harsh, mid-morning sunlight woke me up. I rolled away from it, and remembered my guest in the living room. Silence told me he was still out. I hoped he eventually made it to the couch.

Hunger made me sit up. My shirt was inside out, and backwards. I fixed it as the small bite of a headache made an appearance. Like a marooned sailor, I made food and water a quick priority. Standing up, they became a priority after aspirin.

The same creaky boards followed me to the kitchen. Their noise made Liam stir. As an apology, I poured a second glass of water. It was handed off with more pain killers.

"How was the floor?" I asked.

"No offense, but the couch is better."

In silence we rehydrated. I glanced at my reflection in the off TV. Attempting to fix any of the mess sounded much worse than walking around in it. I decided to leave it be.

Hangovers, even light ones, leave me fuzzy on how decisions were made and plans were executed. My companion was stuck in a permanent state of exhaustion. Together, we somehow managed to get dressed and make our way out of my apartment.

A couple of blocks away sat a small cafe. At the time, I was certain it was a diner. Both of us needed something hardy and lots of coffee. Neither of us had the energy nor focus required to make either one.

Stumbling into the front door, we realized the restaurant was a frequent brunch stop for Saturday morning patrons. We were quickly seated within a plethora of couples. Anyone could tell we weren't together. Just as easily, anyone could tell we were hungover. Thankfully, no one knew it was from watching our nerd show.

The menu offered organic and heart healthy options. This wasn't what we had been looking for, and I apologized. The selection we made was better than nothing, but just barely.

Conversation was slim. Perhaps it was from our state of being or lack of time together. I quietly took a few hearty drinks of my mimosa.

"How can you handle more alcohol?" Liam mumbled from a cup of coffee.

"It usually helps me the morning after." I remembered then my sunglasses were still on, and took them off.

"You know, that's really more of a myth."

"Makes me feel better." In defiance I took another sip.

"Well, I'm not a doctor," Liam sat up straight. "I just do all the work of one for half the pay."

I switched to water.

"How is the job here?" I was relieved to find something to talk about. All discussion of *Eternity* was worn out the night before.

"It's fine. Not bad." He thought for a moment. "I've been in better places, but I've also been in much worse."

What I ordered, but not what I imagined, was placed in front of me. I could tell Liam was having the same thought. From what I guessed were the eggs I removed a basil leaf. Complete lack of bacon had us both disappointed.

"Do you know where you'll go next?" I poked my weird eggs with a fork.

He shook his head. "I don't know how long I'll be here. But after this-" he paused, not wanting to say what 'this' was. "I think I'm just about done with traveling."

Salt and ketchup made our meals edible. Coffee helped me get it down. A few bites in, my head began to clear up. Slowly, my body was returning to normalcy.

"How's your work?" Liam had made further progress on his breakfast than I had.

I hesitated, searching for the right answer. No one outside of work had asked me about work in months. Was it going well? The app was going well. I wanted to love it.

Recently, it had been a stepping stone to something more. Amelia had told me about corporate and the shiny job that waited for me there if I could just jump high enough. The app was a trampoline. Anytime thoughts of making the jump crept into my head I had quickly pushed them away.

Stepping into the daydream was like a vice. It felt wrong. Imagining that life was the good kind of wrong that you enjoy while it's happening, but when it ends you feel nothing but guilt. This was my first chance to share my secret daydream.

"I might apply for a corporate position in New York." I felt like I opened a closet to show off a Christmas present. Liam paused to listen for more, but I didn't have more to say.

"Cool. That sounds like a lot of fun."

Was it fun? It seemed like it should be. We're always told to go to school and get a job and move up and make more money. That's what I would be doing. I would be moving further away from family, not that they were close then. I didn't have friends to keep me there.

"I don't know." I replied. "I haven't talked to anyone about it."

Liam put his fork down. He noticed my concern, and gave me his attention.

"Do you want to live in New York?"

"I don't know," I said. "I haven't let myself think that much about it."

"You're allowed to have a life, Tessie."

"I know. It just doesn't feel fair to think about it."

Liam looked away and sighed. He couldn't focus on anything a few months down the road either. Unlike him, I had a family to fall back on.

I wanted to think about the future. More than imagining myself there,

I wanted to imagine Matilda there with me. Before we had joked about being roommates somewhere, we just never took it seriously. As lightly as I had considered it, not having the option any more hurt.

A part of me clung to an impossible hope of an organ donor showing up and giving Matilda the new heart she so desperately needed. I wondered how hard it would be to find a list of people waiting for hearts and another list of organ donors and where they lived. Liam worked in a hospital, so that was a step towards finding it.

It was insane to even think about, but I couldn't help wondering if I could find a list of organ donors, track them down, and see if they were good people. I could kill off anyone who was bad. Then Matilda and the other good people on the list would be better and could live the rest of their lives and be happy. In my life I had maybe shot a BB gun once or twice. But sure, I could get away with murder.

For a while we sat in silence. The café slowly became more crowded. Our plates were emptied and taken away. Two checks appeared, but we both continued working on the thermos of coffee given to our table.

"Do you remember the prank you guys pulled that one year at my parents' Christmas party?" Liam finally spoke.

"Which one? We did pranks every year."

"I think you guys were starting high school. Mom and Dad had invited this," he searched for the right words, "asshole. I don't know why he was there, but he was some jerk that lived down the street for a while."

I combed my memory for the event. One piece came to me. Matilda and I had been extra ruthless to the man who complained about bikes on the sidewalk and stared at the jogging housewives.

"That tall guy," I answered. The man had been slightly above average height. Matilda and I had to stand on the staircase to make it work.

"You guys threw raw grains of rice into his hair," Liam smiled, remembering more details.

"He was across the room from us, but he kept looking straight up like an idiot." I laughed. Matilda had asked me for help going after the jerk neighbor. I was happy to do her bidding, but he had said something less than polite to our mothers. No idea what it had been. I was ready to go after him.

"Why did they invite him?" Liam wondered.

"Maybe they didn't, and he just crashed the party." We laughed. "Matilda put laxatives in his punch."

"No she didn't." He paused, remembering his sister. "Did she?"

I nodded. "I think that's why he left early."

"I miss those Christmases."

I glanced Liam's way. In all features, he was practically identical to his sister. Simply because of his health he wasn't as pale, but the dark hair and bright eyes were the same.

As soon as Liam turned sixteen he had a driver's license. Immediately, he was instructed to drive a used car and take Matilda and me to school. This continued until he graduated.

To us he seemed incredibly advanced. He was the very grown up big brother who could drive a car. We would sit in the back and keep our rowdiness on a lower level, because in our eyes an adult was there. When we were old enough to drive, he was in college. Somehow the big brother grew even bigger in our eyes. He was a real adult then. He was headed to an important job, and would do adult things long before we would.

That morning as I sat across from him, the years between us felt much smaller. Instead of being Matilda's big brother that was always around to fix things or drive us to school, he was just another confused person. He suddenly seemed twenty years younger. His life wasn't more put together than mine; he was just as tired and unbalanced as I was. That terrified me.

The café materialized around me. Most of the crowd had faded away. The coffee was gone. Our waiter eyed us, patiently waiting for us to pay and clear the table. Liam hadn't moved. He was still thinking about the Christmas Party.

"I think we were the reason that guy moved." I tried to lighten the dark air that had fallen around us.

"It wouldn't surprise me." His eyes stayed on something in the distance, mental focus unchanged.

"The house looks exactly the same," I noted.

"Yeah, she didn't do anything to it," he said. "I'm going to miss it."

"What are you going to do with it?"

"I don't know."

Eventually we reached Sunday evening. The time between our hangovers in the café and returning to Matilda was a bit of a blur. Somehow less communication occurred. My apartment became a quiet world where nothing was discussed. The only sounds came from the TV as we sat motionless on the couch.

Reality had come to visit. While it stayed it gave us nothing but uncertainty and fear for the future. One fact about the future was very clear, without Matilda, we had no one.

As promised, I picked up her donuts on the way in. She greeted us at the door, as full of sass and cheer as always. The red door swung open and there stood a smiling Matilda. Somehow, she looked paler than before.

"You're the best!" she greeted me, taking the box of donuts.

I reached out and hugged her. For a moment we stood still in the front room. Matilda's arms wrapped around my back, and I took in every piece of the moment I could. Her hair smelled like coconut. Under my fingers, backbone lumps were poking through her shirt. The hall clock ticked. I hugged tight and she did the same.

"Three days is a long time, huh?" her voice was weak in my ear.

"Yeah," was all I could manage before letting go.

"So did Liam annoy you that much?" she joked.

I shook my head. "He was a great, temporary roommate. He happens to like *Eternity*."

Matilda rolled her eyes and carried the donuts to the kitchen.

"Not that nerd show again."

"It's not that nerd show. It's the nerd show." Liam entered the front door and carried his bag upstairs.

Donuts were popped into the microwave. Matilda began to talk about how quiet things had been and the help of being free from distractions. Recently her quiet, hermit life had been interrupted by having her brother move back in, she was rather happy to enjoy the solitude again.

Later Matilda led the two of us through the house showing off the work she had done. Side projects that had been abandoned in the past were picked up and finished. Three completely new paintings now joined others in the downstairs closet storage.

In the basement she had welded one small sculpture. A life size cat stood in the middle of the room. When the wind blew, his tail spun.

"Cats' tails don't spin like that," Liam said.

"That's not the point." Matilda told him.

"What is the point?" he asked.

"To look cute. God you're such a boy. I bet before long three adorable, old ladies will be trying to buy this for their garden."

Back upstairs she showed off the last painting she finished. Total, over the weekend she finished six paintings and a sculpture. I'm not an artist, but to me that's quick. I doubt she slept much.

An easel and tarp had been set up in the front room. The latest painting still rested inside. Matilda had always been one to paint abstract. Her work often had bold colors and different shapes that could look like a dog or a flower or an apple tree depending on your mood. This one was different.

Three bold colors split the canvas like Neapolitan ice cream. The top was dark black, the bottom was red, and white filled in the middle. From the top right corner to the bottom left stretched a thin slash of pale blue.

Matilda didn't linger on it. She told us she hadn't moved it to the closet with the others because it wasn't dry. Then she changed the subject to donuts and returned to the kitchen.

For most of the evening, Liam and I remained silent. Having been alone, Matilda had no trouble filling the empty space with talking. We just took in her words. We were both almost scared to blink, because missing a second of her being there with us felt like a tragedy.

In those three days, we both had a sample of life without Matilda. When we finally came back to her, three days had felt like a year. We had a sample of the distant future, and were left terrified. It was another realization of our numbered days and how few we had left.

I memorized her look. The everyday look that I had seen so often I forgot how much of a treasure it was. Her hair was pulled back in a messy bun. A loose, paint stained shirt hung from her pale body. Sharp collar bones emerged from the wide neck, more prominent than ever before. Bright eyes bounced with each word. Red lips rolled and danced as she hardly stopped to take a breath.

Wine was poured for the three of us. Liam and I only spoke when we needed to answer a question. We didn't hear half of what she said. We just wanted to make the seconds last longer as we sat still, completely captivated by her presence.

My ears rang with the sound of ticking. An imaginary clock relentlessly echoed in my head, telling me that the time was limited and slipping away faster than I could experience it. I wanted to run away and forget any of this was happening. But at the same time I wanted to pause the evening and spend forever sitting in the kitchen listening to Matilda talk about anything.

The crutch that kept me from breaking down that evening was Liam. When I glanced at him, he was in the same state as me; silently taking in every moment of his sister that he could. We both realized we weren't going through hell alone.

I had a friend.

7 2) THE ZOO TRIP

A pro to dying is the relaxed expectations everyone has of you. During those last few months Matilda did very little work. Most of her time was out with me or Liam doing odd things or just enjoying an afternoon. I'll admit I left work early a few times just to watch old movies on her couch. Matilda took her spot in the sectional's corner and we huddled under throws for a couple of hours.

Other days we were in donut shops or parks. We would eat a beautiful sandwich or an elaborate dessert, and then I would sit for a few minutes as Matilda struggled to get the lighting right for a good photo. Obscenities were often hurled at trees off a path or ducks in a pond. I dug my feet into the crunchy gravel on the path and waited patiently for her to finish. Outings were rare, and grew continually less frequent.

In those days she never woke up before ten. When I offered eating out she suggested food that was delivered instead. A usual day was wrapped in a throw on the couch.

Two blankets bearing Disney characters had become permanent installments in the living room. Cocooned by their bright colors and fuzzy fabric we viewed *Pride and Prejudice* for the second or third time that week.

When she wasn't with Liam or me, Matilda did a lot of sleeping and Wikipedia reading. Every so often she was presenting new facts she had read about or discovered in page after page of scrolling. A desire to learn was still present. Some of her time and facts covered a string of obscure animals and random people from history.

Occasionally, her thoughts came about during other conversation. Liam's stories from the hospital had a tendency to run disturbing or disgusting. Whenever one began to emerge, Matilda cut his words off with information on ocelots or children's author Roald Dahl.

"Hippos mark territory by defecating," Matilda proclaimed, cutting off

Liam's story.

That was the third fact about hippopotami of the evening. The trend of studying exotic animals had continued to grow over the weeks. After some time moving through different South American jungle creatures, she began explaining what she learned about the inhabitants of the African Savannah. From Matilda's non-sequiturs, I had learned a great deal about giraffes, lions, and something called a springbok.

A quick search showed Liam and me that it was a small, tan and black antelope.

"They are adorable, and jump twelve feet in the air."

Her intentions, even though she didn't come right out and say them, became a little clearer one afternoon. For once, we weren't watching TV. Instead, we were camped in the front room attempting to be productive. I had found an excuse to work from home, and sent some emails from the couch while Matilda sat at her desk. I glanced up to see her graphics work had been put away. Instead she browsed a webpage with cheetah prints on the edges.

"What's that?" I joined her side.

"Just a zoo. They do backstage tours," she gave a sleepy answer, but I knew she was interested. Her larger, recent requests had stopped her from asking for favors for a while. "They let you pet some of the animals. It just looked cool."

"It does look cool, we should do it."

"No, we don't have to," she tried to be modest. I had already commandeered the mouse and scrolled until I found a phone number.

Soon I was given an automated list, and pressed numbers until I was put on hold. Bouncy jungle music began playing in my ear. While I waited to speak to a human, Matilda made small attempts to stop me.

"We don't have to."

"If you want to do it, we're going to do it," I told her.

"But it's expensive, and I hate to make you go to all the trouble."

"Shut up. It's not a trouble," I silenced her.

Tiredness hung in her eyes. It wasn't even lunchtime, but she looked like she had been hard at work all day.

"If they ask, what animal do you want to pet?"

Finally, Matilda smiled and said, "an otter."

After moving a tall painting of a tree and a tea cup away from the glass door, I slipped outside to the patio. Matilda had been playing music from our high school days while we worked, and I didn't have the heart to tell her to pause it. Cat had been enjoying the sunshine from a chair by the table. As I appeared, his head turned to me. Instead of running away, he paused, considering staying around. I took one step out of the door and he showed me his butt as he trotted off.

Red tiles stretched across the patio ground. I started a slow circle on them, first rounding the glass table then pacing along the driveway side. The hold music reached the bridge for the third time. Occasionally, a roar or a bird call was mixed in. Finally, a human voice was heard.

"Hi, I am trying to schedule one of your backstage tours that include petting otters."

"Are you interested in The Backstage Experience?" A deadpan voice told me a price. Her numbers made me gulp. I shook back the thought.

"Yes, I would like to do that please. And I need to schedule it as soon as possible." I heard a computer click lazily. In sync with the key clicks, I bounced from tile to tile.

"The next private tour isn't available until January, but every Friday they do group tours for 20 people."

I stopped bouncing. Nothing could make me subject Matilda to sharing her otter snuggles with other people. Irritation began to grow, but I held it back and kept my voice calm. "Okay, well that is unacceptable. I need a private tour within the next week."

Clearly, this woman had been going through a rough day. I had no aim of taking my stress out on her. Lack of tours was not her fault. I forced my voice to sound as polite as I could; she tried to help me out.

"Sometimes they schedule more tours if there's enough demand. But that doesn't always happen."

"Look," I sighed, and took a seat at the table. "I hate to play this card, but my friend is dying. She's too old for Make a Wish, and she really wants to pet an otter. So please, is there something you can do to help me out?"

"Is this like *A Walk to Remember* thing?" her voice changed to speculation.

"Sure."

"Let me make a call." She put me back on hold. Frustration was kindled by dragging my finger across the glass and leaving a streaked smudge. Soon I had the tune and order of animal calls memorized.

"I found an opening," her sudden return made me jump.

"Thank you!" I almost shouted. "When?"

"Friday at two thirty." I shot out of my chair, thanking her a hundred times.

My appreciation was nothing compared to Matilda's. Her fatigue melted away as she grasped me in a hug.

"Thank you," she whispered.

On the drive back and forth from the beach, we had exhausted most road trip games. We had tried various forms of alphabet games, license plate decipers, and apps that promised to keep us entertained. All of them had eventually lost their thrill. Luckily, it was just over an hour the zoo, which was just enough time for simple conversations to not wear out.

Matilda settled into her spot in my passenger seat. Per usual, she navigated and DJ'ed. She was good at chatting, but simultaneously skimmed a magazine of bridal gowns.

The parking lot was laid out by animals. After passing through the gate, attendants pointed out where to go until we were parked in the tiger section.

"Remember that," I told her, pointing to a faded painting of a tiger at the end of our row.

"Done," Matilda replied.

Sunshine spilled over the world without a single cloud to stop it. Pink bears made an appearance over Matilda's eyes. Miraculously, her hair made it into a ponytail. I tried pulling my hair back too, but a nubby, short ponytail was no match to her natural, black waves.

At the ticketing booth, a young woman behind glass took our names and spoke into a crackly microphone. She slid lanyards with badges across the counter to us. "Take these, and Emmet will meet you by the restrooms on the left in just a few moments."

Cartoon animals surrounded a bold Tessie Fletcher- Backstage Guest. I slid the lanyard over my head; Matilda tied hers to the belt loop on her shorts.

"Have a wild time!" the employee's well-wishing was enthusiastic, but rehearsed.

"What a terrifying statue," Matilda said. "It's like they're saying, 'welcome to the zoo kids. We're here to teach you about nature and scare the shit out of you with the gorilla that ate Tarzan.'"

A large, unrealistic gorilla statue sat next to our bench. Eyes the size of tennis balls glared into the crowd of guests entering the zoo.

"Still hate monkeys?"

"I will always hate monkeys!" she almost shouted. "Because they're terrible, Tessie! Usually they never see a banana; they just live their life in unkempt terror as they fight each other constantly. They're dirty and pornographic and terrible!"

"A gorilla isn't a monkey," I began.

"Shut up."

The crowd began to break as a young man walked towards us with confidence. He was completely covered in khaki, and mud from zoo days past had stained his hiking boots. A nametag and large radio on his belt told us he was a person of power here. At least, he believed he was.

"I think this is us." I tugged Matilda up with me as I stood.

A Teddy Roosevelt hat shaded a thick beard and dark eyes. It was difficult to tell where khaki ended and skin began as arms and legs had seen many sunny days without SPF.

"You guys must be Matilda and Tessie!"

"What gave it away?" Matilda held up her lanyard. I nudged her.

"I'm Emmet, and I'm going to be showing you guys around the zoo today," perfect white teeth smiled over every word. "It's the perfect job for me, because I love animals."

"Oh this sounds promising."

"Be nice," I hissed.

If Emmet heard Matilda's comment, he pretended not to notice. He turned around and began leading us to an employee door. The new view of our guide changed Matilda's perspective.

"Yeah, okay I can be nice."

Behind the view of guests, a golf cart was waiting for us.

I hopped into the back seat of the golf cart, letting Matilda have the passenger seat. We zipped out from between the buildings and onto a backlot.

"Most of the vegetation consumed by our animals is grown on property," Emmet explained. "We're coming up on a few of the fields now. This time of year is a great chance to see how full they get."

The cart slipped onto the back road that circled the zoo. Green filled the space beside us. Row after row of odd plants stretched over the empty acres. Tall chain link fence surrounded everything to deter greedy local wildlife or even curious humans.

"The entire zoo is plotted out like a map. Animals from similar parts of the world all stay together. We're going to the North America sector to see a barn. Now I know that doesn't sound too exciting, because we're in North America now, but we'll see some great friends over there."

From my spot in the back I only caught glimpses of the buildings we passed as they rolled away behind us. I doubted the view was much better from Matilda's spot.

Emmet called each of the buildings a barn. They were only a barn in so much as they held animals. The surprisingly clean, concrete and steel looked nothing like the red barns from children's books about farms. High fences suggested privacy from the sounds and sites of the backroad we were on.

The cart stopped beside a building that was no different to the others we had seen. We climbed out and slipped through a perfectly ordinary door. Inside we were met with a delightful family of otters.

Five or so slipped all around an enclosure. Every moment, a new head popped out of a different window of the wooden house. Several scampered across a log bridge while more swam in the pool below it. At the sound of a clicker, they all rushed to a corner of the enclosure and waited for a keeper to pass off their food. Together, they were like a chorus of dog toys. All of them squeaked in an unearthly, cute sound.

"Two families of otters live here," Emmet explained. "Today B family is out where guests can see them, so A family is getting a day off. One of them is going to come over and say hi in a minute."

"We get to touch it?" Matilda held her breath, waiting for an answer.

"Of course, most of them can be pretty snuggly."

The two of us squealed with excitement as a slick otter in a harness and leash was brought to us. His handler offered us treats to coax him over, but we didn't need it. Right away, he was in Matilda's lap and climbing up her shoulders. Longer and heavier than a house cat, he filled her arms.

"This is Spike," the handler explained. She passed off a treat to Matilda, but Spike quickly had it. "He is five years old, so pretty grown up, but still acts like a baby."

Matilda laughed and rubbed Spike's head as he held still. That only lasted a moment; he was soon circling her shoulders again. She stretched out in the floor so Spike could travel her crossed legs.

"Can I take some pictures for you?" The handler offered. Matilda passed off her camera. I watched them both from Emmet's side.

"Thanks for doing this. She's going through," I paused for the right words, "A rough time."

His face dropped, "Oh you're the one from the *Walk to Remember* phone call."

"Yeah." Apparently word had spread about my desperate plea to help a friend. I glanced back at Matilda and Spike. The otter had knocked her pink sunglasses from her head. With some help, they were on his face.

"Tessie, look!" Matilda called. "He thinks he's people!"

"Let me make a quick call," Emmet stepped to the side and took the radio from his belt. "Maybe we can see a few more barns."

"Really? Thank you!" I smiled.

"Hey, it's no problem," he replied. "Today is not a busy day for me, and you guys are a lot nicer than most of the people that come through. And you're not asking stupid questions."

"Wait," I touched his arm before he slipped out the door. "She hates monkeys."

"Got it," Emmet smiled.

After goodbyes to Spike, we returned to the golf cart. I found my place in the back seat just before it jolted into reverse and zipped back onto the road. Instead of going back the way we came, we continued on the outer road.

"I called some people, and I think we can go to a couple more barns today," Emmet said.

"Really?!" I had told Matilda the tour only included one barn, she understood our guide was going out of his way to be kind to us.

"We won't peak in the baboon section. I hear you're not a big fan." He nodded to a series of barn as we passed them.

"No. Damn dirty shits."

"Matilda," I tried to stop her language, but Emmet interrupted me.

"It's fine, we're backstage. Say whatever the hell you want."

Even after her online research of animals across the globe, Matilda was not nearly informed as Emmet was. She would ask one question about an antelope, and Emmet had ten extra facts she hadn't heard yet.

At the second barn, a set of fire escape stairs took us to the door. A second story entrance was required to be face to face with the giraffes inside. We joined a keeper who was offering grain buckets to two females.

Heads the size of suitcases came up to us. Matilda and I scratched ears and ossicones while we fed them from our hands. Heavy, velvet lips rubbed my palms clean of grain pellets.

"These are reticulated giraffes," the barn keeper told us. "They have bigger spots."

More facts about Ibuni and Lily were listed off, but I didn't pay much attention. I was mostly focusing on excitement of petting a giraffe. Dark eyes watched me from under long eyelashes. Matilda noticed them too.

"I wonder what they would look like with mascara."

"I've honestly always wanted to try it," the keeper replied.

Our backstory had spread to most of the employees. Each one that talked to us was incredibly kind. They answered any questions we had and offered to take pictures.

Soon we found ourselves in another barn. This time we leaned against a cool, cement wall. Just ahead of us thick, metal pillars stretched fifteen feet into the air. One of the gates across the barn was unlatched, and two keepers slowly pushed it open. In strode a ten foot tall, African elephant.

"This is Dina," Emmet began making introductions. "She's getting a bath today, but afterwards we should be able to say hi."

Dina stopped in the center of the room as buckets and hoses were brought near her. On cue, she lay down and a bath began. Saggy, grey skin was soon covered in white suds. An ear bigger than a blanket lifted straight up and was scrubbed down. Tiny eyes closed in relaxation.

"We only have ladies here," Emmet went on. "Elephants are matriarchal. They run in a heard with one female in charge. Bull elephants are usually seen alone, but occasionally run in bachelor groups. Dina is our second biggest girl. Her mother, Rafiki is the herd's matriarch."

Dina got up and lay on her opposite side. Scrubbing began all over again on the second half of her body.

"How do you run a breeding program without any boys?" Matilda asked bluntly.

"Artificial insemination. In elephants, it's the best way to ensure success." Our guide was unfazed by the question. "Two more should deliver calves next summer."

After her body was clean, Dina stood up. She lifted a back foot and rested it on a stool. One of the keepers began filing the skin on the bottom of her feet.

"Wow," I said. "An elephant getting a pedicure isn't something I ever thought I'd see."

"They need it, walking around barefoot in the dirt all day," Emmet smiled. He glanced my way and I smiled back.

When her feet were finished, Dina was led to our spot at the fence. Tentatively at first, I reached through and stroked her trunk. The dark skin was sturdy and rough. My fingers fell into the crevices as my hand glided down her trunk. Standing directly in front of her, I realized just how big she really was. Elephants are known for being the largest land animal, but you don't quite realize how big that actually is until one is less than a meter away.

"Elephants really do have an excellent memory. That's not just a cartoon joke about elephants never forgetting," As Emmet's facts began; I stepped aside and let Matilda meet Dina.

"After an elephant passes away, every elephant in the heard that knew her will stand beside her body and touch her. The one that knew her the longest stays there the longest. Not long ago some researchers had been following a heard for a few months. The elephants could recognize the sounds of other elephants, even the ones that had died."

I watched Matilda silently stroke the elephant's trunk, taking in the words. Emmet realized it too and changed subjects. "Did you know elephants hate bees?"

Like the elephants, the white rhinos had large pillars between us and them. Again I was surprised at their size. A lovely girl by the name of Lola had a shoulder taller than my head. Stubby legs carried her around the stall a few times until food appeared. A six thousand pound, barrel of a body came to a stop beside us. Her wide, flat mouth scooped up the hay we tossed in front of her.

Eventually, her body was close enough to scratch. Lola's skin was rough, but not nearly as much as Dina's had been. Our hands scratched her ears and under her belly, the part we could reach at least. A tiny tail swished either side of her round, white rump.

Lola's face was bigger than a spare tire. Protruding from it was a short fat horn that looked hardly threatening or even valuable. Not everyone agreed, and the white rhinos were endangered for it. To me, Lola was more like a gigantic, poor sighted golden retriever. She knew to come when her name was called, and liked being scratched on the belly. Any danger was simply them moving too fast and not seeing where they were going, hence the pillars between us.

As a wrap up, Emmet brought us to a display section used for the larger tours. A few smaller animals were brought out for a meet and greet. Since there were only two of us, the benches for onlookers were left behind and we stood beside a stool holding an ocelot.

Less friendly than Spike, Zelda spent her time pacing the area as far as her leash would allow. Only once could my fingers catch the edge of her silky fur. Soon she left and was followed by a North American red fox.

Emmet excused himself as a middle aged man showed off the last animal of the day. The dashing boy's name was Albert, and had a love for the treats we gave him. Somewhat advanced in years, he was happy to sit still and be snuggled. He made me want a fox of my own.

All too soon, Albert was taken away from us. We watched as black feet trotted away, and a slick orange tail slipped behind a door. Our tour was finished.

"Did you know it's almost six?" Matilda said. "We need food."

Emmet appeared, carrying two bags from the gift shop. "I'm sorry to keep you guys out so long, the shop closed on us."

"Oh don't apologize, you went out of your way for us," I offered with a smile. Indeed, the tour had gone much longer than I had planned, and was more extensive than either of us had hoped.

"Well, please accept these from us." He passed off the bags. "We really hope you had a good day."

Word had spread pretty far about our situation; our bags were stuffed with merchandise. Matilda examined the contents of hers as we walked through the thinning parking lot to the car.

"We have a water bottle," she revealed plastic bottle with a lid shaped like a lion head. On the side were three large, green arrows encouraging zoo guests to reduce, reuse, and recycle. Matilda plunged her hand back into the bag and found a stuffed animal. "Aw! He got me an otter!"

"It looks like Spike!" We turned into the row of cars marked as the tiger section.

"Thank you. This day has been amazing." She smiled. "Now let me see what's in yours."

In the car I searched for anything nearby that had decent food. Matilda rifled through my bag and discovered a similar water bottle, as well as a stuffed giraffe."

"I'll trade you," I offered.

"Hell no, Spike 2 is mine forever."

Soon we were on the road towards home and, more importantly, a stop for food.

"Oh my gosh," Matilda breathed, "He left his number in here."

"What! Why?" The car jerked and I quickly slipped back into the lane. "That one must be yours."

"No this is the bag he handed you," she laughed and rattled the water bottle.

"Why? Why would he do that?" My hands stiffened around the steering wheel.

"Because you're hot, you should call him."

"No, he lives an hour away. He's way too crunchy granola, and he had a long beard. Who knows what's under that." I kept my eyes on the road and bit my lip until it hurt.

"So?"

"If men can be picky about hair on my legs and armpits, I can be picky about hair on their face."

"Yeah," she agreed. "He probably has poop from every continent on those shoes." She grew silent as we both mulled over the situation for a few seconds. "But, come on, you saw the same khaki covered butt that I did."

"I'll think about it," quieted her on the subject. Momentarily.

We found a family restaurant in the next mile and milled inside. The place was completely covered in wood paneling. The ocean was the obvious theme from the anchors, nets, and photos of ships that peppered the walls. Yet the menu did not offer much in the way of fish.

Feeling frivolous, we ordered bright blue drinks in gigantic glasses. Pineapple wedges speared by plastic swords hung on the edge. With my highlander level of daily consumption, the amount of alcohol in the glass was not taking hold of me. I kept sipping water to stay level headed. Matilda was a different story.

Quickly she was leaning aggressively to her right. After three sips she had taken to staring into space. I quickly lost track of how many times she thanked me. Before long, the conversation turned back to our guide and the unexamined number waiting in my souvenir bag.

"I should have called more boys and taken a few more chances." I could see the ghosts of past crushes glaze Matilda's eyes. Like any young woman, she would pine after the occasional gentleman. Rarely did her attraction escalate to the point of making a move.

As her best friend, I knew all the details of Matilda's relationships. Mine had not been much different.

"Promise you'll at least give this guy a shot." Her gaze had turned towards me. I knew she was trying to help, but my thoughts had not lingered on Emmet as much as hers had. No doubt she wasn't thinking of him for herself, she just wanted me to have someone later.

"Okay. Promise." I smiled at her before downing a bit more of my drink.

The blue liquid in Matilda's glass was gone before I reached the halfway point of mine. I slid the glass across the table and offered her the rest. She accepted it, and kept talking.

"At least I don't have to break some poor bastard's heart. Or make him feel like shit for going after another girl when I'm gone." She laughed at her own joke. I smiled politely, unable to shake the pain that Matilda was so careful to hide.

As each other's only close friends, most of our time across our nearly thirty years was spent together. In hindsight, our excessive bffing might have kept us both from serious relationships. But I wouldn't trade a minute of it for an extra boyfriend or date in my life.

8 10) WEDDING DRESSES, PHOTOSHOP, LIES

Returning to work after our animal tour was harder than coming in after the beach. Working Monday after you took Friday off is like trying to swim when you have just finished a huge meal. You know that you have to make it to the other side of the pool, but you just want to lie still on a lawn chair and enjoy your swollen tummy. Nothing is worth the effort, and all you want to do is curl up into a fetal position and take a nap.

I was struggling to focus on my project. The allure and excitement of designing an app had vanished in the harsh light of a vacation hangover. Amelia had been distant for a few weeks. I knew I needed to haul ass to get her attention again, but I couldn't get myself to do it. For the most part I was working on daily projects and polishing up final notes. All of it felt like a waste of time. I wanted to sit on the couch with Matilda and watch *The Golden Girls*.

Each evening I drove straight to Matilda's house and had dinner with her and sometimes Liam. After dinner I finished whatever bottle of wine we opened and stayed as late as I could manage. We had found nirvana in the sleepy pile of blankets on the couch.

Matilda had taken to eating whatever she wanted. Other meals showed up if Liam was there. Any night he didn't work he was cooking. Any time he wasn't, we were eating pizza, chicken, and lasagna. If it was more work than throwing something frozen in the oven, we didn't want to eat it.

One afternoon I sat at my desk calculating how early I could excuse myself to leave. Any chance of working those last two hours was gone. The sound of my phone startled me out of planning. Matilda was calling.

"Hey," her voice sounded half distracted, "I need you to take Wednesday and Thursday off next week."

"Okay, I'll try to move some things around." I opened a calendar. "Can we do Thursday and Friday instead?"

"No," Matilda was blunt. "It has to be Wednesday and Thursday. I made appointments"

"What's going on?"

"I'll explain tonight, can you come over?"

"I was already planning to." I highlighted the days on the schedule.

"Cool. Oh, and pick up some pizza. Liam is working and I'm tired of stir fry and salmon," I could hear her clicking the computer mouse as she brought up a page to place an order. Our local favorite had been offering online ordering options for a couple years, but never managed to work out all the kinks. She grunted as the page crashed. "I'll order it, but if you want wine bring it yourself. You drank me dry."

"Stalk a better liquor cabinet."

"Why would I bother? You always have enough at your place. I never have to worry about it." Matilda cursed under her breath. "This keeps adding olives. If you pick it up, and it has those Satan toe rings on it, punch them in the face for me."

"Will do."

A couple of hours later I was opening the red, front door. Matilda's computer was on in the front room and playing songs from our road trips. She was waiting for me on the couch, a basket of pink and gold explosion sat on the coffee table.

I glanced down at a rolled up tee shirt, a wine glass, and a button. All of them bore the same three letters in a large, bold print.

"What's up?" I was unsure where this night would take me.

Matilda ceremoniously stood, and took my hand, "I have something to ask you."

"Can I put this pizza down first?"

"No," she didn't break eye contact.

"Okay."

"Tessie. We have been friends for over twenty years. You were there for every Christmas, every birthday, and every important life event. You took me on a cruise. You helped me hide my white cardigan from my parents when we spilled grape juice on it. Remember? We weren't supposed to be playing with the glass tea set but we did anyways."

"Yes, I remember," I assured her. "We buried it at the bottom of your Barbie box and it was never seen again."

"You were there for graduation, my first job, all of my crushes, the cardigan cover up of 2001, the popsicle cover up of 2002, and it only makes sense that I ask you now." Matilda got down on one knee. "Theresa Philip Fletcher."

"That's not my middle name."

"Don't care. Will you do me the honor of being my fake Made of Honor in the fake wedding of me and the luckiest man alive, Micah

Farnham so that I can try on a wedding dress and get free food and feel like a princess?"

"Yes. Yes a thousand times."

We laughed and hugged. Matilda took my face in her hands.

"This is the happiest day of my life."

"Let me put down this pizza, my hand is cramping up."

We moved to the couch so that I could open my present and Matilda could show off her plans. A large binder was dropped onto the table with a thud. Burlap and butterflies surrounded the words *Wedding Plans*.

Matilda flipped the front cover open. An image of a white sand beach dominated the page. Near it was a close up of a ring. I turned to see a similar one on Matilda's hand.

"Where'd you get that?"

"A store at the mall for twelve bucks. If we're going to get free perks, we gotta sell this. Let me fill you in on everything I've put together so far."

Scraps of fabric and corners of other pictures stuck out the edges of the binder. Glitter letters were present on each page. Hours of work had gone into the project.

"We have been dating for a year and half. He proposed on the beach earlier this summer."

I glanced at the corner of the page. Matilda was hugging the movie star on the same beach. She noticed me staring at it.

"Made that in Photoshop."

"Nicely done."

"Thanks." She was unfazed.

The next page was full of honeymoon plans. Pictures from our cruise filled the page, and a second image of her with arms around the celebrity's chiseled torso.

"What the shit, is he shirtless in that picture?"

"Yup," she stated.

"Where did you find that?"

"I dug deep on the internet and put my skills to the test." She showed me her phone, "I even made a selfie one."

Sure enough, Matilda was cheek to cheek with Micah.

"That's impressive, and you are insane."

"Yeah, I know. But I have it ready if they want to see the groom." She returned her attention to the binder.

All I could do was smile. She continued her detailed explanation of wedding plans while I started eating. A nearby country club had been reserved for the first Saturday in May. The ceremony would be on the front lawn and the reception inside. Her colors were gray and baby blue. A swatch of fabric was pinned to my picture on another page.

"It matches your hair and brings out my eyes," was the most feminine sentence to ever come out of Matilda's mouth. I just agreed and started slice two.

"Isn't he a bit older than you?"

"Yes, but we don't notice because of how very mature I am," Matilda slapped the next page open.

It had pictures of cakes and flower designs. The glue behind the images was seeping out of the edges and making the pages stick together. With a wrist flick, she flipped the page and a song list appeared. Beside it was a very strict *Do Not Play* list.

"I could always write the name Matt really well, so I thought that's what we could call him. I can't just say Micah Farnham, they'll think I'm crazy."

"Right, because you definitely aren't." I said. She continued, unfazed.

"Exactly, you can't just go in and try on wedding dresses at a sophisticated shop unless you're actually getting married. They're really prejudiced against single people."

"What are you going to tell them when you don't want to buy any of the dresses you tried on?" I was on slice three, Matilda was still just half way through her first.

"I've practiced the, 'I don't know, it just doesn't feel like *the one* you know?'" Her voice dropped on the word *one*.

In our middle school years we found our sexual awakening with members of the same band. I can't even remember the name of it. It was some sort of rough, punk group. We each had a different member we swore we would marry.

Post school afternoons were spent in either her bedroom or mine. Either one had the same posters papering the wall. Weddings with boys that had been thrust into young stardom were planned. We had locations, dresses, and bridesmaids selected. Plans were never as detailed as the spread Matilda prepared for an imaginary wedding with a movie star just to try on wedding dresses.

On Wednesday I donned my maid of honor shirt. Matilda wore a shirt that said "bride" in a matching font under her flannel button up. We took my car downtown on the agreement it was easier to park than the tank. About three blocks from the bridal shop I found a bare meter. After a painstakingly large amount of quarters, we marched back to the shop.

Glass doors opened to an immediate lace paradise. A sweet aroma of flowers was in every breath, and creepy, headless mannequins displayed their dresses. We paused to take in their unusual pose, and didn't notice an employee approach.

Like a puff of fart, a smartly dressed woman suddenly existed beside us.

"Do you have an appointment?" We took in the black pencil skirt and blonde hair that had been pulled into the world's tightest bun.

"Yes, Matilda Day," she replied from behind the encyclopedia sized binder.

A lipstick smile changed the woman's entire demeanor, "Of course, follow me. I'm Megan, I'll be helping you both today."

"It's going to eat us!" Matilda panicked as we followed the woman to the counter.

"Hush, she can smell fear and lies," I hissed back.

A bottle of champagne and two glasses were retrieved from under the counter. With a quick pop the glasses were filled and handed to us. The brand was cheap, but sweet. Add in the fact it was free and I gulped it down.

"What's the full name?" Megan asked.

"Matilda Day," she said.

"Yes, but what's his name?"

"Matt." Matilda really had practiced.

"Matt what?"

Matilda hesitated. She hadn't practiced enough. In her carefully plotted fantasy lie she had forgotten a rather sincere detail, her groom's fake last name. I saw her eyes dart to the side. The tin foil on the open bottle was in shreds that bordered on violent if touched.

"Sharp." Matilda's voice ended the awkward silence, and she broke into fake laughter. "Matt Sharp. I'm just not used to saying it."

Megan laughed, "Well, get used to writing it too. It'll be your name."

Matilda's smile disappeared; I knew the poor woman was in for it. Before I could give a warning, Matilda snapped back.

"No. I'm not changing my name."

The same, lipstick smile from our entrance returned. "Of course, let's get you started."

A binder appeared before us that rivaled Matilda's for size. Magically it opened to a page of models in white. Words describing cut and style were tossed around and I didn't understand what they meant. I drank another glass of free champagne.

Before long, we were lead to a fitting room. Squishy, pink carpet begged me to take off my shoes, and I complied. Then I found my place on a large, puffy sofa. Megan wheeled in a rack of complete whiteness. Together we flicked through the hangers before Matilda disappeared behind purple, velvet curtains.

"Maid of honor?" Megan asked as we waited.

I hid a burp, "Yes."

"Do you know what she wants you to wear?"

"We… Haven't discussed it past color yet."

"Let me know and I can pull a few things," Megan's smile was getting more believable.

"Matilda," I called, "What do you want me to wear?"

A muffled voice answered, "Whatever you want, babe. You know the shade of blue."

After giving my figure an eye, Megan disappeared. I glanced down at my jeans and shirt. No doubt a judgment had passed over us from the sales clerk. I took a mental note that if I should ever get married, I would avoid this particular shop. Then I felt myself pause.

I returned to reality as Matilda emerged in a white avalanche that rivaled Cinderella's ball gown for space. Lace straps poked out of her shoulders like triangles, but they were no match for the maelstrom of lace that wrapped from her waist to the floor.

"I think I had a dress like this for a Barbie once," I told her, filling my glass for the third time.

"Oh my gosh, it's heavy! There is so much fabric here, who needs this much fabric?" Matilda struggled to the full length mirrors for a better view. "If you squint it looks like a whipped cream can exploded."

"I'm glad you're not serious about this one, it's terrible." I did my best to smooth out the skirt. Fluffed to its fullest potential, the dress took up even more space.

Matilda glanced at the landscape, and then promptly sat in the floor. Most of the skirt stayed afloat, circling her in a great, white reef. She glanced at my reflection in the mirror.

"Look, I'm a mushroom!"

As she stood up I passed off her glass. The bottle had reached empty.

When Matilda left to get into dress number two, Megan returned with a much slimmer rack. The same shade of blue from the notebook was shaped into five dresses of varying styles. I pulled a long, slim one and slipped into the dressing room opposite Matilda.

Soon we both were in new dresses. Matilda's second choice was much slimmer. It wrapped around her curves without a trace of lace.

"You look pretty!" I pointed to her more flattering choice.

"You look like your car!" she laughed.

I turned to the full length mirrors. The shade of blue indeed matched my bug parked down the street.

"You made a great choice of colors, because I have an awesome car."

"You have an awesome car because I picked it out for you."

We stood together at the mirrors and admired our choices. Megan opened a second bottle and handed off fresh glasses. Numbers and package explanations were repeated to us. I didn't listen, I was watching Matilda.

When flannel shirts and graphic tees are ninety percent of someone's wardrobe, you rarely see them dress up. I could count on one hand the number of times I saw Matilda in a dress. That day she looked so beautiful.

My admiration was halted by her next question.

"Do you have any dresses with pockets?"

I couldn't stop myself from laughing.

"I'll look, but I don't know of any off hand." Megan was not amused.

She slipped out of the room, no doubt taking a break from us. Matilda admired herself in the mirrors for a moment longer before returning to the dressing stall.

I retrieved another blue dress and slipped away too. My second dress was strapless and ended at my knees. Matilda's plans were right, the color was flattering. Feeling pretty, I stepped out to meet Matilda.

As she emerged from the purple curtain, any thoughts of my own attractiveness were gone. The dress was lovely. The flattery almost lifted Matilda off her feet as she glided to the mirrors.

In the newest, almost sparkling dress, Matilda stood straight and tall in the mirror. Proper lighting made her look even more beautiful. No details about the dress stayed with me. Hell, I don't even know if it had straps or sleeves or nothing. I just remember she looked absolutely stunning, and thinking Micah Farnham didn't deserve her. I glanced at her reflection; her big eyes were beginning to swell.

"Wow," Matilda breathed. "I don't remember ever feeling this pretty."

I stepped closer and placed my hands on her shoulders, "You're more beautiful than a female Jon Hamm."

She laughed, the joke worked, but a single tear still escaped down her cheek. A hand wiped it away as quickly as it appeared.

"This is all society's fault, her voice grew stronger. "Girls are trained to believe they have to have a prince and a white dress. If they don't get it by thirty, they think there's something wrong with them."

"There's nothing wrong with you," I assured her.

"Except for my faulty heart."

"Stop, I'm serious. Instead of setting up a home and having babies you had a career. How many artists get paid to do what they love?"

A halfhearted smile brought, "I only sold two paintings."

"And that's awesome! So many gave up before then, but you didn't."

Her eyes were dry, but her face was still solemn. She looked hard at her reflection. Pale fingertips glided over the details in the white fabric. The dress deserved a moment to just be appreciated for its intricate perfection.

"Society is terrible for making me want this."

"Maybe," I admitted. "But I think that at our core we all want lifelong companionship, and it's natural to want something that makes you look pretty. Now we might not be lovers or anything, but we're pretty great companions."

A grin began to spread across her face, "You're the best maid of honor I've ever had."

"Thanks," I had to laugh. "Also, right now you are planning a wedding with your celebrity crush. How many people get to do that?"

"Yeah, but I don't get the sex part with him."

"Well," I thought for a moment. "We'll write him a letter. I hear he's very charitable."

Finally, Matilda gave a genuine, cover your face from embarrassment, laugh. I couldn't bring myself to laugh with her. Grief stabbed my heart like a knife. Two feelings fought each other to hurt me the most. One was watching Matilda cope with never having her own wedding. As intense as her opinions on society were, planning a wedding was something we all at least deserve to dream about. But that wasn't as hard as realizing she wouldn't be beside me when I planned my own.

Someday I would be in the same situation, a book of details and a date set ahead of me. Friends would be nearby as I stood there in white, deciding on a dress. Matilda wouldn't be near me. If she wouldn't be there, then I might as well do it alone. My heart broke at the thought of ever doing it at all without her.

Any feeling of hurt for my suffering instead of what Matilda was going through gave me a wave of guilt. It was like someone pinned me to the floor with a lead blanket. I couldn't get up, and I didn't want to. I needed to feel the pressure of the guilt, because I deserved it for thinking so selfishly. I had no right to be sad for my situation, I needed to be sad for her.

I filled my glass with the last of the second champagne bottle.

"You okay to drive?" Matilda questioned as she stepped into the changing room.

"Yeah, don't worry," I assured her mothering. "This is some weak ass shit."

After a lie about finances and Matilda's convincing, "None of them just felt like 'the one' you know?" we were out the door. The appointment pushed us well into lunch time.

Matilda complained about hunger, but the painful thoughts took away my appetite. A bucket of fried chicken joined us for the ride home.

Once on Matilda's couch, pieces were divided up between us. I poured whiskey into the glass of soda on the coffee table.

"Dude, it's like two in the afternoon," she said. "Pace yourself at least a little bit."

"That cheap champagne was a tease," I explained. I returned the bottle to the liquor cabinet in the kitchen after an extra gulp. Matilda had begun flipping through channels on the TV and hadn't noticed.

The changes stopped on a reality show about wedding dresses. Matilda made a comment about the intrusive pressure that exists everywhere for women to get married. Yet we didn't switch to anything else

"You looked a lot prettier than her," I stated.

"Thank you."

Two women and what felt like one hundred dresses later, the chicken was gone. The couch sucked us up with soft blankets, and we settled into a food coma. Unable to move to get the remote, we kept watching reality shows.

"Why did I need to take tomorrow off too? Are we going to another dress place?"

"Oh no much better," she replied. "Three different caterers are coming over to present their wedding deals."

"Yes! Nothing is better than free food." Even with a full stomach I felt excited.

"Free food, free hors d'oeuvres, and free cake," she sighed. Sleep was creeping in.

The lazy afternoon turned into a lazy evening. By nightfall we were sluggish to the point of me not wanting to drive home. I took residency in the guest room.

The next morning, Matilda insisted we couldn't eat breakfast. She claimed that every ounce of stomach space must be filled with culinary delicacies. Bargaining and threats got me coffee and one slice of toast.

When the first chief finally arrived at eleven, I was ready to eat him. We sat down on the same side of the dining room table. A white table cloth was spread before us. He entered from the kitchen with a tray and two plates were set down. To call them half portions would have been a generous statement.

A long explanation was given. I didn't hear it, because I was eating every possible bite. The samples were like taking a food pill. Matilda scratched meticulous notes. Every bite she had was savored and described. She had questions for each items, and the cook was happy to give a lengthy answer. My plate was empty before Matilda finished half.

After samples of finger foods and a slice of wedding cake that was much smaller than promised, Matilda gave a practiced answer.

"I enjoyed all of it, and your prices are fair. The only thing is I still have to hear from two more options today."

The caterer understood and remained professional. He packed up his things and Matilda waved to his van as he drove off.

"That was not enough food after fasting all morning." I complained from the table.

"I'm sorry," Matilda returned to the dining room. "The next one will be here in like twenty minutes. I promise that they will food." She shrugged, knowing her answer made no sense.

The second caterer was much like the first. The presentation was lacking in spectacle, but the food was a little better. It was a woman that time, and I think she felt more relaxed around us.

She asked Matilda more about her wedding plans and the groom. Matilda had answers stored away for any sort of question that arose.

"Some advice, don't be afraid to kiss his mom's ass," she explained while opening a wine pairing. I eagerly held out my glass. She filled it and continued, "Get her to like you now. It'll make a huge difference in twenty years."

When prompted, she talked about her own wedding. Matilda asked questions about seating and flowers that had terms I had never heard before. They asked my opinion on one of factors I didn't understand.

"Uh, I agree with whatever Matilda thinks is best."

"Well you are perfect at your job," the caterer laughed.

That round we had much more generous portions of cake. Matilda flipped through images of the decorative options. I found myself sharing opinions of tiered circles of sugar heaven.

Matilda's wrap up was even more convincing that time. They shared smiles and laughs as she showed the caterer out the front door.

As the door closed, Matilda's smile faded from her face. Her expression was suddenly blank. In the natural light of the front room she looked paler than normal.

"Are you okay?" I joined her at her side, but she didn't turn to face me.

"For a minute I forgot it wasn't real." After a sigh, she went back to smiling, "All right! Round three. Let's see what this sorry bastard has for us to eat."

9 4) GAS STATION AND NEW FRIENDS

In late August that year an unholy heat wave passed through our area. Stepping outside was like sliding into a hot tub full of jelly. Turning on the air conditioning hardly brought an ease to anyone. As Mrs. Day used say about rough fixes, "it's better than nothing, but just barely."

The only remedy we found was lying in the basement floor of Matilda's home. Makeshift creature comforts were carried down with us to make the coolest section of the house more tolerable, and to justify our time cut off from the world. Sculptures and paintings were shoved to one wall to make space.

An old TV was set up against one wall. Because of its age and location, hooking up cable or internet was impossible. We were stuck watching DVDs. Our small arms, combined with weakness from the heat, had us bringing down bean bag chairs to sit on. The only couch small enough to fit down the stairs was in the front room, and after several tries lifting it was determined an impossibility. The old bean bag chairs were better than the concrete floor, but just barely. Every forty five minutes we stood and flipped them over so we could sit on the newly cooled side.

Pride and Prejudice wrapped up for the second time that weekend. Credits rolled up the screen, but we didn't move from our spots. Empty soda cans and candy wrappers littered the floor around us.

The sight took me back to our evenings in the family space upstairs. While games, seats, and various other pieces changed across our childhood years, one staple remained: the TV and the two of us falling asleep in front of it on a weekend night.

I stretched out my foot, almost expecting to feel the sandy colored carpet under me. Instead, I was met by the chill of the basement floor. My body soaked in it. After a moment, I repositioned myself to find a fresh, cool spot.

"I need a slushie," Matilda said after a moment.

"Me too."

"I don't know if I can stand up."

The chairs offered very little support. With the distraction of Mr. Darcy, we had gone a while without flipping the bean bags over. Our bodies had stiffened and welded to the hard floor.

After a moment of rallying, we stood together. Moans of pain shot out as our bodies wrenched back to straight. A thousand years of age settled into my joints and muscles.

"How did we ever sit on these all night?" I had to turn my entire body to look at Matilda.

"I miss childhood," she squeaked.

A few struggle filled minutes later, we were up the stairs and headed for the front door. Opening it was like stepping into an oven. We shuffled to my car and instantly cranked its AC. My bones thanked me for sitting in a proper chair, but the black vinyl seat seared my skin.

Sidewalks were barren. Parents seemed to be encouraging their children to stay indoors.

Thankfully the best gas station for slushies was close. I parked beside it in a miniscule section of shade. Inside we were swallowed by cool air.

Matilda cursed when we approached the slushie machine. "Why don't they have cherry life? This store is a part of that same chain from the beach."

Begrudgingly, she still filled a large cup with frozen, sugar water. Our tongues steadily becoming bluer, we wandered through the store. The heat waiting for us outside insisted we skim every aisle of junk food and take our time.

"Get whatever treat you want," Matilda said from behind her pink bears. "It's on me."

I scooped up a women's magazine and we made our way to the register. A similar publication sat with mine on the counter. As we were rung up, Matilda eyed the clear display case bellow our purchase.

"Give me five scratch offs too," she called to the man across from us.

"Which ones?" He was only half interested in us. The temperature had added a glaze to not only his sleeveless arms, but his distant eyes as well.

"Those," she pointed to a roll. "They look the prettiest."

Her selection process unnoticed, Matilda was passed the tickets along with her receipt.

The back of the convenience store held a single table and booth. Usually, a perch for nothing but fading, fluorescent light, we took the spot. For a few moments, we silently enjoyed the cool and our reading material. I think Matilda and I kept the magazine industry going with our weekly purchases.

"Mia Turner and Stanley Reed split up," she finally spoke.

"Called it." My eyes remained on an article about Manhattan apartments.

"Oh she was cheating on him with her costar Angie Comstock."

"Eek. Talk about a scandal."

"Ha," she glanced up at me, "I thought my wedding planning was screwed up."

She turned a few pages and was quickly caught up in another article.

"Micah Farnham is in Portugal studying for a role." She closed the magazine, content with her celebrity news. "That's my man."

After fishing a quarter from her purse, she set to work on her scratch off tickets. Each one was closely studied front and back before she began.

"Scratching this shit off is the best part," she explained with a loose grin. "I don't even care if I win or lose."

Her thumb and finger set into scribbling away grey dust. Small mountains of the stuff began to grow on either side of the paper. The card was eventually cleared, and she won nothing.

"Damnit."

The same rigor went into the second ticket. Flakes of dust began to spread across the table. I brushed it away.

"Wonder how they make this," she pondered aloud. Her fist didn't slow.

"Not sure." I brushed away more dust.

"I just won fifty dollars!" Beaming, Matilda held up the ticket for me to see. "Just like that! How fun!"

After more scratching and more piles of dust, Matilda found two more losses and a ticket for fifteen dollars. She examined the tickets and the rest of our purchases from the day.

"Well that was a bit anticlimactic," she mused. "Now that I've scratched all the grey stuff off, what fun is there?"

"You won enough to pay for all of this and dinner." I closed my magazine.

"That's true, I'm feeling pizza." Matilda gathered her things. "Want to have it delivered and stay the rest of the evening?"

We made our way back to the car. The heat slapping us in the face the moment we stepped outside. At the car I struggled to find my keys and unlock the door.

Matilda gazed past me into the distance as I searched. Her mind had gone somewhere else. The doors opened and she stopped me.

"Get the air started, there's something I want to do." In an instant she was inside.

I turned the air up to full blast and rolled down the windows. Even in the shade my car had quickly turned into a hell box. Across the small parking lot I could see shimmers of hot air rising off of the asphalt. Matilda appeared at the passenger window.

"I have to try one more thing, but you're not allowed to do it with me." She displayed a red and white carton of cigarettes.

"What the hell?"

"I know it's stupid and bad for you, but I just have to know what it's like. What makes it so cool?" She popped out of the window and began fiddling with the plastic wrap. I joined her behind my car.

"I never thought it looked cool," I stated. I knew this sudden event was a bad decision, but a part of me wanted to see where it would end.

"Bully for you," Matilda muttered with one cigarette balanced between her red lips. She reminded me of someone's great aunt living out her retirement years in Florida.

"The brown end goes in your mouth," I instructed.

"Really?"

"Yeah, that's where the filter is." I leaned against the car's trunk.

"But that's the gross looking end." She removed the stick to inspect it. Agreeing she had been in error, the filtered end came to rest on her lips.

After a struggle with a lighter, the stick was ignited. Matilda took one breath in, and made a sour face. Coughing began. The cigarette fell to the ground. She coughed again. In frustration, the carton thudded against a nearby dumpster in an angry throw.

When she finally caught her breath, Matilda leaned against the car's bumper. Her eyes closed as she swayed to catch her balance. It might have been the taste of a single puff, the way she lost her breath, the insane amount of sugar from her slushie, the ridiculous heat, or a combination of the four, but Matilda dropped blue vomit onto the pavement.

"Don't tell Liam," she muttered.

"Of course not," I offered her a warm water bottle from my back seat. She rinsed her mouth and we took our seats in the car. "Should I drive?"

"Just let me sit for a minute." Matilda's eyes closed as she let the cool air wash over her. "This would be a great image for one of those anti-smoking ads. I'm dying and everything. I mean, not from smoking, but still."

After a moment, we began the drive home. Matilda's intention to order pizza was not deterred. Having won the lottery that day, she justified splurging on delivery, breadsticks, and dessert.

We could tolerate the ground floor when we returned. Reality television gathered all of our attention over the course of the late afternoon and dinner. Another marathon about expensive wedding dresses was on, and Matilda explained how hers had been better than any of the choices on screen. She sat crisscross in the corner, without a blanket for once. I could feel myself relaxing as I put my brain on autopilot and let myself enjoy just sitting on the couch with her.

"I don't think there are any more things to do," she stated calmly.

"What do you mean?" I glanced her way, but her eyes stayed on the T.V.

"I just think I've done it all," she shrugged. "We took a trip, we saw the animals, and now I like the idea of sitting on the couch and watching dumb T.V."

I searched for a response. She couldn't just be done. Despite our small adventures across the past few months there was still so much left to do. Surely she would want to clean out her attic or go hiking one day. Nothing came to me worthwhile enough to merit a debate. I found myself retreating from any argument.

"If that's what you want," said a Tessie-ish voice that didn't feel like my own.

"Yeah," she sounded like she was telling she finished the last of the milk, not that she was finished with life. "I'm just going to enjoy life while I have it. Sitting on the couch with you and eating dinner with Liam when he isn't working sound like good days to me."

She finally looked at me and smiled. I half-heartedly smiled back.

A work day waited for me in the distance. With a flimsy excuse, I left a few minutes later. Inside my car I couldn't make myself drive home. After a few minutes of silence, I started the engine and began driving forward.

No particular destination came to me. I drove straight. If the road split I randomly picked which way to go. Without music, my blue car drifted quietly through a suburb near my childhood home.

As blocks began to tick past, the street evolved into a spacious area. Houses slowly moved further apart and away from road. I couldn't focus on them or anything else I passed. My eyes stayed on road ahead of me.

After the Peppersburg Carnival I told myself to stop pestering Matilda about any trips or life events that needed rushing. Even though she said she was done, I couldn't stay quiet about it. I knew there had to be more that I was missing. At least one more project left for us. Something that would require time and planning and would give us nothing but happiness after. I wanted to hold hands like children and jump off a cliff of perhaps into a lake of memories.

I kept asking myself if I had failed. As a friend, it was my duty to create memories and give Matilda whatever she wanted or needed as she went through this rough time. I wondered if by not knowing what to do for her next I had failed

Beside me, an email lit up my phone. It was work, and I didn't want it, so I tossed the phone into my back seat.

The sun was gone. The night offered a relief to the unquenchable heat that had taken hold of everything. On the slow road, I lowered the roof of my bug and let the wind cover me. I undid my stubby ponytail and let my hair become a tangled mess behind my head.

A constant call of the wind across my ears lulled my thoughts.

We were eight again. On the side patio of the Day home a soft chill rested on our bear arms. Matilda was holding a pretzel stick dipped in chocolate. I had one too. We both shivered and sipped Cherry Life from a wine glass. It was a Christmas party.

Looking up at the sky, we begged for it to snow. A few stars told us clouds were gone, and a Christmas party snow wouldn't happen that year. We still hoped.

A stoplight woke me from the highway hypnosis. I had brought myself downtown. Unwillingly, my autopilot setting brought me close to my apartment.

I looked up at the clear sky. No stars were visible in the metropolitan area. I found myself wishing for a snowfall. I wished for a wish, and for a chance to figure out what to do. Matilda thought she was done, but I knew she wasn't. What I didn't know was how to show her that, or what she was missing. One more thing, that's what I kept thinking. There is one more thing she needed to do.

A text saved me.

I had ignored the buzz of five new emails. Worried that Matilda wanted to know if I made it home, I responded to the light ding coming from my phone.

The only reason Liam had my number was from group texts with Matilda. Both of them would include me in plans for dinner or an afternoon. Then during her three day art bender, he asked for directions to my apartment.

Can we meet?

In a few minutes I was walking into a local watering hole. Matilda and I had stopped in a couple of times before. Nothing about the place was particularly exciting. Our only ventures there were late nights when almost everywhere else had closed.

Liam was resting on a stool by the bar. A few empty glasses littered the seats nearby him. I scooted them away and sat down. Scrubs hung from Liam like they were tired too. Matilda had mentioned he was working a couple of extra-long shifts. Tiredness had been dialed up quite a bit. He leaned on one arm, ready to fall asleep.

"How's it going?" I began.

"I don't know," he sighed.

"Did you want to get food or something?" I tried. My dinner had been two hours before, but I could easily talk myself into a light, second course.

"I ate dinner already." He took a sip of brandy on the rocks.

I glanced at the empty martini glasses. "Was it just olives?"

"Those aren't mine," he managed a smirk.

The bartender found his way to us. Tall, bald, and strong the man looked like a hairless bear. Despite his stature he had a knack for moving silently through his dimly lit domain. Harsh demeanor kept anyone from being rowdy. His broad shoulders and stern face made him bouncer and mixologist all in one. Anytime I had visited, the shabby place stayed quiet. Patrons knew better than to poke the bear.

Once a glass of whiskey and cola were passed to me I managed to break the silence.

"Are you going to talk to me about what's bothering you? Or did you just not want to drink alone?"

"My baby sister is dying." He was blunt; thumb and first finger twirling the glass below him. Melting ice clinked.

"My best friend is dying." I threw back the drink I had. A quick burn relaxed my muscles. Both empty glasses were quickly refreshed.

"I hate saying this, but I have to fix myself. I sure as hell can't talk to Matilda about it." Liam tried to sit up on the stool, but quickly slouched again. I took another drink, not buzzed yet and not ready to give any advice or comfort.

"I know I should be sad for her, but I don't know what I'm going to do when she's gone" he sighed. A chill swept past both of us at the thought. "I know saying that is selfish, or whatever, but I just don't know what I'll do. There's no more family left. My only friends are drinking friends scattered across a few states. They don't even know I have a sister."

Guilt fell on me. In my evening of depressed driving I hadn't even considered my family. They waited a few quick hours away. In a moment I could call them or visit. If it came to it, I could move there. As my life was crumbling away around me I had one net catching me. Liam had none.

"The sliver of a life I have is going to go when she does. I'll do what I did last time, just get sucked into work and stay lonely."

I rolled my eyes. "My god, Liam, I'll be your friend."

Surprised, he stayed silent.

"Yes, this sucks, and our lives are about to change forever. But you sure as hell aren't alone in this." I finished my second drink. The bear returned, and asked if we wanted more. I shook my head.

"Thank you." His voice was timid. "But do you know what's happening to you after this?"

I remembered the ignored emails that ignited my phone. Anything from work could afford to wait, but anyone wanting to climb that ladder would know that nothing could wait. I wanted the New York apartment, but in that moment at the bar I wanted to smash my phone on the counter. I wanted to run home and be hugged by my mom. I wanted a corporate job with a big paycheck and I wanted my best friend to be an adult with me.

"I have no idea," I finally said. "Anytime I think about what I'm going to be doing a year from now I feel bad for doing it."

"Me too," he confessed. "But we have to at some point."

I regretted turning down drink three. Liam's glass was still half full. I thought about taking it.

Liam had slouched onto the counter. His mint green scrubs swallowed him up.

"They say that you're supposed to be there for them and make them comfortable and happy." He gazed into his low glass.

"She seems content," I shrugged. "Tonight she told me she was done."

"Done?"

"Sort of like there wasn't anything else elaborate to do. And then she kept watching reality TV just like the past few months." My glass was also empty. I looked around for the bartender to refill it.

"Are we doing enough though? She is losing fifty or more years she thought she had, and we make her feel better by letting her decide what to eat."

"There has to be something else." I bit my lip. Tired from the heat and the long day, I couldn't stretch my imagination very far. "One more thing she doesn't know she wants. Something we can all do that isn't just for her, but for us to remember her."

On cue, a spirit of Matilda appeared from behind the bar in the form of a can of Cherry Life. She was talented enough to haunt us before death.

The bartender had returned, but I forgot all about refilling my own glass. The bright, red can was in his firm hand as he filled a wine glass with the soda. A young woman waited for it a few feet away.

"Where did you get that?" I asked, nodding to the empty can. "I only see those further south."

"Distribution center," he replied. My glass was refilled. "It's a little over an hour away. Most stores around here just don't want to haul it that far I guess."

I was ten. Matilda and I stood on the side patio with our own wine glass Cherry Life. I could see gentle snowflakes joining us. A gasp escaped my young body at the sight.

"Close your eyes!" Matilda called.

Together we made silly wishes. Combined magic of Christmas, the snow, and our earnest hearts ensured that they would come true. I think I wished for a dog that year. In a blink the bar returned. Fading fluorescent lights and stained carpet reminded me I wasn't ten anymore.

Realization came. The thought electrified my heart and ran through my arms and legs then out of my fingers and feet. I turned to Liam, unchanged by my burst of inspiration.

"Let's throw a Day family Christmas party."

10 OFF SEASON CHRISTMAS PLANNING

"Like the parties that Matilda tried to throw twice that completely flopped?"

The quiet bar suddenly felt brighter. Shadows fell away as a thousand ideas rushed into my head in a sudden brainstorm. I needed to write them down. A small stack of napkins sat within arm's reach.

"This will be different. We're all a few years older, and can make better decisions and plans. Plus you're here, the extra person will help." I found a pen and roughly scratched the word "Christmas" on one of the square napkins.

Liam hesitated. Only a minute earlier, thoughts of loss and acceptance left us both on the verge of inconsolable. In my inspiration, sadness had fallen away. Excitement found its way in.

"Tessie, this is a nice idea, but we don't have until Christmas," he said.

"I know," I replied. "That's why we're going to do it next month." I scratched down the word "September."

Ice clinked in Liam's empty glass. The man bear was nowhere in sight, and hopes of a refill were low. I kept my attention on the napkin as "tree" and "pretzel sticks" were added to the short list.

"Why does it have to be a Christmas party? I know you want something else, but is this our best option?"

"Christmas is her favorite holiday," I declared. Liam's lack of enthusiasm was getting frustrating. "Why do you think she tried twice to do this before, or flew out to wherever you were just so your small family could be together?"

He was quiet for a minute. I abandoned the napkin for a document on my phone. Several emails were waiting for my attention. I ignored them, reminding myself it was still Saturday. The ideas were typed up and more were added.

"Isn't Christmas everyone's favorite?" Liam asked. "Like on all the Christmas specials of TV shows where there's some big fight about Christmas. And they have to make it good, because Christmas is one person's favorite. But who's going to say a different holiday is their favorite?"

I finally looked his direction, and ignored the stab from two eyes identical to Matilda's.

"Thanksgiving is my favorite."

Our thoughts were better aligned the following morning. Liam didn't require much more persuasion in the plan. We agreed to present the idea to Matilda and get her opinion. If for some reason she didn't like it, I would drop the idea.

First thing I did was jump in my car and drive over. All three of us were still in pajamas in the kitchen. Matilda's hair had balled into a rats nest on the side of her head. In her few minutes of consciousness, it was untouched by brush or detangle spray.

"Just like before," I explained. "The music, food, and a present we pass out to everybody."

Sleepiness disappeared and excitement filled Matilda to the brim, "I love it, but we have to have all the classic food like before. Like those macrons."

"Those things were good," Liam added.

Soon we were all in the front room. Matilda dragged in her easels and set them up along the wall. Large, dry erase boards were propped on each one so that lists could be made and plans executed. It was the most organized I had ever seen her work. I was so proud. In black marker I wrote out the list I had built so far: food, music, decorations, gifts.

"Come on, don't use black," Matilda said from her desk.

"It's what you had ready."

"There is a plethora of colors right here," she explained, pulling a handful of makers from a drawer. "For the love of God, use at least one different color per board. I will not let you make this planning boring."

I swapped black for lime green. On the second board "food" was printed in all caps. A pink marker added "pretzels" and "Cherry Life." Matilda later included "macarons."

"First, we need a date," Liam spoke up from the couch. "Something far enough away to let us get invitations out, but no so far that they forget they're invited before it happens."

"September 28th," Matilda opened a design program on her desktop.

"Why then?" he asked.

"I just like it," she shrugged.

An excellent way to get everything you want done for Christmas is to not actually celebrate it on Christmas. Provided you can lower your standards a bit. In years past, Matilda and I had complained about any store that set out Christmas supplies before Halloween. That year we complained that they didn't.

One quick trip to the attic told us most of the old decorations were useless. Lack of use and time in storage had worn out long strands of garland. Lights were crushed. Most other decor was either broken or too old. We turned to the internet for decorations that weren't as old as we were or heavily coated in dust.

After a large order of garland, fake snow, and Santa figurines was assembled, Matilda handed over her card. I glanced at the price, hesitant. We had offered splitting costs of the party together, especially since it was a collective plan to pull it off.

"First of all, in a few months I'm not going to need any of this money, but you guys will need yours," Matilda said. She began typing in her card number. "Second, this can just be part of my share."

"Decorations" was scratched off the master list of party needs. I erased the board that had been dedicated to listing all the memories from childhood we were attempting to recreate along the doorways, banisters, and empty shelves. In the cleared area I wrote "Gift." That time I used an orange marker to avoid being scolded again.

The front room had become a hub of planning. Several pages were spread across Matilda's screen as she navigated between searching musicians and closing decoration shops. Liam was sitting with his laptop, attempting to find a rentable, air conditioning unit.

"What sort of gifts did your parents have before?" I asked as I switched to a purple marker.

"One year we did coasters," Matilda said. "But never in my adult life have I used one."

"There are plenty of useful things you haven't used in your adult life," her brother answered from the couch.

I put coasters on the list.

"What about like a corkscrew? I think we did that once."

"I don't know, some of the people I want to invite don't drink," Matilda replied.

We paused. Our list of guests was on a spreadsheet on Matilda's laptop. For the most part it included neighbors that had been around for a while and a few old family friends that kept in touch. Neither of us knew who she was referring to.

"I want to invite some of the people from my church," she explained. "And the older ones don't drink. They don't have a problem with it, but I want the take home gift to be something they can use."

Never before had Matilda mentioned anything about religion or church. I thought back to every Sunday in the past year. When she wasn't talking to me, I assumed she was sleeping in. Racking my brain, I thought I remembered Mr. and Mrs. Day attending regularly, but I wasn't certain.

"You've been going to church?" Liam was just as surprised as me.

"No, Liam, I've been out jogging for two hours every Sunday morning. Guys, I'm dying of course I've taken up religion."

"I guess that makes sense," I offered. "You have been really nice."

"Yeah, well being nice isn't enough to get to heaven. You guys can come with me if you want. They have free coffee, and Jesus is pretty helpful."

"But today's Sunday," Liam said.

"This project is important to you guys," Matilda explained. "I'm not going to hell because I didn't go to church one Sunday."

She turned back to her desktop, seemingly ending the conversation. I erased corkscrew from the list. Attempting to draw focus back, I added "bookmark" to the very short list.

"What about like a gift card?" Liam said.

"No, one wants that." Matilda didn't even look away from a page about cookies.

"A gift card is so disposable," I explained. "It has no memory value and shows that you put zero thought into a gift."

"I've given you gift cards. You liked them."

"No, honey," Matilda finally faced him. "They sucked. I love you, but they sucked."

For a while, Liam was quiet. Matilda and I continued to bounce ideas of magnets and tiny snow globes between each other. Unsure, we left that white board and moved to one labeled "Food" in pink.

Knowing the area a bit better, that list was much fuller. Chocolate pretzels, punch, cookies, meatballs, and cheese fondue gave us a start.

In years past, Mrs. Day had made everything herself. Two days and a night were devoted to the kitchen. Professional level hors d'oeuvres filled the dining room table. The spread belonged in a Christmas edition of *Better Homes and Gardens*. In her rush to make every aspect of the evening perfect, she hardly ate a bite.

Mr. Day always came through the house before guests arrived, photographing decorations and a fluffy dressed Matilda. Living across the street, I was always there early. I can remember each year as I stepped into the house. The place was a wonderland, with Mr. Day standing on a dining room chair to take pictures of the food his wife slaved over.

The list on the whiteboard had grown. Two columns of pink words ran from top to bottom. More ideas were squeezed into the space along the edge.

"We can't cook this," I stated. "Who can we get to cook this?"

"The caterer from my fake wedding! The good one!" Matilda said. "I felt bad for not hiring her at all. She was so nice."

"Will it be weird explaining why you're not married?"

"No, I'll just tell her the truth and that I'm dying," Matilda searched for the caterer's number. "It's worked to get just about everything else I've needed."

A local bakery had to be contacted for the French macarons. That was the only treat Mrs. Day didn't make herself. Matilda never touched them at the parties before, but she insisted they had to be there again.

The room grew quiet for a while as we turned to finding local musicians. A pianist was a staple to Day Christmas parties. The old grand in the front room hadn't been played in years, but every party had someone resting there for a few hours playing Christmas music. Speakers and a playlist were another option. But Matilda wasn't ready to give up.

"Ma-Tessie," Liam's voice interrupted our silent searching.

"What the hell did you just say?" Matilda spun away from her desk.

"A combination of your names."

"Never do that again," she said.

"Screw you, Day. I'll give endearing nicknames whenever I want."

"What do you need?" I ended the debate.

"I found an AC unit we can rent for the night," Liam spun his laptop around for us to see. "September is usually pretty warm, and bodies in the house will make it a lot warmer. An extra chill will make things Christmassy."

"Not a bad idea, Li-Day," they were both silent. "Do you hear how annoying that is?"

"Shut up."

We returned our attention to finding a pianist. A couple years before, Matilda had sold a piece of art to a hotel downtown. They always had someone sitting at the grand piano in the lobby. Beyond that, there was a mall that often had live music, and a large, catholic church. The three of us split to make cold calls.

I stood in the kitchen, maneuvering through a rough, automated system to get through to the mall. A recording listed options for stores, and I waited through the long list for any sort of office contact. The clock on the stove told me it was noon. My stomach told me I should be eating lunch.

On the patio, Cat had grown curios of Liam's existence. He hopped onto the glass table and rubbed his head against a resting arm. For the first time, I saw Cat let someone pet him.

Eventually I made it through to the mall office. Several rings and a voicemail reminded me it was the weekend. I hung up, and opened a pizza app.

Matilda appeared. "I got one!"

"Great!" I held up my phone. "I ordered pizza."

Liam entered. Cat stood at the glass door, checking the area inside. When his eyes fell on Matilda and me, he turned and patted away.

"I didn't find anything," Liam said.

"That's fine, I did," Matilda answered. "It's a local guy who takes these kinds of bookings a lot. But we have to pay extra for him to tune our piano. I don't know when it was played last."

"He doesn't come with his own piano?" Liam looked puzzled.

"No. Why would he?" Matilda opened the fridge.

"Guitar players bring their own guitars," he said.

"It's a damn piano, Liam, he can't just throw it in his trunk." She passed me a soda.

"You talk to Jesus with that mouth?"

"Cussing isn't a sin, read the bible."

"That's probably up for debate."

By that evening, Matilda had invitations ready for the printer. The date was listed across the top in bold, swirly script. Less prominent were the words "Christmas Party." They weren't needed quite as much, considering the red and green theme Matilda had selected and ran with. Details about the location and time filled one side. On the back she included a note.

> *Friends,*
>
> *Let's come together and celebrate the most wonderful time of year three months early. Wear your sweaters, drink hot chocolate, have a merry evening. Without the stress of the season, enjoy one last Day family Christmas Party.*

"One last" was like a gut punch. I just nodded and told it looked good.

As more and more plans fell into place I found it difficult to focus when I was at work. Not that it had been easy to concentrate in the recent months. Amelia still wanted to hear my ideas for the company app. I found myself answering each email later than the one before. She had set up a tentative date in a couple months. I could deliver a pitch if I convinced her the idea was in good enough shape in the coming weeks.

I had been paired with a graphic designer from another branch. Emails bounced between us of sketches and ideas for color schemes. After three weeks, I didn't know if Cameron was a man or woman, and by then I was too scared to ask.

Amelia wanted a solid, fully formed plan before a pitch was made to some select higher ups. Until then, she instructed that most of my time be spent organizing the set up and color scheme while the non-sexually specific Cameron took my ideas and made them pretty to look at.

That afternoon I was given two different versions of the food diary's main page to pick from. The images were identical except for an accent swoosh of color running along the upper left corner. One was a soft red, the other yellow, they matched two of the colors that intertwined on the Osiris logo.

Several minutes were spent staring at the images side by side on my computer screen. My body was still as my eyes grew tired staring at the diary twins. Any care for the specifics finally fell apart. I hit reply and told Cameron red because it was fewer letters to type out.

"Afternoon, Tess!" Glen and his smile appeared at the doorway above a tie covered in smiling french-fries. "How are you feelin?"

"Everything is good," I smiled. "Just a little sleepy. It's that time of day."

"Well make sure you coffee up before five. We have a little staff meeting," he laughed. "Don't put everyone else to sleep!"

I gave him thumbs up as he strolled away. Despite my appreciation for Glen and his cheeriness, the thought of sitting through a meeting that afternoon made me want to spin around and jump out of my window. Instead I looked back at my desk.

Our local social media pages were staying updated. A picture of radishes had gained a surprising amount of attention that day. I went through and replied to comments with positive answers. Each one was a complete fabrication considering my desire to leave that afternoon through any means possible.

Daydreams of a hamburger floated by. I paired it with the fries from Glen's tie, and thought about a hard soda to wash it all down. I calculated how quickly I could leave the office, eat the whole meal, and return in time to answer any new emails that came through.

By the time I thought of the closest place, how long the walk would take, and if I could eat while walking back the phone on my desk rang.

"Miss Fletcher," the almost mechanical voice of our receptionist said, "there's a Mr. Day to see you."

"Uh, okay," I mumbled. I never had an office guest, and even less often did the receptionist call me. The sudden grown up responsibility left me off pace.

I was brought back to reality by seeing Liam appear at the door. For once he was out of scrubs, and in jeans and a t-shirt. A yellow sticker adorned his chest with "visitor" printed in all caps above his signature. It matched the large envelope he was carrying.

"I didn't even know we had those," was my only greeting.

"This place is more boring than I imagined," he said, closing the door. "And I imagined it as pretty boring."

"What would make it less boring?"

"I don't know, fake grass maybe? You guys grow plants and stuff." He closed the door and took a seat.

I imagined the addition of fake plants to the office outside my door. Trees in corners and lines of plastic grass along cubicles clashed with the fluorescent lighting and worn, carpet floor. For our company's product, and encouragement of healthy living, the work space did not match.

"So what's up?" I asked. "I've never had a guest before."

"I found Santa," Liam said. He passed the envelope to me, using a rather serious tone despite talking about hiring a Santa Claus for our out of season Christmas party.

"When I called the mall, they wouldn't give me any information about their old Santa."

"Old Santa?" I asked, struggling to unhook the tab at the top of the envelope.

He took the envelope back from me and opened it.

"Three years ago their Santa retired," Liam explained. "They have a new one, but the old one is the same guy my parents always hired."

A headshot slid out of the envelope and onto my desk. Perfect teeth shined from the midst of a white beard. Bright eyes, small glasses, and the red hat completed the ensemble.

"He grows his own beard. The guy's legit."

I examined the picture closer. Indeed he was legit.

"How did you find all of this?" The opposite side of the photo had a copy of his resume. He was officially licensed as a Santa. Apparently that's a thing.

"I set up an interview in their offices. It wasn't hard to get, I just looked at their positions and applied with your resume."

I would have been frustrated, but I was mostly bewildered at how he got my resume. Overshadowing both feelings, I was impressed.

"As soon as I had an opportunity, I got on a computer and looked through their old pay stubs," he explained.

"Are you a male nurse that moonlights as a hacker?" I finally spoke up.

"It wasn't that hard," he continued. "I found the largest paycheck that only occurred during November and December. It repeated on the same dates several years back, so I printed the latest one and slipped out the front door before anyone saw me."

A second piece of paper contained a full name and home address. It also told me my estimate for how much mall Santas were paid was wildly low. Not that the topic had crossed my mind that often.

"Wait," I let common sense have a moment, "what am I going to do when the mall calls me asking to hire you?"

"I didn't give them a real number. At least, it didn't belong to any of us."

"Okay, you thought of everything."

In our plans for Matilda's party we tried to make everything perfect. To us, perfect was keeping things as close to the original party thrown by their parents as humanly possible. By our best assumption, past attempts to hold a Day Family Christmas Party failed out of unfamiliarity. Slight differences of no live music or gift for the guests ended up making huge changes.

Losing power the first time didn't help either.

Now the three of us had made careful plans to revive the parties that fizzled out years before. Yet Matilda had made no mention of having our own Santa. While he had been a staple of the event before, in our current plans she never mentioned him or seemed to notice his absence. Based on Liam's unusual appearance at my office, I assumed we were being discrete.

"So I think we should go talk to this guy, and convince him to come out of retirement for one night," Liam smiled.

"Right now?" I glanced at the time. It was already 4:30, and recently I had remained strict with work. In our planning I had not needed any afternoons or whole days off. I knew I'd need a lot more time off down the road, and I was trying to save up.

"Yeah, sure. We're already together," he stood up. "I can drive."

"Okay," I smiled, ready to create a fantastic surprise.

We soon pulled to a stop in front of an average, two story house. A chain link fence surrounded the yard, and worn patches of grass told me a dog was usually in the area. The surviving grass and potted plants were kept meticulously clean. I counted six on either side of the porch steps as we approached the front door.

"Wait," I spoke up before we rang the doorbell, "Turn your phone of before we go in."

"Why?"

"He's an old guy, if our phones ring while we're in there it's over."

"Right," Liam pulled his phone from his pocket. "Gotta make sure this doesn't ring when no one calls me."

The man who answered the door looked exactly like Santa on vacation. Some places have the Christmas decorations of a Florida Santa wearing a golf shirt and sunglasses. Something similar stood before us.

Palm trees were scattered across a blue, button up shirt. He was wearing faded, cargo shorts and soft flip flops. A full, white beard stretched down to his chest, and made up for the lack of hair on his head.

"Are you Jehovah's Witness?" He stood up straight, curious of the strangers on his porch.

"No, sir," I smiled, not sure how to proceed.

"Mr. Higgins?" Liam spoke up. I let him take the lead.

"Yes, that's me." The man finally smiled back.

"Several years ago my parents hired you for Christmas parties, until they passed away. I was wondering if we could talk to you about it for a minute."

Mr. Higgins smile faded, but didn't disappear. From Liam's age, he could tell losing both parents had been a tragedy. I could tell Liam tacked on that fact for sympathy points. It worked. The door opened wider and Mr. Higgins stepped back.

"Come in."

We shuffled through the front door together. The inside of the home matched the outside. Any shelf space held one or two centered figurines. A lacy, runner stretched across a coffee table where two neat stacks of magazines sat on either side of a candy bowl. Another pile sat on an end table between two recliners. A muted TV was running a 24 hour news channel.

Old photos of children stair stepped down the opposite wall and met recent photos of grandchildren. Above all of them was an aged photo of Mr. Higgins. His hand rested on a woman's shoulder. The living room was the epitome of a grandparent's dwelling.

A bichon frise patted in from the other room. By the state of his eyes and lack of energy, I could tell he matched his owner's age (in dog years). He took his place on one of the recliners as Mr. Higgins sat on the other.

"Please sit down," he instructed.

Liam and I sat mechanically on the couch. I felt myself sink further into the cushions and watched my knees rise. Despite sitting several spaces apart, the sinking couch was rolling the two of us together.

"What can I help you with?" He asked, shutting off the TV.

"Well," Liam began a seemingly rehearsed speech. "Like I said, my parents hired you every year for a Christmas party. When they passed away those parties sort of fizzled out. We want to recreate them now."

Higgins nodded. His eyes had moved to the dog beside him. Dog was scratching too much. Even if he was listening to our story, I could tell he was calculating his home's risk of a flea infestation.

"It was always pretty big," Liam went on. "We had a piano player and lots of guests. The

Day family went all out."

"I'm sure it was wonderful," Higgins replied. "But, I'm sorry, before I retired I did a lot of those parties. I don't specifically remember yours."

"I understand, and that's totally fine," Liam glanced my way for help. I shrugged with nothing to offer. "But now we're trying to recreate one of those parties for my sister. Every year, it was always you there, so it really should be you now."

He finally looked back at us. Our plea was not particularly exciting, but he remained polite. Liam had one more card to play, and I could see him holding onto it until the right moment.

"I have a few friends that are still in the service." His description made us pause. "I'm sure they'd do a great a job for you. Most of us learned from the same place. If you mentioned me they'd cut you a deal."

Liam's desperation was growing.

"Thank you, but it really does have to be you."

"I understand," Vacation Santa sat up in his recliner. "But nowadays I just like spending Christmas with my grandkids. I wasted a lot of time at parties and in the mall. God, I hate that mall."

"It's not at Christmas," I finally spoke. "It's next month."

For the first time since we arrived, the man really looked at us. He seemed to take in our features trying to figure out how crazy we were.

"What?" he said after a moment.

Liam saw his chance, and dropped the sadness bomb. Like Matilda, he stole an opportunity to get everything out of her final days.

"My sister is really sick, and she's not going to be around at Christmas." The monologue sounded verbatim to a Hallmark movie. "We just want to give her one more awesome Christmas. Like when we were kids."

"Is this *A Walk to Remember* thing?"

"Actually it's more like *Beaches*," I said.

Higgins sighed. We had hit the right spot in his heart. We were almost there. I glanced at Liam, ready for him to wrap it up and win. He nodded back.

"Does she know you came out here?"

"No," Liam replied. "We wanted you to be a big, last surprise."

"My old rate was $25 an hour after the booking fee, but that was a few-"

"Fifty," Liam interjected. "And you can have your pick of the left over alcohol."

"That's nice of you, son, but I don't drink."

"Food then."

Higgins sighed again. He glanced towards the pictures on the wall. I followed his eyes as they lingered on the picture of him and a woman who could only be his wife. The wedding band was still on his finger.

"What the heck," he finally said. "You guys are trying to do something nice for someone you love."

The rest of the conversation was very calm. Logistics of the event were sorted out. We both thanked him and shook hands before heading out the front door. Once we were both seated in the car with the doors closed, we let loose.

"We did it!" I cheered. A matter I didn't know existed that afternoon had become the greatest victory of the week.

"We got Santa out of retirement," Liam started the car, bouncing in his seat.

"We got Santa to come out of retirement and do us a favor. We're awesome."

"This needs to be a secret, though. I think." He turned onto the road and began driving back towards my office.

"Sure," I replied. "This will make it fun."

I turned my phone back on and an explosion started. Texts flooded in with missed calls. Every single one was from work.

A shiver ran down my back. In the hot car I was suddenly very cold.

Where are you? We have a meeting.

No one has seen you in an hour.

Did you have a guest? He didn't sign out.

Glen had called three times in the mix. The receptionist called once and left a voicemail. I was in no hurry to listen to it.

For the rest of the ride I stayed completely silent. I dreaded returning to my office. A nauseous rumble purred in my stomach on the straight road. Throughout my childhood I had avoided punishments by avoiding breaking rules. Correction from adults terrified me. The fear had only grown with age.

Inside of our building my legs wobbled as I walked from the elevator to our door. At that point, the place was quiet. Almost everyone had left for the day. I slipped inside, hoping I could avoid any possible lecture or frustration.

The single, sliver of luck I felt was from the fact the meeting I missed was within our own office. No one from corporate or other branches or even the farms we covered was going to be there. Losing trust of coworkers was awful, but not nearly as troubling as hurting a higher up.

A single light was still on. A faint hint of it glowed from under Glen's office door. I sighed with relief. He was most likely gone, and even if he was around I could easily get my things and leave without notice. Later I could send an email about an emergency and be in the clear.

It was an emergency, I reassured myself. Favors for dying friends counted as emergencies.

In my office I kept the light off. I knew that the sunlight from the window I could gather everything and be outside again before any knowledge of my presence floated across the office to Glen.

My escape was stopped by a figure in the doorway.

His French fry tie was gone along with his smile. I had never really seen Glen with a serious expression. Even during a slight crisis he kept a calm demeanor and upbeat attitude.

"You disappeared," he said. His face didn't change.

"I'm sorry," I tried to give a small smile. "I had a bit of an emergency."

The serious expression remained on Glen's face. My smile left.

"You missed a meeting," he remained in the doorway. The shadows of the dark room behind him created a menacing person I had never seen before.

"I'm sorry," I said again. "Can I just get an email of the notes?"

"You can get an email of some of the notes, but that's not the point."

I shifted my weight, not sure how to respond.

"I understand that Matilda is sick," Glen continued. "You've had to head out early and take days off here and there. That's fine, but you can't let work slip up with it. No one knew where you were today, which is bad enough. But in that meeting everyone covered a month's worth of work from each department and made plans for the next month. You wasted your coworkers' time waiting for you, and you've wasted more of their time answering all of the questions you will now have."

"I'm sorry."

"Don't let a hard time destroy you." He gave me a cold look. I bit my lip, afraid to show this new version of my boss that I was afraid.

"It won't happen again," I replied.

"No," he was cold, "it won't. I'll see you in the morning."

Glen left the doorway and returned to his own office. When I heard his door close I started breathing again. I may not have been given any punishment, but I was in trouble.

I quickly slipped through the desks and towards the front door. At the reception desk, a clipboard was out. The guest sign in sheet still had Liam's name and no sign out time. I thought of Matilda.

If she were with me, and had witnessed my scolding, she would have scratched in a hand flipping the bird in the tiny, white box. Matilda was not with me. Since I lacked her art skills and complete carelessness for image, I didn't draw it in myself.

Outside, my phone buzzed; Matilda texted me.

Liam is cooking food, so you should come over.

I smiled and headed towards Matilda's, leaving all thoughts of work behind.

11 1) GETTING A CHRISTMAS TREE

Dusty attic smell always reminds me of Christmas. As a kid, about the only time we went into our attic was to retrieve our tree, ornaments, and decorations. Sometimes Mom or Dad might have stored things up there. Old toys Tara and I outgrew or unwanted pieces of furniture were carried up the ladder. Whatever time of year that happened, I still thought of Christmas.

When the three of us dug through Matilda's attic I got a whiff of that dust smell. It helped the feeling of party planning. That past week I had been playing Christmas music at any opportunity. The temperature was in the eighties, and even Mariah Carey couldn't make me feel seasonal out of season.

"I'm telling you, there's nothing up here," Matilda called from below the trap door.

"I know Mom and Dad had an artificial tree one year." Liam was delicately perched on a box mountain. He opened a plastic bin then passed it to me. "More decorations."

"I have been living in this house and you haven't. I'm telling you there is no tree here."

Matilda took the box from me and began climbing down the ladder. Liam parkoured over a baby crib full of unrecognizable clutter and opened another box.

"In that time, how often did you come up here?" He closed the lid and opened another.

"None." Matilda's head appeared at my feet.

"Exactly. Shut up." Liam opened the last big box in the space. "Damnit."

Soon we were all standing at the bottom of the ladder in the second floor hallway.

119

"So now that we can all agree there is no tree in this house," Matilda shot a look at her brother, "where are we going to get one?"

"Tessie, is there one at your place?" Liam asked.

I shook my head, "I always just went home to my parents. I never really decorated that much."

"Even if there was, I don't want to use it," Matilda sternly declared. "We said we're throwing a Day Family Christmas party, which means we're getting a real tree that will burst into flames if we don't water it."

Bringing home a tree was part of the excitement. The party always happened on a Saturday. On Friday afternoon, Mr. Day would come home with a gigantic tree. Together they all decorated it while watching *A Muppet Christmas Carol.*

The blue Subaru station wagon would pull into their driveway, a tree tied to the roof. Mr. Day would always get one so big that it would hang off each end of the car. Like a postcard image, he would untie the tree while the rest of the family watched and help bring it in. Tara and I would watch the live action Norman Rockwell unfold from our living room window.

Soon after, the two of us would beg Mom and Dad for a real tree. Mom would go on her rant about pine needles and the mess they made. Ten minutes later, my sister and I gave up. By middle school, we had our mother's lecture on living trees memorized, and any hope of having our own was abandoned.

I had never wondered where Mr. Day got the tree each year. It just happened, like gravity or the sun setting. You experience it so much that it just becomes a staple in your life with no curiosity to its origin. As soon as the staple disappears, life seems permanently altered for the worse.

Mysterious Christmas tree markets would not be popping up in front of grocery stores or in vacant lots for at least another two months. Possibly longer. We were a week from the off season party.

Online searching got us a number for the local farmers market. According to the organizer on the other end of the line, the vendor information was classified. Over the next couple days we did more online searching. Christmas tree farms are incredibly allusive.

The three of us sat around the dining room table one evening with laptops and phones. In planning for the night, we had veered to the three of us searching for Christmas trees. The room had become a control center for the planning of a singular outlet of our event. Phone numbers were endangered. Anytime we actually found a farm to call, they either didn't answer, didn't call back or just said no.

"How can someone who makes the most joyous part of the most joyous holiday be so hard to deal with?" Liam's head was almost absorbed by the rumpled table cloth. "Christmas tree farms should be held to the same standard as mall Santas."

"Wow. You should sick the freemasons on them."

He rolled his eyes at me.

We were all silent. Effort with no return had run us down. Matilda was being unusually quiet from her spot at the head of the table. One red lip was bit in concentration. Behind blue eyes you could almost see small gears turning together.

"There's something else we could do," she finally said. "If we did it right, it wouldn't be illegal. Okay, maybe it would. I don't know trespassing laws, but they probably wouldn't come after us."

Liam and I shared a glance. "What?" he finally sat up straight.

"We could steal one."

By our estimate, the closest farm was forty five minutes away. We knew we couldn't leave earlier than midnight. The strictest cover of darkness was necessary.

"I've never been a part of a caper before," Liam appeared in the hallway. His dark hair was concealed by a darker hat, and long black sleeves hid his white arms.

"I'm glad we get to have our first caper together." I had dressed similarly. We were all taking the plan seriously.

"My best friends are losers." Like her brother, Matilda wore a black toboggan over her already black hair. In the dark apparel her skin was even paler.

All three of us had tucked black cargo pants into hiking boots. We looked strikingly similar to bank robbers from any given superhero cartoon. Like the other two, I concealed my hair in a hat. Knowing it was going to be a long night, we had all just finished coffee. At that point we were fidgety making final adjustments to our caper clothes.

"We look cool." Liam noted.

"No, honey, we don't." Matilda scolded. "Now everyone take a pair of gloves."

The forecast said it would not get lower than sixty that night, but we all complied. Even in the cool house I was starting to get warm.

Preparations had been taken rather seriously for a Christmas Tree Caper. Over the past three days, each of us had taken cash back at various gas stations and stores. Together, we had at least twice what a good tree would go for at a market. We hoped our generosity would deter any charges of trespassing or mild theft.

I had made a point to wipe down each bill when we counted them and packed the envelope. It was folded and securely buttoned into my thigh pocket.

"I don't understand why we can't just go to an ATM," Matilda had asked.

"Because they can trace that!" Liam had taken the planning a little too seriously.

In the garage we prepped the tank. We agreed it was the only one of our cars that could tow a tree of the size we wanted. Matilda opened the hatch back, and we discovered a slight problem. The SUV was old, so the rows of seats were completely removable. They didn't fold into the floor like anything made after 2002. The only seats inside were the driver and the passenger. There were three of us.

Over the previous years, Matilda had transported several sculptures, paintings, and art supplies. The entire space was needed, so the middle and back rows of seats had been out for a while. In our meticulous planning, we didn't think of having enough seatbelts for everyone.

"Where are the seats now?" I asked, getting irritated.

"Yeah," Matilda paused. "I don't have any idea."

"Think!" I tossed the rope I'd been carrying into the car.

"Oh pressure! Thank you, that is really going to help me remember."

"Guys, I'll just sit in the floor." Liam climbed in, ending the discussion. "Everyone calm down and let's just rob this tree farm."

"Technically this is a burglary," I corrected. I patted the money pocket with my gloved hand. "If you can even call it that. We are paying."

"Tessie, I'm worried you're not taking this burglary seriously." Matilda closed the trunk, and Liam rolled backwards to avoid being hit by the door.

I climbed into the passenger seat. Matilda soon joined me, and dropped a rusty hand saw onto the floor between us.

"I'm not going to Clark Griswold this."

Matilda backed out of the garage and turned around in the driveway. From the open garage door, Cat gave us an exasperated look. He soon trotted off into the night.

In a few short minutes we were away from the crowded suburb and weaving through back roads. Everything was dark. I felt invisible if I leaned into the passenger seat. We were all quiet, as if we felt the need to be sneaky miles from our destination.

Houses and buildings were spread further and further apart, until one only appeared every half mile. The GPS took us up hills and around sharp curves. What would have been lovely, rural view by day turned sinister in the darkness. Our view of shadowed trees and excitement of trespassing kept us on edge.

Something moved at the road's edge. We gasped. A raccoon hurried away from the car.

Eventually, we reached a dirt road. Based on its sharp cut off of the main road and downhill, we didn't take it. Matilda turned around and parked across from it. The nose of the tank faced home, ready for a peal out and speed away. Loaded with a rope and a rusty saw, we began our walk.

"If anyone falls behind, leave them for dead!" Matilda hissed as she scurried down the steep bank.

"Or we could just meet back at the car," Liam said.

"That's less exciting, why would you even suggest that?" she led us off the dirt road and into some tree coverage. In silence we crept through the farm.

Beside us, short pine trees were planted ten feet apart. The first ones we saw must have been three feet tall. A second row ran parallel to the first, the trees slightly taller. The perfect stacks were fuzzy, green chess sets waiting to be played. More and more rows appeared, each one lined with trees taller than the last.

Soon a sea of trees stretched before us. It rolled across the field and up the opposite hill. Just before the top, trees stopped along a grass shore where a dark house slept for the night. Spruce, pine, and fir might have been visible in the daylight, or to an eye that knew trees. In the darkness it was all a tangled labyrinth of almost Christmas.

On cue, the moon appeared from behind clouds. In the new light we examined rows until we found something close to what we were looking for. Without any real knowledge of the measurements of Matilda's home or car, the best we could do was guess.

"Will it fit?" I asked. A plump tree had held our attention for a moment.

"There aren't any seats," Matilda said. "And if we have to we'll open the back window."

We agreed, and got to work. Calling the handsaw dull would be an understatement. After several long minutes of work on the base, Liam hardly made a dent.

"Are you that weak?" Matilda asked. "Would it help if I got out a nail file?"

"It might, miss doesn't have tools," he grunted. I was handed the saw and knelt down for a turn.

"I have tools," she explained. "It's just that none of them are applicable to this situation."

The rest of their debate was lost to me. Cutting down a tree with a dull saw is indeed strenuous work. I was thankful for the thick gloves. They did more than conceal fingerprints. Every few slides the saw would get stuck on a knot in the trunk. Several hard tugs and shoves broke the wood loose. A third of the way into the tree I gave up.

Matilda took a turn. Profanities buzzed in time with the saw. Her thin back and shoulders bounced as she threw her whole body into moving the work. Soon she was out of breath.

"This is impossible," she moaned. The blade was stuck firmly in the center of the trunk. Our progress had taken a solid thirty minutes.

"We can't exactly stop," Liam began his turn. "And if we did we'd have no tree. That isn't an option."

The tag team method continued. The weight of the tree began to pull it sideways, and sawing slowly got easier. Matilda and I laid out the rope, ready to tie up the branches as soon as it fell.

"Do you know how to tie up a Christmas tree?" I asked.

"No," she said. "I just know we need to do it so the branches don't break or something."

"Move," Liam's voice interrupted us. Snaps and cracks filled the air as the tree slowly fell and landed with a thud.

"Finally!" Matilda began to gather branches under the rope.

"How does this work exactly?" Liam asked.

"No idea, I'm just making it look like the ones Dad always brought home."

A weight shifted in my pocket. The envelope.

"Shit," I whispered, looking to the house. "Did you guys see a mailbox anywhere on the way in?"

"Shit," Matilda returned. We both strained our eyes in the darkness, searching dirt road we followed in. On top of the hill, twenty feet from the house stood the mailbox.

We glanced at each other.

"Where else could we leave it?" she wondered.

"Thanks for the help, guys." Liam bear hugged the tree, trying to gather the rope.

"Shut up, this is more important," Matilda's voice rose.

"You guys get the tree together and start towards the car. I'll go drop the money off, and catch up with you." I started down the line of trees to the dirt road.

"Thanks for the help with the heavy lifting," Matilda called after me. Liam huffed, still hugging the branches alone.

"I'm doing the dangerous thing, it evens out." I croaked back.

I told myself it wasn't really dangerous to leave something in a stranger's mailbox in the middle of the night. I didn't believe it. Sticking to the trees, I hurried towards the house. As the hill grew steeper I slowed down. Eventually I was walking.

The envelope of cash was silently tucked into the box. I breathed a sigh of relief. I was done. I turned around to head back towards the others.

A deep, loud bark broke through the air. I was sprinting. Some kind of magic kept me from falling on my face as I raced back down the steep hill. I didn't look back to see if it was in pursuit. Even though I ran further from the house, the barking didn't get any quieter. I imagined an old timey farmer appearing at a window, dressed in a nightgown and pointing a shotgun in my direction.

I leapt down the last section of hill and ran along the dirt road. Two figures with a tree in tow appeared ahead. It bounced between them as they struggled to run down the road. In seconds I caught up to them. Barking rang in my ears.

Matilda lifted what she could from the top half. Liam had taken the bulk of the weight at the base of the tree. I jumped in beside him, and together the three of us bounded up the next hill. The barks were mixed with howls.

The tank came into view, license plate gleaming like a finish line. With a click, the trunk began to open and overhead lights filled the car. Matilda stuffed the key back into her pocket, never breaking pace.

Pine needles stabbed my arm through my thin shirt. Even with gloves on, my hands were getting sore from the rough bark of the tree. My arms locked around the weight they carried.

Our feet hit pavement. In one final bound we all flew into the trunk. Matilda was in the driver's seat in an instant. The top of the tree brushed her face as she scrambled to start the car. Liam closed the back door as I fell into the passenger seat. Tires spun in gravel and we sped away.

Once again, we took sharp curves and glided up and down hills. This time we zipped through each one. Matilda floored the gas pedal, and the engine roared as we ascended each hill.

"Everyone okay?" she asked after a few moments.

I felt my heart pound in my chest. My sides screamed from running, but I had to smile.

"Yeah. That was kind of fun."

We continued to rush through the night. The darkness turned from sinister to a protective blanket. Slowly houses began to emerge around us. Matilda eased off the gas, and we were soon surrounded by civilization.

By some miracle, the tree was in fantastic shape. The three of us stood around it in the living room. Every branch and needle looked impeccable. All we could do was admire it quietly for a moment or two.

"That might be the wildest thing I've ever done," Liam declared. Matilda and I shot him a glance. "My life hasn't been very exciting."

"Well, I don't think I've broken the law before," I said.

"Even though we paid for the tree that caper was trespassing and sort of stealing. But I doubt anyone will come after us for it." Matilda smiled, admiring her work. "Let's get some wine."

Soon we were all sipping on a red. Selection was made simply by it being the easiest to grab. I refilled my glass as the other two argued.

"Is it a spruce?" Liam twirled one of the branches between his fingers.

"I don't know," Matilda took a drink.

"Or is it a pine?" He plucked a few needles.

"I don't know." She took a second drink.

"Well, what do you know?"

"Not trees, obviously!"

Too tired to do anything else, but enough endorphins pumping to keep us from sleeping, we settled down on the couch for some TV. Another show about wedding dresses was on. Matilda insisted we hadn't watched it, even though it looked the same as every other one. She said each one was different, but I couldn't tell. Instead, Liam and I talked her into our standard movie choice.

"Okay," she sighed. "But you can't get mad when Tessie and I quote the whole thing."

"Sorry, that is going to happen," I told him.

We didn't last much longer. Matilda and I gave the only reactions along the way. Well delivered sass often got a "yes," from one of us. Anytime the music peaked, we both "da da da da da da da da'd," in unison.

The next morning I found myself wrapped in a fleece blanket, still on the couch. The DVD main menu burned my eyes from the large TV. Someone had muted it several hours before, but not spent the same level of energy to hit the power button.

Matilda's calves had intertwined with mine. I wouldn't be standing up for a while. Next to us, Liam's face had been absorbed by a pillow. There was no sending him to make coffee.

For a moment I took my companions in. I wanted to remember enjoying the feeling of just having them both close by. As I lay still on the couch, I told myself not to count down the few times left of being with Matilda, but to feel every part of this one instead. I loved the sound of her faint breaths into the throw pillow, the matching look of her and Liam's disheveled bed head. I even loved the slight discomfort of her shin bone digging into my calf.

Another wonderful adventure had been added to our long list. I knew only a few more were left.

12 3) CHRISTMAS PARTY

The tree in the living room became much less lonely as other decorations appeared around the house. Garland wrapped the banister on the stairs and skimmed the edge of shelves and doorways. Ceramic Santas and wooden reindeer appeared in newly empty spaces. The house opened up quite a bit when we moved Matilda's finished pieces upstairs. Meanwhile outside trees remained full and green, and the temperature refused to drop below seventy five.

While the edge of summer lingered in every other corner of our lives, inside the Day home it was the week of Christmas. Hand towels had small wreaths woven into them, and scented candles with names like "cranberry custard" and "snow kissed pinecone" were taking turns being lit.

I lit "midnight winter" and set it on the coffee table. The last stretches of garland needed to be untangled before stretching them across the final doorways in the house. Matilda had been complaining about being tired, so I joined her on the couch for an easy job.

Instead of *Pride and Prejudice* or her reality shows, an old Christmas movie was playing in the background. It was black and white and unfamiliar to me, but Matilda mentioned it. So it was playing.

A painting of snow, trees, and a country church covered the blanket on Matilda's legs. Years before, I had seen it drape across the couch the day after Thanksgiving. Decorating was a slow process, but Mrs. Day began it like clockwork each year. Seasonal throw pillows and blankets were always the first to show up. It wasn't exactly a rule not to use them, but if they were out another blanket was used first. I was glad to see Matilda with it that day.

Keeping happy memories afloat without stirring up grief was a balancing act. The work to do both had kept Liam from grieving himself over his parents or I think even his sister. Their back and forth had remained a steady, dickish but playful repartee.

"You can't use that blanket," he appeared in the living room with a large postage box. The socks had arrived.

"It's a blanket, and I am cold." Matilda pulled the blanket up to her chin.

"Then get one from the basket, no one can see the picture if you use it."

"Not using a blanket as a blanket is like throwing out food instead of eating it. You're ruining its only goal in life and destroying its dreams."

"That's not really a blanket, though, it's like a decoration," Liam explained.

I silently detangled garland.

"That might have been Mom's rule, but I'm dying and I want to use the Thomas Kinkade blanket."

"You can't use that excuse forever," Liam said. He carried the box to the kitchen to unpack the party favors.

"No shit," Matilda yawned.

I tried not to smile. If they caught me laughing at them their silly banter would suddenly turn to a heated defense of each other. The same thing had happened to other friends growing up, and the week before to a young man delivering pizza. Unless you came out of their mother, you couldn't make fun of a Day child.

My phone buzzed. It was my parents.

"Hi, honey!" my dad's voice was loud enough for Matilda to hear. She smiled.

"Hi, how's the watch?"

"Wrapping up the summer bunch. Winter birds will be all that's around soon. In a couple months I get to put out the fatty food." I could tell by his tone Dad was leaning to look out the nearest window. "Can't wait to see you in a few days!"

"Yes!" I suddenly remembered the sheets on my bed were old. I'd need to swap them out; Mom would know if I didn't. "You still have that spare key to my place, right?"

"Yes, GET OUT OF THERE!" He shouted and banged a fist on the window. That only happened when mourning doves ate from the songbird feeder.

"Great. I probably won't be there, but you guys know where everything is."

"Thanks, honey. I just wanted to check in, and make sure you didn't forget about us."

"Of course not," I mostly hadn't. "But I haven't been home so food there is slim."

"That's okay," he laughed. "We just need coffee."

"Tell Mom and Tara I love them."

"Will do. Love you. Tell the kids I love them."

I hung up and turned to Matilda, "Dad sends his love."

"I heard," she said. "Love him too."

Silently I considered the list of RSVPs. Including my family, it was still rather short. Half had responded, and not all of them were yes. I hoped the rest were just bad at answering and good at showing up.

My fears weren't alone. All three of us were nervous by the short list of confirmations, but none of us voiced any concerns. We feared failure; we just all hoped we were wrong. In the back of my mind I formed a disaster plan to keep the evening good for Matilda should no one be there.

When we first scheduled the party, I requested the last two days leading up to it off. In that time, I left work at work. Plans for the app or the presentation were left behind in my office. I refused to let myself even think about it.

After clean sheets were stretched across my bed, I disabled work notifications on my phone. Now was Matilda's time, and I could make them wait. Coffee was stocked, and blankets were folded neatly on the couch for my sister. Duffle bag in hand, I left my apartment behind just like work.

In the recent weeks I was usually crashing on Matilda's couch or in the guest bedroom. The only difference for the coming days was preparation. I would have a toothbrush and sleep in my own clothes instead of Matilda's spare pajamas.

When we were young, every Christmas party played out fairly similar for both of us. Our mothers would lay out a nice dress for us to wear. We would be scrubbed down in the bathtub before getting stuffed into the fluffy dresses. Last, our hair brushed and pulled back in some way with a themed bow. As much as Matilda and I hated frilly dresses and our having our hair styled, arriving to the party made everything change.

We were suddenly sophisticated in our abundance of lace and velvet. For at least the first few minutes, demeanor completely changed. We considered ourselves "very fancy ladies," and if anyone added the word "young" we were insulted.

The day before our own Christmas Matilda and I went shopping. Any of the dresses hanging in our closets would have been acceptable, but we both wanted something special.

That morning we decided to head to one of the nicer department stores that were usually frequented by middle aged women from the higher end of society. The air was a little chilly; Matilda described it as a fall tease.

A flannel shirt was unbuttoned over a plain, black V-neck. A large scarf topped everything off. All of it was to distract from the swollen abdomen sticking out over her jeans further than usual.

Her usual lipstick was swapped for a darker red. Both of us spent extra time getting ready, perhaps out of wanting to look our best for trying on new dresses, perhaps out of feeling like our outings were slowly more limited. There was an unspoken need to make them feel special.

"Does anyone here actually stand at the door with perfume samples?" She asked as we entered. "Or is that one of those myths like valet parking?"

"Valet parking is real."

"I've never seen it."

The fall collection was already filling the women's section of the store. Together we zigzagged through racks of dresses, letting the material graze our palms. Sequins, silk, and lace hit my fingers before we began skimming through options.

Matilda retrieved a black cocktail dress and inspected the tag. Hair had been wrangled into a bun on her head, and the pink bears sat in front of it like a tiara.

"Wait," I said. "No looking at price tags today. We just get what we want because we like it."

"Deal," she replied, tucking the tag back into the fabric. "But actually I need to see what size this is."

I don't remember much more of the afternoon buying dresses. I do remember how happy she was the entire time. Much happier than the day she tried on wedding dresses. For once her hair did what she wanted, and stayed perfect for the day. I can still see her odd, darker lipstick, remaining perfect despite a coffee break halfway through. She had grown tired pretty quickly.

When she finally stood before the mirror in the dark, purple dress she had selected she said something along the lines of, "This is really nice, you should bury me in this." I changed the subject.

While much of that day was a blur, I do remember the scramble of that evening and the following morning. Like overstretched mothers, Liam and I wanted everything to be perfect. The three of us finally decorated the stolen tree while watching a human version of *A Christmas Carol*.

"Poor guy, we stole him and didn't even put any clothes on him," Matilda said from the couch. The same blanket was draped across her legs as she untangled ornaments.

"If you think about it he's the lucky one," I explained. "He got picked and put on display before any of his buddies this year."

"Hope they weren't mad that we took it." She set the box beside her and leaned back into the couch cushions.

"If they even noticed it was gone," Liam's voice came from the corner behind the tree.

"My gosh," Matilda sat up. "I legitimately forgot you were back there."

The lights on the tree were suddenly illuminated.

"Thanks, brother."

I had settled into the guest bedroom. My clothes were hanging in the closet or in the drawers. In the bathroom just beside it a lot of toiletries were scattered about. The two days had felt much longer, but in a happy, fun way.

The house had felt like a second home since I was a child. As Matilda and I became adults with full time jobs, sleepovers weren't any less frequent. But in those days around the off season party, and somewhat later, it was more like home than my own place.

Upstairs the family space was bursting with paintings. Any work of Matilda's that wasn't mounted to the wall had been carried up and delicately put away. With the newly freed space in the corners, spare chairs, and walls, the house could hold a dozen extra guests.

Jittery panic and excitement woke me up the next morning. Downstairs I found out I wasn't the only one. Liam had been awake for a while.

Mrs. Day was strict with cleaning. Even when we were little toys couldn't be left out. Weekly, the house was swept and scrubbed. The floors looked more than clean after being scrubbed and polished. In her years alone, Matilda kept the place tidy, but deep cleaning became extinct. As I walked to the kitchen for coffee, I was blinded by shine on the hardwood and baseboards.

A pile of cleaning supplies sat beside Liam. He stood over the stove, scrubbing out each burner with a magic eraser. I never realized they were dirty until I saw them clean.

"Oh good," he glanced my way. "As soon as Matilda is up I can vacuum upstairs."

"No one's going upstairs; you don't need to worry about it."

"I go upstairs." He finished the last burner and moved to the counter.

I poured coffee into a mug and examined the kitchen. Everything was gleaming from his work. Mrs. Day would have been proud.

"How long have you been up?"

"Just a couple of hours." Satisfied with the kitchen, he dropped the sponge into a bucket of supplies.

I glanced at the microwave clock. It wasn't early morning, but it wasn't late either. Liam's dedication had found a way to surpass mine.

"Wow, this looks really nice," Matilda appeared. "Thanks." The two exchanged a smile.

Later, Matilda and I set out to pick up the food from the caterer. After the events of planning her fake wedding, she felt obligated to place a rather large order with them.

A couple weeks before, she sat down and called the woman up. Once again, playing the dying card got her exactly what we wanted. The caterer completely understood the situation, and was happy to hear from us again.

My tiny car was filled to the brim with food. The two of us slid into the front seats. We had to push them forward to fit everything in, and the steering wheel was uncomfortably close to my stomach.

"That could not have gone better," Matilda said. I silently hoped the caterer wasn't our single stroke of good luck for the whole event. It was eleven in the morning, eight hours until our night began.

I backed into the driveway and close to the garage to make unloading easier. Matilda hopped out to open the door, and let out a tiny shriek.

"Where is my car?" She stormed into the empty garage and turned a circle, as if she had missed the gigantic, black SUV somehow. I continued backing in as Matilda ran inside the house.

"Liam!" She shouted from the kitchen. "Where's my car?"

My concern was more for the cold food in my own car. So I began unloading as Matilda stormed through her house looking for her brother. I texted him.

Did you borrow the tank?

Trays were slid into the industrial fridge. Even after holding half of the food, it was mostly empty. Finally the desserts were brought to the kitchen island. My phone buzzed.

Yes, I had to run an errand. Be back in a couple hours.

"That bastard," Matilda picked up a tray to carry to the dining room. "Why didn't he take his stupid, electric car?"

"It's actually a hybrid."

"Half electric car then."

We left the half assembled food options to start getting ready. Like young girls getting ready for prom, we had hung our dresses on the back of the bedroom doors. Nail polish and make up was scattered across the guest bed, and we stood before it all in bathrobes.

The spare AC unit had been placed in the basement. Earlier that morning I made sure to turn it on. Cool air had been pumping into the house for a couple of hours, but we were yet to feel it. To be safe, I turned down the main AC for the house. That day was hot for fall. We wanted as close to winter as possible.

When I emerged from the bathroom with wet hair, a chill wrapped around my ankles and ran up my spine. It was perfect.

Soon Matilda and I were in the guest bedroom, wearing sweat suits and sorting eye shadow. Pallets of powder have a way of overflowing across the years. Together we compared colors to our new dresses until the familiar shake of the garage door hummed under our feet.

The tank had returned with Liam in it. Every inch from the passenger seat across the seat-less floors to the hatchback was packed full of bottles of red soda. We emerged in the garage to see Liam stumble from the driver seat. Two empty bottles fell out with him.

"You cannot buy Cherry Life locally," he explained walking to the back of the car. "But you can buy it in balk from a distributor just a couple of hours away."

For once Matilda was silent. She joined her brother at the trunk and stared at stacks and stacks of Cherry Life soda.

"This was the smallest order they let me get."

"I'm sorry I called you a bastard for taking my car," she whispered.

"No worries."

Soda was stocked everywhere. The remaining two thirds of the industrial fridge were packed full. We shoved them into the kitchen fridge. The wine cooler in the basement was stuffed. Eventually, the final stacks had to be left in the floor of the garage.

"I quite literally have a lifetime supply." Matilda finally let herself smile. She pulled the closest bottle from its plastic ring and opened it. "Water isn't going to do me much good now anyways."

We each opened a bottle. All of us accepted this seemingly impossible task of consuming what felt like an infinite supply of cherry flavored drink. The option was added to the drink selection for the night.

"I have to shower," Liam announced. "I smell like ass."

The pianist was supposed to arrive half an hour before things began. This was a precautionary measure for any early guests. It was also to make us feel Christmassy. At twenty till, he had yet to arrive.

Despite our efforts of watching old Christmas movies, elaborately decorating, and stealing a Christmas tree I could tell the feel of Christmas wasn't with us; probably because it was late September.

While it was supposed to be fall, the weather was hardly acting like us. That day the temperature hadn't dipped below sixty degrees. The house had a pleasant chill, but outside was t-shirt comfortable.

I stood at the food spread by the dining room table making last minute adjustments to our set up. A wooden, husband and wife snowman sculpture joined the platters of cookies and tiny sandwiches. Four different times I moved them around a bowl of Chex mix.

Liam and Matilda were still struggling with bottles of Cherry Life. They discovered taking off the plastic rings helped to stack the bottles closer together in the fridge. Matilda insisted on cutting up all of the rings to save wildlife.

"It's bad enough we are sending these to the dump," she explained, sharply pointing her scissors towards him. "The least we can do is save some birds and turtles."

Fifteen till. No pianist. Liam appeared at my side.

"Santa's car just pulled up. Get him upstairs while I distract her."

I glanced out the window to see Mr. Higgins walking up the sidewalk.

As before, he was wearing a bright, Hawaiian shirt and cargo shorts. He carried a large duffle bag, and, except for the full, white beard, held no resemblance to Santa Claus.

The others disappeared into the garage. I rushed to open the door before he could ring the doorbell. It swung open to reveal a surprised, old man.

"Mr. Higgins?" I motioned him inside.

"Jerry is fine," he stepped into the threshold.

"Okay, thanks again," I pointed up the stairs. "Just up there and to the right. There's a bag of party favors there too. Can I get you anything?"

"Oh, the surprise," his face brightened as he remembered. "No, thanks, sweetheart."

In a silent flash he was up the stairs. I paused, unsure which was more unnerving: a strange man getting dressed in the room I had been using, or that same strange man calling me sweetheart first. I was stopped by someone else standing in the still open door.

"Liberace!" I smiled and pointed at him.

"No," he was blunt. He wore a standard, black suit, and had hair combed back. It all matched his serious expression.

"Ah, that would be expensive." No response. "Just there, thanks."

He sat down at the piano in the front room and a clunky, tuning began. It sounded terrible. A fear ran through me. Our last big hurrah for Matilda wouldn't be ruined by guests or a power outage or bad food; it would be one shit of a piano player.

I spun around, searching for Liam. We could send the lame, piano guy away. I would grab some speakers from Matilda's workshop in the basement, plug in my phone, we would have Christmas music. The first error of the night had arrived and I was ready to fix it.

Then it all stopped. He began playing a lovely rendition of *Good King Wenceslas*, and everything was better. Not just the music, everything was better.

On a hot September evening, I suddenly felt the chill of December. Reindeer and Santas that had just been wood and ceramic were suddenly beautiful. I could smell the sugar cookies and the cinnamon from the cider punch. I felt pretty in my new dress. It was like hearing those notes on the piano flipped a switch and made it Christmas.

The doorbell rang again, that time Matilda and Liam arrived to open it. Two groups of four entered all at once, making the house feel alive. They all either wore elaborate Christmas sweaters or dressed for a cocktail party. I didn't know any of them, but they knew the Days. Everyone shared smiles and hugs before passing in a whirlwind to the dining room.

A second group entered. One couple was middle aged, and wearing matching sweaters. The wife hugged Matilda and patted Liam's face. I stood to the side and avoided any acknowledgement. The next guest caught me.

Mrs. Parrish, I think it was Mrs. Parrish, took hold of my hand. She had lived in a house down the street as long as I could remember and had been retired longer than I'd been alive. She could have a conversation with anyone. Every Halloween she gave out full sized candy bars. It was impossible not to love her.

"Tessie Fletcher! How are your parents?" She leaned on my arm and relieved the weight from her cane. "I think of your mother every time I clean out my junk drawer."

"Very well, thank you. They should be here soon."

"I was so excited to hear about your little party. I remember you girls riding your bikes up to my house every day. You both just looked so cute."

Amongst Mrs. Day's strict rules were no bikes on the street. On the rare occasions Matilda and I did ride them, we were confined to the driveway. With the countless children waving to Mrs. Parrish, it would be easy to confuse two little girls for another group. I smiled and listened to her memories.

Small groups began forming in the dining room and living room. The three of us were still by the door, the incoming flow of guests tying us there. I held my breath. For the start we had a decent crowd, but we could easily use more. A new car was parking out front. I was getting hungry.

"Tessie," Matilda pulled my gaze away from the plate of pretzel sticks. A couple close to my parents' age stood with her. "This is Mr. and Mrs. Vernon, they go to my church."

"Tessie!" Mrs. Vernon shook my hand. "We have heard so much about you. How is work going? Managing Facebook for a company must be fun."

"Yeah," my mind drew a blank on what I did for a living. This stranger's kindness caught me off guard. "Posting pictures of carrots and things."

Matilda stepped in, explaining how I wrote for the blog and worked the other social media pages. For a moment I didn't recognize her. She was standing so straight and tall, her hair tamed by a flat iron. The conversation sounded so grown up as she introduced me and talked about my career. It was the singular taste I had of seeing my best friend as an adult.

The Vernons slipped away with polite well wishes. I watched after them for a moment.

"I gotta be honest, those guys were nicer than Glen," I told Matilda. "When you said church people I expected uptight, quiet women."

They're not actually like that at all. The Vernons have taken me to the doctor a few times. And most Sundays they've fed me dinner."

We soon drifted away from the door and into the atmosphere of the evening. I made circles with Matilda around the main floor of the house.

Just like when we were kids, we had on our nice dresses. The only difference was our height and the wine in our glasses.

More guests began to flow through the door. In a moment, I was swept into a dual hug with both of my parents. Tara waved from behind them.

I couldn't remember the last time I saw her well-dressed. To the best of my memory, she had been very young, but in my mind she was always five. That night she wore a nice dress and kept every hair in a perfect curl.

"You look too old," I said from over my mother's shoulder.

"You're one to talk," she smiled back. "You're holding a wine glass like a forty year old mother of three."

"This looks excellent," my mother said when they finally let go of me.

"Thank you, did you guys find everything at my place okay?"

"Yes, go enjoy this, but we want to spend time with you before we leave," Dad patted my head before a neighbor pulled him away.

In the years since their move, my parents had been back to visit very little. Several times a year I drove out to see them. Yet to our old friends it was like they had never left town. Dad was swept into a conversation next to the piano. Mom made her way to the kitchen with a woman who lived around the corner. I glanced at an abandoned Tara.

"Don't worry," she assured me. "I can find people to talk to."

Matilda appeared beside me, refilling both of our glasses. A small smile had crept onto her face as the first people arrived. It remained throughout the night, a content, pleased smile that came from the underlying happiness we had created.

"Thank you," she told me. "I guess there was something else I needed to do."

The bustle of conversations around us was silenced by Liam's voice. Much like his father in years past, he took a spot by the bottom of the stairs and called attention with one sentence.

"Do you guys hear something on the roof?"

Matilda spun around to face him. Just in that moment, Mr. Higgins began to descend the stairs. In his red suit he was completely transformed. A large, decorative sack was swung over his back, and he waved while giving the house a greeting.

Her jaw dropped open and eyes widened. In her heels, still clutching a half empty glass and a bottle of wine, Matilda began to bounce up and down from excitement. A giddy laughter flowed from deep inside her. The adult I had seen all evening disappeared. In return, I didn't see the usual Matilda, but the child from that Easter picture. She rushed out of the room to greet Santa.

"Nicely done," I told Liam.

"We both did it," he said with a napkin full of macarons in his hands.

"The party, yes," I agreed. "But Santa was all you. That's the happiest I've seen her months."

Santa milled through the guests. For a while Matilda was glued to his side. Everyone seemed to like being given fuzzy, red and green socks. At least they were better than gift cards.

Across the first hour, the house kept filling up. I tried to glide through the rooms and make a decent count, but didn't get far. As best as I could tell, most of the people we invited showed up. Food supplies were lasting well. I tried to encourage people to drink bottles of Cherry Life.

In the living room, Matilda and Liam had settled into the couch with a group of people old enough to be our parents. Mom had joined at the end of the couch. Everyone was listening to a woman talk. I paused for a moment on the words, "she looked beautiful in her dress."

The woman continued, "She didn't cry at all. She was just excited, and she could not stop giggling." Matilda leaned in, hanging on every word of the story. The woman smiled and took Matilda's hand before she continued. "You look just like her."

My mother's hand reached up and took mine. I glanced down to see her watching me watch Matilda. She didn't say anything, she just smiled at me. I wanted to smile and cry at the same time. In the moment I didn't do either one. I told myself there would be enough time for crying later.

The doorbell rang again. I hurried to answer it, not wanting the others to lose a moment of the story. This worked out, since the guest at the door was for me.

Khaki and hiking boots had been replaced with a dress shirt and penny loafers. Had it not been for his full, bushy beard, I wouldn't have recognized him. Despite the zoo's distance, he had driven to Matilda's home for a Christmas party with people he didn't even know.

"Tessie!" he smiled.

"Hi!" my mind raced, searching for his name. Just as I was about to say it, he spoke up.

"Emmet."

"Yes," I answered. "From-"

"I work at the zoo," he remained on the doorstep.

"Yes. Please come in," I opened the front door further.

An air of awkwardness came with him. Not knowing anything about him besides the fact he worked at a zoo, I struggled for something to say. I pointed out the food and mentioned Santa.

"This is fun, an out of season Christmas party," he tried to make conversation. I wanted a drink.

"Yeah, Matilda likes Christmas a lot."

"So she's still alive. Everything okay?" As soon as he asked, he kicked himself for the question.

My eyes narrowed. I wanted to punch him, but my hand relaxed.

"Excuse me," I said instead. "I have to go… drink some wine."

I slipped off to the kitchen and left Emmet on his own. Dad was talking to Liam about life since they had moved. Liam seemed to feign interest at the talk of the small town.

"The community is strong. Tara had no trouble settling in."

Luckily, Dad was uncorking a new bottle and smiled at me. He poured two glasses and slid one my way.

"This was for your mom, but it looks like you might need it more."

"Thanks," I took a long sip.

"You've done a great job setting this up," he said. "Don't let one person spoil any of it."

My father was occasionally omniscient.

When the wine was gone, which did not take long, Matilda appeared with Cherry Life to refill my glass. One more piece of the tiny checklist remained undone. Cherry life and pretzel sticks in hand, we slipped out onto the side patio.

Cat was nowhere to be seen; no doubt because people were in his home. Most likely he had gone behind the garage or under the house. It would be a couple of days before any of us saw him again.

It was much easier to stand outside when the weather wasn't freezing. Yet without the snow some of the magic felt lost. I gazed up at the sky, wishing for a shooting star or some other unexplainable image to christen our evening. Together we gazed up at the sky, stars barely visible from our spot in the suburb.

"Thank you," Matilda said. "It's like Mom and Dad are here again, for one more moment."

I kept my eyes upwards. I was almost scared to look at her. Simply hearing her voice made it feel like any scourge of the evening or close coming end was nonexistent. There was nothing ahead; just us, lifelong friends, enjoying our own piece of a Christmas party.

"I made a stupid list."

"You did?" I still looked at the faint stars, but I could feel her eyes on me.

"There's just one thing I didn't get to do."

"What is it?" I finally looked her way. "Let's do it."

Special moments and memories were pushed aside. I wanted to give her whatever she needed. If a party with all of our old friends and neighbors didn't complete her final wishes on earth, I would do anything to make her happy. I thought of the list of murders again.

"No, it's dumb." She took a bite of pretzel.

"Come on, let's do it," I said. "We can figure it out. I'll figure it out."

"Tessie," she finally looked at me. "It's okay."

Her coca cola red lips gave a faint smile, but her crystal eyes began to water. In the faint light from the window her face seemed paler than usual, but the last month had driven into a fainter shade of white. She was a Snow White struggling to keep tears back.

"It's okay to cry," I whispered.

"No," she touched her eyes with a free hand. "It's not. We only have a little bit of time left. I can feel it. And I don't want to waste it crying or being sorry. I just want to spend as much wonderful time with you as I can. I can't leave you much, but I won't leave you bad memories when there's enough time to make good ones."

We remained silent after that. Stars grew blurry from my clouded eyes. I closed them, and swallowed any feelings back. If Matilda wanted us to be happy, I would be happy. Tears were for later.

Soon my glass was empty. I didn't want more cherry flavored soda. That evening the only alcohol that had been out was wine. I knew I could slip into a cabinet and find something stronger. I needed it.

"I could use a second round of food," I finally said.

"Hey, as much as that caterer cost, we're each having at least three rounds." Matilda downed the last of her soda. "Let's get back to these losers."

Before we piled a second plate full of meat balls and cookies, we both slipped into the downstairs bathroom. With some double sided tape, we secured two googly eyes to the underside of the toilet seat. In our list of pranks, it wasn't exactly high, but it was simple and quickly accomplished. Like any good prank it left the receivers bewildered.

With two very full, plastic plates, we took seats on the staircase. From the right spot, we could keep eyes on everyone in the living room, front room, dining room, and hallway around the stairs. Everyone was milling around us, and from the fifth or sixth step up we were just above head height.

Matilda dropped something into my hand.

"Pretend like you're eating. It hides that you're holding them."

I glanced down at a small clump of silver BBs. Less than ten rolled in my palm. It was more than enough.

"Where did you get these?" I asked.

"I found a box of them in Liam's closet. They were from back before he got all spooked by guns."

Every so often we glanced up from our food, found an unsuspecting victim, and tossed a tiny metal ball into their hair. Half of them didn't even notice. A few winced for a second, and returned to what they were doing. Several looked up in the air in confusion. Our childlike game lasted for only a few minutes.

The fun wasn't really in doing silly things. It was in remembering how it felt to pull pranks when we thought they were very clever. Tossing BBs was another moment of the evening to feel like little girls again.

Working through the second plate of food was harder than I thought. Eventually all that was left were two macarons. I wanted to finish them off, but offered them to Matilda instead.

"No thanks," she tossed her last BB. "I don't really like them that much."

We descended the stairs after they were gone. A couple of guests were beginning to leave. The night had passed its peak and was beginning to slow down. Most of the food was gone. The Cherry Life had barely been touched, yet the recycling bin was full of empty bottles.

"One more prank," Matilda stopped me at the bottom of the stairs. "I told Emmet you were interested in him, so have fun with that."

She pointed behind me. I turned to see the zoo guy approaching. Looking back, Matilda had already disappeared into the living room. There was no escaping this conversation. I drove into the skid and hoped for the best.

"Hi again," he offered.

"Hi," I smiled politely. "Enjoying yourself?"

"Yes, look," he glanced at his feet. I felt a little bit of pity. He was trying. "I'm sorry for how I phrased things earlier. I was nervous and not really thinking."

"It's okay," I reassured him. "Happens to all of us."

In hindsight, I think Matilda was worried about me. She didn't want to leave me alone, or perhaps she felt a little guilty for all of our time spent together. My dating life was never complex, but in that last year especially there was nothing.

I glanced over Emmet. Besides his overgrown facial hair, he was rather well groomed. He also worked with animals every day, which was a definite plus. My mind fell into an idea of, "oh, what the hell?"

"Will you let me take you to dinner sometime?" he asked.

"Sure," I sighed. "Would you like my number?"

He left after that with my number saved to his phone. Not being an idiot, he waited a few days before texting me. Me being an idiot, I didn't answer.

The night quickly dwindled. Guests slipped out one by one. As Matilda hugged and said goodbye to the Vernons, Liam wrote a check in the kitchen to Santa. Shortly after, Mr. Higgins slipped out the side patio door with two cases of Cherry Life in tow.

Finally my parents were the last to leave. They hugged all three of us, and each took more Cherry Life.

"Well done," Mom said. "Very well organized."

"Thank you," I smiled. "Lunch tomorrow? I need to see you at least a little before you leave."

"Yes, honey," Dad hugged me again. "We'll only steal you for a minute."

As soon as they slipped out the front door the three of us collapsed into the couch. Suddenly my feet began throbbing in my flats. Except for the few minutes on the steps, I had been standing all evening. I tried to recollect how many faces I talked to and the food I ate, but the glasses of wine were blurring it all together.

"Man, that piano player was a drag," Matilda said laying down. "He can play a piano, but don't invite him to any parties."

She laughed alone at her joke. Her face was buried into the rumpled, Kinkade blanket.

"Who was that guy with the beard?" Liam asked, glancing my way. A napkin of macarons was spread across his lap.

"Don't worry about it," I snapped. Quickly flipping the subject I added, "Matilda, your church people were nice."

"Right?" she sat back up. "I love those guys. You should have my funeral there."

"Don't talk about that," I said.

"Hey, it's my funeral. I think I should get a say on where you're going to have it."

We all glanced around at the littered plates, napkins, and cups. Food had already been taken care of by my mother. Without any instruction, she jumped to put away perishables in the slim fridge space. Tara had been given the job of putting plastic wrap around everything else. Messines still lingered.

"Absolutely no cleaning up," Matilda read my mind. "Everyone upstairs and in bed."

"After a nightcap," I added as I stood. I needed more than a little bit of wine to ease the pain in my feet.

13 6) THE TWO HUNDRED

After the party I met my family for a meal. I couldn't do more with them before they all had to drive back. Instead of talking I listened to stories from Tara. She was starting her senior year and I felt old. I didn't want to mention work.

I told myself telling them about my idea for the company's app would jinx it. If things fell through, it would be easier to not bring up the situation at all than to explain why it didn't work out. That pitch was coming up, and my thoughts were focusing on it again.

All too soon they were gone and life was falling back into its normal routine. All trace of their presence was gone from my apartment. Mom's years of orderly dedication had rubbed off. The only evidence was the blankets on the couch. Tara had folded them better than I did.

The weather began to change, but that was all. Every Monday morning we had our coffee at the regular stop. The café was back to serving only the tables inside. Matilda parked crooked and I slipped in behind her. We talked about celebrities and looked for men walking by on the street. Winesdays were as scheduled. Liam was never around. Matilda convinced him to find something else to do, and we had our girl time. Things felt the same.

If she didn't text, I assumed Matilda was with Liam or working. She still made posters and ads for the same company. Welding equipment was in full use. Paintings appeared once and a while in a hallway or closet. Matilda stopped thinking of random things to do. I wasn't pulled out on afternoons to buy a dress or eat fifteen donuts. When we did get together, it was for our regular times in the week.

I began to like work again. Projects that felt dull and flavorless in the summer had a sweet excitement in the fall. I remembered why I had my career. Without realizing it, I would begin a section of a project in the afternoon, and when I glanced up from my desk almost everyone had left for the day. Quite by accident, I was working late any night I had no plans with Matilda.

Amelia noticed too. She started coming by once a week. Verbal encouragements were thrown at me and I collaborated on big ideas.

The words, "second chance," were never said, but that's what she gave me. Another presentation emerged that was noticeably similar to the one I flubbed up at the beach. Again I was making a presentation Amelia would give. Only this time everything was proofread three times and I turned it in early. Less than an hour after I sent it, I got an email that just read, looks great. She was happy.

That afternoon I left work early to get to Matilda's. No one had mentioned it, but we all knew the six month mark was upon us. Without specifying the reason, the three of us made plans to spend the evening together.

Dinner was calm. We watched a movie and stayed together as the night wore on. Each of us found another excuse of something else to do. After we retrieved winter clothes from the attic, cleaned out the spice cabinet, and polished the hard wood surfaces of each room, we were at a loss for activities.

By half past eleven, we were seated around the edge of the dining room table with an old board game. It had been discovered during our excavation in the attic. Quietly we moved plastic pieces from space to space on faded cardboard.

Midnight came, and we held our breath. Nothing happened.

"Well it's not an exact science," Matilda's voice broke the silence that had wrapped around the house. "Today has been a good day. I have energy and we're doing stuff. They told me I would get sick and be in bed. I'm fine."

The last two words came as a blessing. Matilda's declaration promised months of health in our minds. Everything was okay. Our schedules stayed the same. The world looked up. Matilda laughed and threw shade. This ticking bomb had no visible clock, and could tick as long as it pleased. I was happy.

One afternoon, Amelia made her way into my office. That day her smile wasn't a plaster put on for the workday, it was a genuinely friendly smile. She took her usual seat, and I was excited to give her my attention.

"I have some good news for today," she began, skipping usual pleasantries. "Your work recently has really been top notch. Others at the corporate office have noticed."

"Thank you, I've been feeling good about it lately." Sense told me to tread lightly.

"You're ahead of most employees across our region in this position."

"Thank you," I said again.

"In a few weeks we have a shareholders meeting. It's a big group, and they're actually local. So some of the executives have decided to come down and have the meeting here." Amelia listed off the names of higher ups I had never met, but knew of from memos and paperwork.   Terms the company used, that I pretended to understand, were littered in the conversation. Amelia described what this meeting and presentation was going to be about. It had something to do with trading lots of money and help for the company. To the people I had never met in the corporate offices, it was all very important. I convinced her I cared with my side of the conversation.

"I think you should present your idea," Amelia wrapped up her idea with another smile. It was time for me to care. "The right people can stay back an extra hour and they're going to like you. I'll admit, for a minute you had me worried. But I honestly can't wait to see this completed project and your future here."

Auto pilot had kicked in, and I smiled and thanked her. Amelia left satisfied with me and herself, and my work began. Information was handed to me and I did my side of research. I marked a date a few weeks ahead on my calendar. Ideas were becoming real. I needed to buckle down and polish the thought and plans until they were perfect.

It was easy to get wrapped up in the planning. This meeting was going to be held after work hours in our conference room. I had twenty minutes at the end to show them what I had been working on, and that Amelia had helped me sculpt it. Large prints of non-sexually specific Cameron would be put up for everyone to see. This meeting was the rocket that could shoot me to a bigger job.

If such a life change came, I would simply be going from a one bedroom apartment in my hometown to a one bedroom apartment in New York. As I began dedicating time and energy to the meeting on the horizon, I let myself slip into the daydream that had been off limits.

Mom and Dad would rush to visit me. Tara would have a cool, older sister she could stay with on spring break. I could see a future Tessie, walking down a street in high heels and drinking coffee. Maybe a change in scenery would be good for me; especially if things would be changing at home. If they changed at home.

I kicked the thought out of my head. All I needed to focus on was this meeting, and making sure I did my best for it. I told myself it was the only thing on my horizon. Any other future thoughts were tossed into a back closet in my mind where I slammed the door closed and locked it.

With the extra time spent at work, most meals were ordered in for the evenings. The office trash can became accustomed to Styrofoam containers and Chinese takeout boxes. My wallet and exhausted stomach told me I needed a break. The rest of my body agreed with them, and I went home at five one evening.

The amount of money I had thrown at food told me to cook from home. Ingredients that felt foreign sneered at me from the pantry. I scowled back in my pajamas and poured a glass of wine. Why couldn't a satisfying meal come from pouring moscato into a glass?

I distracted myself with my phone. Intent was to find a ten minute recipe using only a frying pan, white rice, and some deli ham. Instead, I texted Matilda.

That day had been pretty normal. We chatted and sent pictures. Things were feeling the way they had before. The only real difference was Liam was around now and then to make us food. I thought about asking him what to make that night.

Fear has a way of disappearing when you ignore it. Celebrating Christmas in September sparked a desire to mesh holidays in a new, offseason tradition.

During occasional breaks my mind slipped to a quiet, personal pet project. I wanted to eat turkey and hang paper hearts. Working title for the event was Thanksatine Day. Matilda would like it. I decided after this pitch meeting was done we could start planning it.

Matilda wasn't answering any texts, and the internet gave me no cooking help. Deep in the icy pit of my freezer I found a pizza. Many moons before I threw it back there for just such an evening. I sighed with relief, and enjoyed my second glass while the oven preheated.

A knock at the door made me jump. No one knocked at my door. Even the landlady just left notes.

Matilda stood in the threshold, carrying a large, flat box. A baggie, dark hoodie made her look smaller and paler than usual. Both of her arms worked to hold up everything. Inside were stacks of envelopes tied up with ribbon. Piles ranged in size.

"Do you want some pizza? I was feeling lazy," I offered.

"No thanks, I'm not hungry." She sighed. "I'm just dropping these off."

"Thanks," I stood back as she dropped the box onto the counter with a thud. I glanced towards one of the larger stacks kept together with pink ribbon. "What is it?"

"My letters. They're very organized, you should be proud. It took a long time."

"How many letters?" I noticed some of the envelopes were stretched with several sheets of paper. Some were thin. There were a lot.

"Two hundred. There's a note on top explaining all of them. So I guess two hundred and one, but a note doesn't really count as a letter. Also it's messy, my hand was pretty cramped by then."

I picked up one of the stacks at the top, the heaviest from what I could tell. Blue ribbon held them together. February thirteenth of the following year was written on the first one; four months from that night, my birthday. The bundle fell back into the box.

"There's seventy three of those," Matilda explained. I cast a wary look. "Sorry, I want you to live to be ninety eight."

I searched for the right words. The peculiarity of the gift caught me off guard, and didn't want to seem ungrateful or diminish her hard work.

"Thank you," I finally managed.

"I just think you might need it, Tessie." Her eyes sliced me in half.

"Do you want to watch something or just stay for a bit?"

"Thanks, but I'm kind of tired," She shrugged. Her frail body was practically drowning in the hoodie.

"Yeah, okay." I sipped my wine, trying to find calm in the uneasiness.

"Can you do me a favor?" she asked.

"Sure, always."

"Stop." She nodded to the glass in my hand. "I can't save you after this."

I placed the glass on the counter.

"Promise?"

"Promise," I nodded, frozen to my spot.

"And for goodness sake, think about church. The people there are actually really nice."

"Okay."

"Okay," she agreed, pausing at the door. "Tessie, I love you."

"I love you too."

The door closed, and I stayed in my spot. The last few moments hardly felt real. If I had seen the Matilda from that night a year ago I wouldn't have recognized her. Recently she had grown even paler, dark bags hung under glazed eyes. As her abdomen swelled she wore baggy clothes daily. They always made her look even thinner. She was a bleached sheet stretched over a frail skeleton.

A harsh beep from the oven woke me from my trance. It was preheated.

After sliding in the partially thawed pizza, I turned back to my kitchen. The ominous box remained on the counter. I carried it to the other room and slit it under my bed. Keeping it from sight meant it couldn't exist for a while. I had too much to do.

A shaky hand poured whiskey over ice and waited for my food. I forced my mind to my office, putting all the focus I could muster into the project waiting for me there.

14 WHEN THE DAYS ARE GONE

Getting ready to present the app consumed my life. My calendar filled with checklists leading up to the day of the presentation. Slowly each day became a darker shade of red, specifying the intensity of the act. Post it notes of every shade of blue lined my desk in rows and columns. Highlighters and pens marked up all of them in my own system of stars and check marks.

Final artwork had been completed by Cameron. Everything was printed on large poster boards that sat together in my office. I thanked him/her and said I would be in contact if any adjustments needed to be made post approval.

Amelia set up the whole meeting. A select few board members would be coming to our office, and Glen was ecstatic. They would sit in our conference room and listen to me explain the value of an Osiris app for the company as a whole.

If things went well, a prototype would be created. Then I would make the same presentation to the entire board while being backed by the first members. Amelia would be with me every step of the way. The most important members of the company would hear my name and listen to me.

Amelia made it very clear that this could be good for both of us. Doors could open that only led to better things. If they liked me and my idea I could move to New York, have a fancy apartment and a bunch of extra money. Matilda could help me decorate it and give me a new painting to hang. Mom would brag about me even more than she already did.

No pressure or anything.

Most nights I was staying late. I set up the poster boards on chairs in front of my desk and matched the images with a power point presentation. All I needed were words.

Carry out boxes filled the trashcan by my door. Every evening the cleaning crew had a different restaurant's logo waiting for them.

Matilda was offering the occasional encouraging text. I was bad about trying to talk. Our conversations were much shorter and spaced further apart. Sometimes I found a minute to send something, but it would be an hour or so before she answered. *Sorry I was asleep* or *Sorry I was busy* was the typical response.

I tried not to think about it. I knew as soon as I made my pitch my calendar would open up again. It would be easy to get away so we could eat donuts and watch one of her wedding shows.

One evening was spent working on packets of information. They said almost the same thing as the sideshow, but everything had to be condensed and fitted to sheets of paper. The one part of the entire project that should have been simple wasn't. Three hours after the office was empty, I still slapped the keyboard in frustration.

My phone buzzed with a text from Emmet.

Hey how are you?

I tossed my phone into the desk drawer and slammed it closed.

The week of the presentation arrived. Monday morning I was already jittery in my apartment. I took one sip of brandy to get my heart rate down. Matilda didn't have her usual meeting, so we cancelled coffee and I went to the office early.

As soon as the presentation was finished, I would tell her about my fancy job possibilities. She would be excited for me. We would spend an hour looking at Ikea furniture and planning for living in a new place. Matilda would tell me she'd come and visit. I would tell her to just move there too.

I never was one for talking about things unless I knew they were happening. That way if it didn't work out, I wasn't faced with the humiliating job of telling everyone that it didn't work out. Until I was accepted to college, I didn't mention that I had applied anywhere. It was safer to not bring any of it up.

The day before the presentation was a Wednesday. I knew that morning that I couldn't make it to our usual wine and magazine pairing. When I texted Matilda I just called it a work thing, and said I was sorry.

Four hours later, she texted back and said she couldn't make it either. I promised Friday evening we could hang out as usual.

Late that night I was still rehearsing what I would say. It needed to sound cool, but grounded. To some I was too young to be taken seriously, so I needed to keep a collected, professional side. I wondered if I should lie about my age. Then I wondered if I should scrap everything and make a brand new presentation from scratch. Around nine I decided to leave it all alone and went home.

Thursday was a whirlwind. While I was the only one besides Amelia who really could be affected by the presentation, the rest of the office was tense from the thought of higher ups being in our midst. Everyone worked harder and things looked a little tidier.

The day seemed to buzz around me. Amelia arrived. We went over everything that had already been covered in our recent emails. Glen sent the receptionist out to get refreshments for the conference table.

It was getting close. I set up the poster boards on my chairs one last time to look at the three of them. They didn't have any mistakes, but I was worried they did. I scanned each one thoroughly before I assured myself they were fine. I didn't believe myself.

I took a deep breath and looked out my window at the front door. In any minute they would be walking in. Then my phone rang.

Liam was calling me. He had never called my phone before.

"Hello?" my voice was weak. I could feel my hands shaking. I prayed my assumption was wrong.

"Tessie," his voice shook. He stopped to take a breath.

"I know," my voice broke as I hung up.

Instantly the structured life that had absorbed me for the past two weeks shattered. None of it mattered. The foundation of my life had been pulled away and I could feel everything collapsing from it. My lip quivered and tears began to sting my eyes. My body couldn't move. Then she came in.

"Tessie, why aren't you set up?" Amelia's face changed when I turned towards her.

"I... my," I couldn't form the words. Any sound I started to make was choked back.

"Oh no, I'm so sorry." I waited for her to step forward and hug me. She didn't move. "Take a few minutes, then I'll help you carry everything in there."

"What?" My shell shock began to wear off. "No, I have to go."

I gathered up my things. I didn't know where I was headed; I would call Liam and find out.

"You can't leave," Amelia stayed in my door. "I'm sorry, I know you're sad, but we just need you for less than an hour. Then you can go."

"What the hell?" my hands rolled into fists.

"You're upset, but you have to get a grip. There's too much riding on this."

I could see my fists swinging in front of me. I wanted to hit this stupid woman in the face as hard as I could. This useless, corporate shit bag was standing there alive and healthy when Matilda wasn't. Instead I grabbed the poster boards.

With one swing after another I smashed them against the corner of the desk. It only took a few hits before they started breaking. I ripped them apart the rest of the way.

"I'm done," I hissed.

With only my purse in hand, I stormed past Amelia. She stumbled back out of the doorway as I raced out of the office. The world blurred.

I was inside my apartment. Things suddenly felt real. The click of the deadbolt was louder than any explosion. Everything was quiet and blank. White walls and wooden floors stared at me. The only trace of Matilda was her painting in the living room.

She would never paint anything else for me.

Everyone thinks that just because someone is artsy, they're super dramatic all the time. While Matilda did write me two hundred letters, she didn't let anyone see her deathbed or cry into her sheets. She only let Liam be there because he was working.

I could kill her for not letting me be near her on those last few days, even if she was asleep for most of it. She was pretty sneaky, keeping me away like that; assuring that my last memory with her would be a pleasant one.

In the sanctuary of my covers I curled up into a ball. I wanted to keep pulling my legs into my chest to make myself smaller and smaller until nothing was left, and Tessie Fletcher ceased to exist.

I hugged my legs until they hurt. I kept hugging until my arms hurt too.

As hard as I tried, I couldn't remember how my life had been before we moved into that house. It was like the world didn't exist before Matilda, and couldn't exist without her.

Everything hurt. Nothing hurt. Silent tears rolled into a pool on my pillow.

Outside my window, the sun slipped away and the world grew dark. It was well past what most would call dinner time. I wasn't hungry. There was no point in eating. I kept my eyes on the window. I couldn't move.

When I fell asleep I slept, when I woke up I was awake. If I stood up, I couldn't feel the floor under my feet.

For a couple of days all I had was a couple of glasses of whisky. I didn't even cut it with ice. I sat on the arm of the couch with my feet on the seat. From there I could stare at the painting and sip my glass.

I thought of all the times Matilda was sick when we were little. Mrs. Day gave her vitamin C pills, she got her flu shots, and anytime the weather had the slightest chill she was shoved into some kind of sweater.

I wondered how no one could notice how sick she was all the time. Why didn't I notice? If I had just said something about it to Mom or Mrs. Day they could have seen a specialist. Matilda would have been given some kind of special medicine. She would have been put on a transplant list sooner. When she turned twenty one she could have had a brand new heart.

Everything would have been fine. Why didn't I say something?

I was a stupid kid.

One day I went to the church for the funeral. I sat in pew and watched other people cry. People I didn't know. Some of them I'd never seen before. When it was over I drove home and crawled back into bed.

Liam disappeared. I assumed he moved on to whatever job was waiting for him next. That's what he did last time. I didn't want to talk to anyone, so I didn't ask.

The next day hunger finally came to me. I opened my fridge and ate anything that was ready made. In my freezer, I found frozen lasagna. As I waited the three hours for it to cook, I ate chips and salsa on my couch.

"Why did you buy that?" I could hear Matilda saying. "Frozen lasagna has never been good."

I can tell you from experience now that blocking something out is never a good idea. Trying to forget a memory or a fact or impending doom is like locking a rabid dog in a closet in the back of your house. Just because you locked it away, doesn't mean it's gone. Every so often it might bark or growl or throw itself against the door like it could break out at any second.

You can't live with a dog locked in your house. I did. In those last few days Matilda wasn't sick if I didn't think about it. When the dog broke out of the closet, my whole house exploded. I was left numb all over.

As I sat on my couch with chips and salsa, I heard the crunch of the chips, but didn't taste them. The TV was on, playing some show I hadn't seen before. Despite sitting there watching it play, it was like I couldn't see it.

I leaned back and saw the purple and gold swirls above my head. My hand stroked the edge of the canvas. The edges of paint were rough. I hated myself for not asking her for more paintings.

I felt like a jug after all the orange juice is gone. There was no reason to leave me sitting in the fridge. I belonged in the trash, because now I was useless.

One thing I did hear was a knock on my door. I stumbled to it, and found Glen standing on the other side. He was carrying a box full of things from my desk. From my best estimate, it was a weekday, but he wasn't wearing a tie.

"I wanted you to get your things," he offered the box. I took it, not thinking to invite him in. "How are you?"

I shrugged. I didn't have the energy to speak.

"I know this is hard for you," he said slowly. "Sometimes emotions make us act without thinking."

"Sometimes," I agreed. My voice was raspy from a dry throat.

"I think we could forgive your moment last week, if you want to come back."

I looked him over. Glen was trying to be nice. No doubt he had spoken to Amelia and a few of the others in our company. Most likely he had defended me, insisted I was a great employee, and convinced them to let me come back. I didn't want a job.

"I need some time," I said.

He looked disappointed, but not surprised. In the moment, if Glen had cried or begged me to come back or even offered me his own job I would have said no. I didn't miss Osiris or the pictures of vegetables waiting to be captioned.

"I'll try to hold it for you, but I can't forever."

I only nodded as he turned away. The front door closed and I dropped the box on the kitchen counter.

Back in my bed, I pulled the sheets over my head. I thought of Lizzie and Jane and the way they chatted late in the evening under their sheet. I thought of the sleepovers Matilda and I had. Even as adults we watched movies and giggled about men. Then I realized, she would never laugh with me again. We would never have a sleepover and be two Lizzies.

Audible tears finally came. I couldn't pause them to breathe let alone quit. They ran down my nose and into my pillow. All I could do was let them happen.

For a couple of days, I ate the occasional piece of lasagna. When the chips and salsa were gone, I made toast to go with it. The food was dwindling. I couldn't form a plan to go get more, or what I would even buy. I began to wonder what I could afford to buy.

My savings were in decent shape. I could last a few months. Checking was okay, but all of our trips and excursions over the past year had taken a decent chunk. The Christmas party didn't help either.

That had been over two months ago. It felt like yesterday.

Matilda died four days ago. It felt like forever.

Eventually I pulled the box of letters out from under my bed. All of them were packaged together in organized clumps. Each clump was collected by ribbon from old wrapping paper stashes or piles meant for hair. Needless to say, Matilda's hair never had ribbon in it.

It was the most organized Matilda had ever been. A rough note sat at the top of the box, listing the inventory. Sitting in the floor of my bedroom, I spread the stacks around me, learning what was there.

Sorry this note looks bad. My hand is pretty cramped from writing two hundred letters. Wow. This paper makes me look so tan.

I touched the dried ink. Elegant swirls declared themselves ugly. I'm not going to share the extent of the letters themselves. She did offer some wonderful advice like *Don't be an ass that ignores people trying to be nice to you* and

Take this opportunity to walk around your apartment naked. It feels great. They were for me and Matilda and no one else. I'll pass on one piece, later.

The two largest clumps had seventy three letters each. The bottom right corner of each envelope held a number. One pile was for Christmas. One pile was for birthdays. According to her note, Matilda wanted to me to read one each year, and expected me to live to be ninety eight.

A smaller clump of three was letters for various break ups. Another clump of three was in case I ever got married, she assured me I would. One was for an engagement, one for the stress of planning a wedding, and one for a wedding toast.

Obviously I would be your maid of honor. So here's the toast I would give.

A stack of four was for having children. There were two for mid-life crises, two more in case I ever mothered asshole teenagers. A large clump of twelve had one for each week over the next few months. One bundle had ten thick letters for whenever I was sad. They were all longer, and meant to be read a few times. Another ten were for times in the years to come when I missed her. At the very top sat a small stack of seven. There was one for every day of the first week she was gone. I was a few days behind.

Extensive planning and hours of work had gone into this pile of letters. Her note assured me it was Matilda's way of being with me through all of it. I think it was more of a chance for her to live out things she knew she wouldn't get to experience.

Even though I was thankful, but didn't want to read a single one. I wanted to sit on the couch with Matilda and watch reality TV. I opened the top letter from the stack of seven.

If you followed my intricate instructions, which you probably didn't, the worst happened yesterday.

After reading the first sentence, I stuffed the letter back into the envelope. Everything was tossed back into the box and kicked under my bed.

I crawled back into my covers. My eyes were out of tears. All I could do was lay still and stare at the wall. I knew I wouldn't be hurting Matilda's feelings by not reading her letters, because she couldn't know I didn't read them. All she was trying to do was help me feel better. It didn't work.

"I can't do this alone," I whispered to no one.

Time became an indistinguishable blob. I hadn't left my apartment in a week. It felt like a month and an hour at the same time. I had no desire to step out of my front door.

One day I found a mac and cheese cup in the cabinet. It was late afternoon, and other than coffee I hadn't eaten anything else. In the same pajamas I'd been wearing for almost three days, I shuffled across the kitchen to the microwave. I opened the door and empty space stared back at me.

There was no half-full coffee mug. Likely, there never would be again. Suddenly I realized how insignificant it was that she left her coffee in the microwave and forgot to finish it. But for some reason I had chosen to turn the cold coffee into a big deal. Our disagreements were few and far between, but they all felt like a horrible waste of time. In that moment I was willing to give anything for another half a cup of coffee with her.

My chest ached. I dropped the cup of noodles and water into the trash and went back to bed.

Real Christmas was a week away.

I called my parents and told them I was going to stay at my place that year. They understood, and asked how I was doing. I lied, insisting I had been eating and just taken time off of work.

Most of my days were spent in bed or sitting on the couch. Occasionally the flow was interrupted by several minutes of tears over something stupid like my solitary painting or a sock. When Matilda had been so much of my life before, she was in everything she left behind. Anything I saw or touched had some connection to her.

One day I sat down with my laptop on the couch. A few searches brought up jobs similar to the one I just left. I was qualified for a few. They all sounded like hell.

I knew that soon Mom would find out about my tantrum. While Mom wasn't one for lecturing, I hated the sound of disappointment that came from her voice. When that disappointed sigh finally came, I could soften it if I at least applied to somewhere else.

Finally, I decided to go get some groceries. With the holiday season in full swing, I knew ordering delivery would be difficult. Clad in sweatpants, snow boots, and a coat I made my way into the chilly air.

Decorations had exploded everywhere. I felt a heavy emptiness without Matilda. We had celebrated our own Christmas together in the warm arms of September. I quit my job. All of these factors kept me from feeling anything close to Christmasy.

At the grocery store, a mechanical Santa moved slowly in the window. I thought of Mr. Higgins and his favor. Did it count as a favor considering how much Liam had paid him? Maybe.

I thought about sending Liam money for Santa. Then I remembered I was unemployed. Also, I had no idea what his email was. I felt my pockets. I had left my phone somewhere in the apartment.

Did Mr. Higgins care that Matilda was gone?

Probably not. Just like everyone else in the world, he didn't care. Her life had been a blip in their long existence. They had all kept moving. Their lives had gone on. Mine hadn't.

My fridge was stocked with frozen pizzas and microwave dinners. Any sort of snack that sounded half way appetizing was added to the mix. I knew I wouldn't need to leave my apartment for at least a week. When the food ran out, I would figure something out from there.

Or so I thought. My phone buzzed.

Emmet was trying again. He asked if I was excited for Christmas. Once again, I lied and told him yes. A small conversation started. I avoided mentioning anything about Matilda. He didn't ask about her.

I kept answering simply because it was something to do. In the past week I had been avoiding contact with my family. There was no one I wanted to talk to, but the TV had done little in the way of entertainment.

Eventually he did ask if I wanted to get dinner the following night. I glanced down at myself. Sweatpants and hoodie had become an indistinguishable blob of grey and green. I couldn't remember the last time I showered. Food stains covered my clothes. Knowing my life was headed nowhere, I agreed I would go.

The next day I showered. A part of me felt good. I found something to wear besides pajamas and spent extra time getting ready. I put on makeup for the first time in days, and brushed my bangs to hide the scar in my eyebrow. Then I felt bad for feeling good. I was supposed to be in mourning, not going on a first date. I tried to shake the feeling away and walked down to my car.

The moment I sat down everything felt worse. There I was, getting ready to go out, and I didn't have anyone to talk to about it. No one was there to help me pick out my dress. No one stalked the guy on social media to make sure he wasn't crazy. I was the only one who knew I was going out for the evening. I would never get ready for a date with Matilda's help.

The tears started all at once. It wasn't just unfair that Matilda's life was cut so short because she missed out on so much. It was unfair to me because I was left alone. My best friend was gone, and without her I had no one.

I screamed. I beat my hands against the steering wheel. Like a tired child, I screamed, I cried, and I hit my fists against anything close to me.

I had been cut short too. I was angry that I didn't have any friends to talk to. I was angry that I didn't try to make any other friends in lifetime because I was always with Matilda. But I didn't want any other friends. I wanted to talk to her.

After a few moments I was quiet. The only sound was me trying to catch my breath. In the rear view mirror I saw the tracks of mascara running in two lines down my face. I picked up my phone.

I'm sorry, but I can't make it. Something came up.

A moment later, he answered.

That's okay. I understand.

I never heard from Emmet again.

The day before Christmas I cleaned up the apartment and myself enough to video chat with my family. If anything was left out of place Mom would question my wellbeing. Wrappers from unhealthy food choices were tossed out. The few dishes I had used repeatedly were cleaned. My box of things from my desk still sat on the counter from the evening Glen stopped by. I tossed it into the closet.

After pulling on a nice sweater and enough makeup to help me fake smile, I called home. Tara answered.

My little sister looked better than I did on any given day. Since she hadn't been crying daily and eating nothing but salt and sugar, she looked like a supermodel next to me.

"Guess what!" she said as soon as she answered. "I'm going to Murphy!"

"That's great!" Her news was the first good thing I'd heard in days.

The university sat just two hours away from my parent's home. She could come home when she needed to, but was far enough away to be on her own. Mom and Dad would be happy with the choice.

"What are you going to study?" I asked.

"Advertisement and public relations," she smiled back.

"Are you going to be Don Draper?"

"Don Draper didn't go to college," Tara explained. "And I am not a man whore."

"Language!" my mother's voice called from off screen. Tara passed the tablet to her.

"Hi, honey, did you get our package?" she asked.

"Yes, thank you. I'm going to open it tomorrow." I glanced at the box sitting on the floor. Discovering its contents were my only plans for the next day. I knew it would be joined with lots of alcohol.

"We got yours, and we can't wait to open it," she smiled at me and I smiled back. "How are you doing?"

"I'm okay," it was half true. That day I had eaten toast.

"Is there anything we can get for you?" Mom was concerned. I tried make my smile convincing.

"Did you get our package?" Dad appeared beside her. He had on a tacky sweater with a large chickadee wearing a scarf.

"Yes, thank you." My smile looked real.

"We wish you were with us, but we understand." Mom's smile didn't look real.

I wrapped up the conversation and gave them all my love. The house was decorated, twinkling lights had framed each of them as they passed the iPad around the room. I looked at my quite apartment. As always, it was white and plain. The late afternoon sun was giving it all extra shadows and gloom.

Plenty of classic Christmas movies could be found on any channel. Instead I put in *Pride and Prejudice*. Alone, I sang the "dadadadadas" in time with the piano. For Christmas dinner I had a frozen pizza and half a bottle of whisky.

My thoughts clouded as alcohol sunk in. My head rolled in a pleasant bliss as my body lost any feeling. I felt better than I had all week. The credits ended, and the main menu appeared. I stared into the screen with no energy to turn it off. After a few minutes, the movie started again and I let it play.

If Matilda were there, she wouldn't have objected. She would have let it play and agreed that it was better than any Christmas movie.

Christmas morning I woke up with a headache. I made myself get water and pain killers as much as I didn't want to. Outside the world seemed quiet.

No one was out. Hardly any cars passed on the street. Everyone was with someone they cared about. Except for me.

I warmed up a cinnamon roll in the microwave for breakfast. In my liquor cabinet I found new bottle of whiskey I had yet to break into. If I started it with my coffee, I could finish the bottle that day. It would be a new record for me. I wanted to fall back into the sweet spot I had found the night before.

Instead I put it in my purse to take it with me. I had been doing plenty of stupid things recently, but I wasn't going to drink and drive. I scooped up my sorry breakfast and headed out the door.

Earlier that year, Matilda bought the plot beside her parents. Her list of grown up accomplishments was rather short, but buying her burial plot was on there. Maybe she did it for the morbid fun of doing it.

Winter had set in. It was cold out, but there wasn't any snow. It made sitting on the ground easier. My ass was still damp and cold.

A gravestone marked Mr. and Mrs. Day's lives. Someone lives a whole life and all they have is a rock saying how long they were here. Matilda's rock hadn't come yet. She just had a marker at the top of her patch of dirt.

I sat alone, staring at dirt beside me. If I didn't blink, the wind chilled my eyes. Cold air filled my lungs with each breath. I wanted to be colder.

"Hey."

I spun around. Liam had the same idea as me. He was dressed similarly in sweatpants and a hoodie under an unzipped coat. All he was missing was the whisky bottle. His eyes even had the same puffiness as mine. They were just as blue as Matilda's, and it hurt like hell.

"When did you get back?" I asked, still sitting.

"I never left," he turned the headstone into a chair. "I took some time off."

"Me too," I said before taking my first sip from the bottle. It was

157

warm going down, and paired well with the cold in the rest of my body.

"I thought you quit," he nodded to the bottle.

I shook my head and took a second drink.

"I'm not strong enough to keep promises anymore."

"Me either," Liam agreed. "She told me not to be sad. What kind of bullshit request is that?"

We sat silently for a while. The whole cemetery was quiet. In the wind the cold gravestones looked even colder. The overcast sky gave the whole place a fitting shadow. I could picture Matilda yelling at her brother for sitting on their parents and putting his feet on their dad's face. Then she would tell us both we were being stupid and send us home.

"I keep thinking of something I want to tell her or ask her," I broke the silence. "Sometimes I have my phone picked up before I remember that I can't."

"The house is really quiet without you guys around," Liam said. "It's impossible not to just be sad there."

"I'm sorry," I answered mechanically.

"Want to come over for the day?" he asked. "If we're going to break promises we might as well do it together someplace that's warm."

I hadn't seen the house since Matilda died. I doubt I'd ever been there before without her in it. When she was gone, the house was quiet and darker. A shadow fell over the whole place. Colors seemed less bright. Even her painting stacked here and there looked faded.

In the front room, Cat sat on the couch. He had curled into a ball, sleeping inside as if he'd always been there. A blue color hung around his neck.

"Cat," I whispered.

"That's Mr. Darcy," Liam took my coat. "Because he doesn't like being around people. Your movie grew on me."

I made my way to the living room. Everything was exactly the same. Christmas decorations had been put away a while ago. Liam hadn't bothered to put anything back up. The couch still held lumpy piles of fleece blankets and throw pillows. Overcast skies gave the room the same shadow as the rest of the house.

We took seats in opposite corners of the couch. He took a bottle of red from the kitchen. I stuck to the one I'd brought along.

"I'll be here for a couple of months," he explained. "The house has to be cleaned out so I can sell it."

Another loss. I wanted to ask him not to sell, or even attempt to buy it myself. I knew either one was impossible. The house I spent my whole live visiting several times a week would soon be gone too. I didn't realize how much that thought hurt until it happened.

For a while we sat in silence. The hallway clock ticked, it was the only sound in the house. I sipped my bottle and pictured Matilda with us on the couch, nestled into her usual corner.

Her hair would be untouched in its usual, messy cascade. Despite being in for the day, she would have on red lipstick. She'd claim Christmas photos as a reason to do makeup, even though she had no intention of leaving her pajamas.

"I miss her," I stated the obvious as I stared into an empty spot on the couch.

"Me too," Liam replied.

"This isn't fair."

"Nothing is fair. Not life, not monopoly, not this."

I couldn't look his way. In those same, bright blue eyes all I could see was Matilda. Their hair was the same, a black mess that never responded to brushes or products. The only difference was the rosy color to his skin. Matilda's might have been the same if she weren't sick from birth.

Then I felt a pain for Liam's sake. Yesterday, in all of my sadness I still called home. A mother, father, and sister talked to me. They told me they loved me and wanted to see me. Liam didn't have that anymore. Just as I felt guilty for mourning when Matilda was still alive, I felt guilty for mourning when Liam had lost so much more.

"What do we do?" I asked, keeping my eyes on Matilda's empty seat.

"We let it happen, because you can't do anything else."

Had she been there, Matilda would have sarcastically thanked him for his comforting thoughts. But she wasn't there, so the room was silent.

I found a moment to smile and asked, "Did she tell you about the wedding dress?"

"Yeah. She showed me the whole book," he laughed for a moment. "Where did she find that shirtless picture?"

"God knows," I laughed too.

"I had no idea she was that good at Photoshop."

Quiet hovered over us again. In my mind I flipped through the pictures Matilda had edited with her arms around the movie star. It must have taken hours.

"Did she ever tell you about painting the wall?" Liam asked. I shook my head. "We used to have this terrible wallpaper in the dining room. Mom hated it, and she wanted something else. But Dad was always like, 'no, we don't need that. It's really fine.' So Matilda asked for watercolors, and said she wanted to start painting. They got some for her, and she set everything up on the table. And she was old enough to know better, she was like five.

"But she just painted all over the walls in there. It must have taken the whole pallet because everything from where the wallpaper started on the bottom to her eye line had paint on it."

"Oh my gosh," I laughed. "Was her entire painting career a ruse to get your mom new wallpaper?"

"Probably," he shrugged. "She didn't even get in trouble. When Dad saw it Mom was just like, 'I've already handled it.'"

I could see young Matilda, most likely stuffed into the same cardigan, dragging a brush across the wall. Her abstractionist style would have already been present as the colors ran together across the grooves of ugly wallpaper. I could see Mrs. Day walking into the dining room and trying not to smile as Matilda stepped back to show off her work.

I wondered why she never told me the story. Maybe it was because her mother told her to keep quiet about it. As wrong as the act was, no doubt she didn't want Matilda to receive any extra scolding. They both knew what she did, and kept it a secret.

I thought about my own secret, and decided to share it.

"I quit my job."

Liam glanced my way, but didn't say anything. I relayed the story of what happened. I explained all my work with the app for the company, and mentioned the childish tantrum I had thrown.

"I'm sorry," he offered.

"It's okay. I wasn't supposed to be there anymore."

"Well," he said. "Until you start somewhere else, do you mind helping me out here?"

"Sure." I knew I needed an excuse to leave my apartment. I reminded myself how little I had been outside. Also, I could tell Liam needed another person around more than I did.

"She didn't write a will or anything, so if there's something you want you can have it."

"Thank you," I replied.

The frail sunlight was beginning to disappear. Shadows from furniture and walls were growing across the floor. Neither of us moved to turn on a light.

"Can we go look at her room?" I asked.

The space hadn't changed since we were in high school. A band poster of our first crushes remained on the wall, crinkled and faded from time. Some of her clothes were still scattered across the floor. Clean shirts spilled out of the overflowing closet. It was like nothing had happened at all.

I stood at her dresser and lightly touched a hair brush. Strands of long black hair were tangled in the teeth. Beside it were two pink bears surrounding dark lenses. I propped them up on top of my head. In the middle was a pile of prescription medicine. I picked up one and read the label. Daily, Matilda had been taking several different pills and never mentioned it. One was fever, another cough, several were to ease pain.

One framed photograph hung on the wall. All four members of the Day family stood together smiling at Liam's pinning ceremony. Mr. Day's hair was just as messy as his children. It would have been a year before they died.

On her nightstand, Matilda had left a gently used bible. Religion never came up until her days were numbered. Sometimes people need a big scare to turn back to God.

The toucan cup from our cruise sat beside it. Mine had been thrown out a long time ago. On the first day of that trip we lost count of how many free refills we'd used the cup for. We covered the cost of the cruise in all the soda we drank. Matilda would have bankrupted the company if they served Cherry Life.

An edge of paper stuck out from under the cup. I unfolded it to see Matilda's neat handwriting lined down the page in a list. She really did write a list, and every item was scratched off but one.

1. Break the law without hurting anyone
2. Pet an otter
3. Feel mom and dad again
4. Win the lottery
5. Get Tessie to stop drinking
6. Write letters to everyone
7. Feel like a kid again
8. Work on art nonstop
9. Have an Art Exhibit
10. Plan a wedding and feel like a princess
11. One more, big trip

"Did she mention this to you?" I held out the paper for Liam to see.

"No," he silently read over the items. His expression fell, "she didn't finish."

I glanced into the hallway. Even from my spot in her room I could count three paintings and a sculpture in a sliver of the hallway. More were piled in the basement and empty family area upstairs.

"What if we finished it for her?"

15 FINISHING THE LIST

Once again, I was spending most of my time at the Day house. With something to work on, I had a drive to be out of my apartment. I had never planned an exhibit before, but a few months ago I had also never planned a Christmas party or hired a Santa.

First, we had to empty out the house. Liam let me go through Matilda's things and take any keepsakes I felt like I wanted. Before we began clearing things out of her room, I gave it a final overlook.

Since mine had been gone a long time, I decided to keep her toucan cup. I dropped it in a tote bag with a couple of her frequently worn flannel shirts. I also kept her sunglasses, and the bible left on her nightstand. Canvas wrapped around the small collection I scavenged from a finished life.

We started upstairs. Two Cherry Lifes, cold from the garage fridge, joined us in Matilda's bedroom. Clothes were folded and dropped into boxes. Old things were tossed out. In a few hours, an empty bed and bare closet were just the scraps of a bedroom.

"Is there anything you wanted to keep?" I asked as we made a pile of boxes downstairs.

"Maybe from Mom and Dad's room."

For the most part we were both silent. Sometimes I caught myself feeling upset, but the systematic folding clothes and dropping them into the box kept me from wallowing. Instead of sitting still and letting my mind sink into place I was able to work with my hands. I had a goal of clearing out the house that I could slowly be working towards.

All the clothes were piled into the SUV. Matilda had been pretty specific about the clothing drive her church had organized. I drove the tank, filled to bursting, and dropped everything off.

Furniture was taken apart. Again the tank was loaded, and we dropped it off at another charity she had selected. One by one the rooms were clearing out. Matilda's was cleaned first, and we started stacking the art in there as we found it. The first unusual piece came from her closet.

After clearing out the explosion of clothes, we discovered three walls and a floor. Leaning against the back wall was an orange canvas. Different shades spread across the back, golden lines and circles hung in one of its corners.

"What is this supposed to be?" Liam asked.

"If you have to ask, you really don't get it." It didn't feel like my own voice.

As long days of packing and cleaning became late evenings, I was sleeping in the guest room again. Planning for an art show felt similar to all the organizing for the Christmas party. Except this time it was actually chilly outside.

I drank way too much of the Cherry Life. Guests at the party had barely scratched the surface of the haul. In the next few weeks, Matilda could have bathed in all of the bottles she drank. Through all of it a large stack was still left in the fridge.

Over a lunch break one day, Liam dropped four on the kitchen island.

"We have to finish this shit off," he said.

"When it's finally gone, I doubt I'll drink it again." I opened a bottle to do my part.

"You're not tired of it yet?"

"No, it really is just so good," I took a large sip.

"I'm already over it," Liam still took one for himself.

"Maybe the nurse people will send you to a few places without it," I opened the kitchen fridge to count the remaining bottles. "Then after a while you'll like it again."

"The nurse people?"

"The traveling nurse people that tell you where to go," I explained. There were twenty more bottles. "I don't know how it works."

"Oh, I'm not doing that anymore."

"Crap, did you resign in disgrace too?" I joked, but worried about both of us being unemployed.

"No," he smiled. "I'm just going to stay in one place. Out in Allensville, actually; where your parents are."

"Why there?" I thought about the small city. They had hospitals and businesses and schools, but nothing particularly exciting.

"They offered a nice job," he shrugged. "Also, your family is pretty much the only people left on earth that I know."

The same was true for me. Tara had been nice enough to pick a college close to Mom and Dad. I was sure they would accept any additional children coming to live nearby, biological or otherwise. My own apartment suddenly sounded very empty.

"I'm sure there are a lot of businesses out there that might need whatever it is you do."

"Maybe," I agreed.

Slowly, the house was emptied. Bedrooms were bare. People drifted in from online sales and handed Liam cash for the dining room table, the sectional couch, and even the piano. Things were drifting away in sweet goodbyes. New people would fill every object with new memories. Someone else would have a deep conversation around the glass table at two in the morning.

One afternoon we sat in front of the TV with a late lunch. The couch was gone by then. In our break Liam had surfed and stopped on a channel half way through *Pride and Prejudice*. For a moment I could take in the story and forget about the life around me that had been puttering by.

The film was still the same. I could still enjoy it. Snappy lines made me laugh and wide shots of open countryside made me sigh.

Cat, or Mr. Darcy, as he had come to be known, seemed to understand what we were watching. He stretched out beside Liam and purred. His life was better, and he still didn't let me get close to him.

Life was slowly thawing. I was back to almost living at the Day house. The contents were thinning. Liam was still cooking meals. It felt like the days with Matilda. Home cooked food was better than the frozen junk I had been eating.

It was nice to have a friend around. He had long strides to being nearly as cool as Matilda, but the interest in our movie helped.

The last of Liam's things were packed into bags and dropped at my apartment, Mr. Darcy included. In his time on the road, Liam had lived from only what could fit in the back of his car. It all stacked very neatly in one corner.

One day I took the cue from clearing out the Day house and turned to my own home. In years past I hadn't hung on to things as much as Matilda had. I could feel a jittery, uncomfortableness to staying put. The tiny town was calling.

Matilda's letters were read more frequently. Next to them sat the box Glen had dropped off. I sat in the floor to clear it out. Notebooks and loose papers were tossed into the trash. So many papers that had been important just a few weeks before were useless. They were tossed out too. Piece by piece I inspected and threw to the garbage bin.

At the bottom a loose pen rolled on its own. I had forgotten about my pen with the Margaret Atwood quote. Before Matilda's death sentence, I had searched everywhere for it. I was certain working without it would be impossible. Until it disappeared, every note and signature was scratched out with that pen.

I rolled the smooth black cap between my fingers. In the finite space a me from a few years before had condensed the poem to three words, "word is power." At the time it meant something. By that day the gold swirls against the dark metallic pen didn't feel very powerful at all. It had been expensive, personal, and important, but for nine months I had forgotten it existed. I had been fine. I tossed it into the bin.

In the final days before Matilda's exhibit, the house was completely cleared. Walls and floors were bare, sticking up like rib cages in a memory skeleton. My second home, Matilda's home, was drifting away. Walking on the immaculately clean floor the same boards creaked, but everything looked different. Rooms felt wider like the walls had taken a deep breath and expanded.

My own apartment seemed shriveled in comparison. The house was fading, but the apartment had died. I looked around at similar white walls and bare floors. In all my time living there, I hadn't made the apartment home. I knew it was time to empty it out too.

The faint signs of life existed in Mr. Darcy. The former outdoor cat and grown accustomed to sitting in the windowsill in the apartment. He was also growing fatter. Not running from every human he saw really cut back on his cardio.

Life came in Matilda's painting. The bright colors drew in any eyes in a world of pale white around it. From my closet to kitchen everything was black or white against a hardwood floor. She was right I did live like a cartoon character.

The couch was the only thing out of line. Since Liam sold his bed on craigslist, he'd been crashing there. Unfolded blankets and crushed pillows never remained in the same place.

Soon it would all be bare too.

When the walls were filled with paintings the house became unrecognizable. Each room had work lined up on the walls. Corners became spots for metal sculptures. Matilda's work was everywhere, but it didn't feel like her house anymore. Soon it would be someone else's.

I stood in the front room in my dress I bought without looking at the price. It was nice to have an excuse to wear it again. The colors were much more fitting to late January than September.

From my spot I watched people drifting in the front door. They were real art people. They were the kind of people that wear big glasses and drape clothes; the ones who know what good art looked like and will spend thousands of dollars on it. Matilda would have made fun of each one of them. She would have called them exotic birds and marveled at our discovery of a new species.

Fancy waiters mingled through the small crowd. Some carried hors d'oeuvres. Some had treys of champagne glasses. All of them wore black pants and white button up shirts. They were penguins shuffling through the peacocks.

"You shouldn't let strangers raid your closet like that," Liam told me in passing.

Alone I watched strangers drift through the shell of the house. Without the people I knew it wasn't the same place, but that was okay. It was a few signatures away from being someone else's.

Each room had a small crowd. I tried to count sold stickers and quickly lost track. People with massive jewelry and scarves that cost more than my rent were kept happy with refreshments. The waiters drifted through the art appreciative crowd without disturbing anyone.

One of them came up to me and offered a glass. It was chilled just right. Tiny bubbles were rolling to the top. I thought about the taste; then I thought about Christmas. Real Christmas was the last time I had a drink.

Matilda was good at keeping things hidden. In her final days, the medicines and pain and her desires to feel complete with the items on her list were secrets. Like the black tank and baggy flannel that hid her swollen belly, she concealed her pain from me. She disguised it all with false energy and unfiltered comments.

She did all of that for me, but for herself too. She insured that the last of our time together was memorable, and unscarred by hospitals.

I politely declined the penguin offering me a glass.

> *Sometimes, at the beach we get knocked down by one nasty wave. We get thrown around, and for a minute we think that this is the end and we won't get up. But then we do, and we're okay.*
>
> *This wave might keep you down for a while. Eventually, you will get up, and you'll be okay. You might still hurt a little, but you'll be okay.*
>
> Love,
> Matilda

ABOUT THE AUTHOR

Danae L. Samms is an enthusiastic creator. Her writing began when she was four with her first play, and continued to grow to a degree in journalism, a blog, and now a novel. Regularly, she keeps up with a blog of unqualified advice on writing and everything else. The only thing she's been doing longer than writing is horseback riding. While horse shoes were never her forte, Danae has spent plenty of time riding and training. Most of that is with her horse Maggie.

Made in the USA
Middletown, DE
02 February 2019